MO FANNING

RAINBOWS AND LOLLIPOPS

Spring Street Books

First published by Spring Street Books Ltd 2025

Copyright © 2025 by Mo Fanning

ISBN: 978-1-7392903-8-2

Book Cover by Charlotte Daniels

mofanning.co.uk | springstreetbooks.co.uk

Thanks to my lovely rainbow Mark
and my joyous lollipop Ernie

thanks...

Rainbows and Lollipops came together faster than anything I've ever attempted to write before. Somehow, I ended up with a first draft in weeks rather than months (or years) and smugly figured I was special. Then I let my fabulous editor loose on the words and realised there were still many miles to travel.

As always, there are so many people to thank for their help, support, and advice. My editor, Sam, who mastered the art of the "shit sandwich" when providing feedback—but who turned what could have been a very different story into something I'm incredibly proud of. To my wonderful (and frankly tireless) publicist, Hannah. To Charlotte, for creating a cover that I personally believe is the best cover ever in the history of books.

To Tina, Matt, Bonnie, Patrick, and Jennie—people who write a billion times better but never make me feel like I don't belong. And to the Faber Gang—Claudia, Dominique, Freya, Merl, Rachel, and Steve—who will soon bring out books that will blow mine right out of the water.

To Mark, who is everything a husband should be and so much more (thanks, YouTube). To Ernie, who is everything you'd expect of a Labrador—and more. More hair. More licks. Just more.

And to you, for buying, stealing, borrowing, or illegally downloading this book. As long as you read it, that's what matters. If you do enjoy it, please consider posting a review. If not, let's never speak of this again.

Try to be a rainbow in someone's cloud

Maya Angelou

readers guide

Rainbows and Lollipops merges traditional novel storytelling with the visual language of television screenplays. The story unfolds across six episodes, just like a streaming series. Each new scene starts with a screenplay-style scene heading. These explain where and when the action takes place.

INT. interior scenes

EXT. exterior scenes

DAY a scene taking place during the day

NIGHT a scene set at night

SUNSET a scene set as the night closes in

CONTINUOUS no location change

SUPER: what appears on the screen

FADE IN start of each episode

FADE TO BLACK is where the titles roll

jake

Two weeks before everything changed, Jake's life had seemed wonderfully, boringly normal. Surrounded by scatter cushions, he perched on the sofa, working from home, reading an emailed complaint from a Horizon Holidays customer whose Düsseldorf mini-break was 'ruined' by a lukewarm in-flight beef casserole.

Tom, pale and dishevelled, stumbled from the bedroom, squinting at the sun, and uttered a weary groan. He'd strained a hamstring at the gym, showing off in front of his new and way

1

too good-looking personal trainer. Luis—said with a lisp to emphasise just how swarthily Spanish and horribly handsome he was.

'Perhaps I should go to hospital,' Tom said. 'Better to be safe than sorry.'

Jake set aside his laptop. 'The best cure is rest. Would you like me to make you a drink?'

'Tea. But no milk. Best to avoid carbs. If I can't work out, I'll balloon.'

'You're not having your usual three sugars, then?'

Tom grimaced. 'I could manage a biscuit. You're supposed to line your stomach if you're taking painkillers.'

Jake patted his shoulder. 'The thing is sweetie, you ate the last of the Jammy Dodgers last night. I suppose I could nip out to the minimart.'

The suggestion was met with a hopeful smile. 'If you're going out anyway, would you mind getting me a bag of prawn cocktail Wotsits?'

Jake grinned. 'So we're lining our stomachs with carbs and trans-fats today, then?'

Tom collapsed into his favourite armchair, scrunching into a ball, and turning his voice down to a sickly croak. 'If they're out of prawn cocktail, the regular ones are fine. And a Mars Bar. And a can of Fanta Lemon. But only if it's been in the fridge. I was reading online about how it's important to keep my electrolytes up.'

Jake shook his head, but reached for his wallet and house keys. When he caught Covid, Tom had been the perfect nurse, tending to his every need, chopping an egg up in a cup. He brought him toast with all the crusts cut off. He'd always imagined them growing old together. Long, lazy Sunday mornings flipping through the papers, solving cryptic crossword puzzles, bickering over whose turn it was to walk the Labrador.

He stepped out of his battered grey felt slippers and pulled on the nearest pair of trainers. 'One fat-bastard junk-food goodie bag coming up.'

Tom frowned, lifted his T-shirt and patted his flat stomach. 'I'm not actually fat, though, right?'

```
INT. TOM AND JAKE'S FLAT - NIGHT
SUPER: '19 JULY 2024'
JAKE lies on top of the bed,
surrounded by his iPad, phone, a maga-
zine, and a spine-up book. It's late,
the blind is drawn.
```

Fate doesn't bother with polite knocks. Fate boots in your door at stupid o'clock, raids your fridge, eats the leftover Chinese and drinks straight from the milk carton. The worst houseguest you never invited, with a particular talent for showing up whenever you think you've got your life sorted. Just to remind you that you're not even close.

Jake shifted in bed, resting his head on Tom's still-cool pillow. Oppressive heat made it impossible to get comfortable, even with the windows open wide, there was just no air. The alarm clock blinked 22:07, each pale blue pulse marking another minute Tom should have been home. Another minute he wasn't.

Once a year, Bowers Estate Agency summoned everyone to a chain hotel just outside Bristol for a day of motivational team building.

'Can't you tell them you're sick?' Jake had said.

'If I don't go, it'll look bad.' Tom had insisted. 'It's all about the networking.'

It wasn't that he didn't trust Tom. He trusted him with his life. He just hated being alone in their flat at night. And the car had been making weird knocking noises. Tom's solution had been to crank up the music, drowning out what sounded like the engine getting ready to either explode or drop out. What if he'd broken down in the middle of nowhere? Down some out-of-the-way country lane. What if the police found an abandoned Mini Cooper near the last reported sighting of some axe-wielding psychopath?

In a last ditch attempt to talk Tom out of spending the night in a Travelodge, Jake had played his trump card: 'It's our anniversary on Friday.'

'Which one?'

'It's been six years since the first time we... you know.'

Tom snorted as he picked out shoes. 'Does Hallmark do a card for that, now?'

No matter, Jake knew he'd won. Tom had promised to drive home as soon as the last whoop-whoop motivational speaker ended his PowerPoint presentation.

The clock ticked over to 22:09.

INT. TOM AND JAKE'S FLAT – NIGHT
SUPER: 'JUNE 2022'

After waiting an hour in a Birmingham pub where Tom had suggested meeting up for early evening cocktails, Jake had taken a bus home only to find the love of his life slumped on their sofa, his eyes glassy, his smile lopsided.

'Did something happen?'

An all-but-empty bottle of Polish vodka sat on the floor.

'Shit. Forgot. Balls.' Tom slurred the words together and tried to sit up, his movements clumsy. 'Sorry. Sorry. Sorry.'

'It's fine,' Jake managed to say, even though it wasn't. He started to tidy, picking up an abandoned tie, smoothing down a creased jacket.

Tom grabbed the vodka, a smile tugging at his lips. 'Lemme make you a cocktail?'

'You sound like you've already had enough.'

This met with a bitter, hollow snort. 'What? You're keeping count. Are you my mother or something?'

Jake heard these exact, same words each time drink took over—blunt weapons meant to deflect and wound.

'Tom, this isn't—' He took a breath, steeling himself. 'I'm not trying to control you, but we've talked about how much you've been drinking...' His voice wavered, and he swallowed, forcing his tone to stay steady. 'You promised.'

And there they were. Two little words with the power to turn any isolated confrontation into all-out war. Sure enough, a spark of anger flared behind vodka-soaked, unfocused eyes.

'Don't start with that again.'

It wasn't worth fighting back. Jake had said everything there was to say at least a dozen times. Instead, he hung his coat on a hook in the lobby and unlaced his shoes.

'I can't keep doing this,' he said, trying not to sound like some sort of drama queen.

A suffocating silence followed. Jake waited for Tom to grab the bottle, but he didn't. Instead, he laughed—a joyless, hollow sound—before sinking back against the cushions, defeated in a way that would crack even the hardest of hearts.

'You're not going to leave me, are you?' Tom's voice came out small and uncertain.

Jake was angry, tired, and heartbroken. But he wouldn't leave.

'No,' he said. 'You're stuck with me, mate.'

He pulled out his phone to order a pizza. With food in his belly, Tom would s0ber up. Tuesday would go back to being Tuesday.

'Pepperoni and mushroom?' he said, tapping at the screen.

Tom let out a breath. 'I'll stop,' he said. 'I'll get help. I promise.'

There they were again. *I promise.* Two little words that could just as easily end whatever war they'd started.

INT. TOM AND JAKE'S FLAT – NIGHT
SUPER: '19 JULY 2024'

A jarring ringtone shattered the quiet, and Jake fumbled for his phone, heart sinking when he saw the caller was Tom's horrible sister.

'It's Tom.' Her usually clipped voice sounded full of wobble. 'There was an accident.'

'But I spoke to him...'

He trailed off, his mind struggling to work out how long ago it had been since Tom had called to say he was on his way. They'd texted at seven. And again just before eight.

Rona's breathing grew ragged. 'They took him into the operating theatre.'

'The operating theatre? Did he break a leg or something? Which hospital?'

'Tom's dead.'

Click and she was gone.

Jake's world slowed down. The floor tilted and the phone slid from his grip, landing with a soft thud. His eyes settled on a framed photograph—the two of them on moving-in day, surrounded by boxes, radiating joy.

Tom couldn't be dead. He called Rona back, but she sent him to voicemail. He needed to speak to someone. Anyone. Hospital switchboards passed him to wards that passed him to other wards, until a voice confirmed the admission of a Tom Carter, in his early 40s.

'Is he OK?' Jake tried to keep his voice calm.

'Are you a relative?'

'I'm his... I'm his boyfriend.'

'Not his husband?'

'We've been together six years. So...'

There was a long, awkward silence. 'I'm afraid I can't tell you anything more. There are rules. Laws. Data protection. You understand?'

Jake had told the woman that yes, he totally understood. That he was sorry for bothering her.

Bile rose in his throat as he stumbled around the flat, his legs weak and unsteady. In the bathroom, he squinted at his reflection, ghostly in the frosted window pane.

'This isn't real.' His voice became a whisper. 'You are dreaming. Wake up.'

He gripped the edge of the sink, his knuckles turning white. The cold, hard porcelain was real. Everything was real. He wasn't dreaming. His chest tightened, his breath coming in shallow gasps. Was this how it felt when your heart gave up? When it saw little point in going on?

He sank to the cold tiled floor, his back against the bathtub. Through an open window, the outside world went about its nocturnal business—a car door slammed, a dog barked.

Someone smoked weed.

```
INT. CITY HOSPITAL - NIGHT
A busy A&E department. All seats are
taken, some people are sitting on the
floor. An illuminated sign indicates
the current wait time is approximately
95 minutes.
```

When Jake's employer ran a staff engagement survey and the results sucked, the HR department at Horizon Seeking Holidays compensated not with pay rises, but with a series of compulsory wellness webinars. An Irish guy in oversize specs, with a fondness for Zoom filters, preached the 5-4-3-2-1 method—a grounding technique to manage anxiety and stay present. You identified five things you could see, four things you could touch, three sounds, two smells, and one taste.

Vending machine. Bunched-up tissue. Antiseptic gel. Angry man. Coffee spill.

The A&E department was all anxious faces and hushed conversations. Harsh lighting stressed the worry etched into every face. Porters pushed trolleys, a tired doctor consoled a sobbing woman, and worried family members paced in tight circles.

Armrest. Phone. The ring he forgot he was wearing. Leg.

Jake's stomach churned, replaying Rona's words.

'Tom's dead.'

All he wanted was an answer. Instead, he'd banged heads with hospital bureaucracy.

'I only want to know if he's alive,' he'd said, and just hearing his mouth form those words didn't seem real. 'I mean... I know he's alive. I just need to know where to find him.'

The stressed-out woman in charge of admissions pointed at a photocopied notice warning of the hospital's zero-tolerance policy.

'You're not a relative. I'm afraid you'll need to step to one side.'

Phone. Door swishing. Another phone. There's always another phone.

What if Rona had got it wrong? Hospitals make mistakes. He'd walk around every floor, open every door, check for himself. And then he'd call a cab and go home, clean his teeth, and climb into bed. And wait for Tom to come home.

Stale sweat. Cheap perfume.

He'd walked over to the lifts and pressed a button, his heart pounding. The doors opened and voices yelled to *stand aside*. Porters wheeled out a grey-faced someone, half-covered by a sheet. Jake jumped out of their way.

And then he saw her.

Rona never changed—tall and slim, salon-fresh blonde hair. Jake ducked behind a vending machine, hoping to stay hidden, but it was too late. She strode towards him, eyes narrowed, lips drawn tight.

'What are you doing here?' she snapped.

He tasted blood, sharp and metallic, as if he'd bitten his tongue or the inside of his cheek.

'I wanted to see Tom.' His voice sounded so very small.

'Tom's body, you mean. You came here to take one last look at the damage you caused.'

Jake flinched. He got it. She was grieving. Lashing out. Trying to find someone to blame.

'Rona, I'm sorry.'

Her expression hardened. 'I'll be sure to tell our mother you didn't intend to kill her son.'

He wanted to fight back but could think of no words worth saying.

'Tom is dead because of you. If you hadn't been so fucking needy—'

'We agreed,' Jake said. 'He was always coming home tonight... last night... yesterday.'

'You dragged him back.' She all but spat. 'You knew he'd be tired, but still you insisted.'

Jake's stomach churned, and he shook his head. What was she talking about?

'It wasn't like that—'

'Of course it was.' Rona interrupted, her voice rising. 'He

9

wanted to have some fun. To get away from you. If you hadn't been so needy, my brother would still be alive.'

The guilt that had gnawed at him in silence now roared in his ears, but Jake forced himself to stay calm. Tom always said to avoid biting back, but anger took over. White-hot anger. The corridor narrowed. The air turned thick and unbreathable.

'I have to see him.'

Her lip curled. 'I've called Amelia. She's on her way. The poor girl is devastated.'

Amelia. The girlfriend groomed to further the Carter family tree. Midway through the third trimester, Tom and Amelia had buried baby Edward with never-worn shoes and an Aston Villa scarf.

'Tom hasn't spoken to her in years,' Jake said.

The words came out sharper than he'd intended. A passing nurse hesitated, looking between them with concern. Rona waved her away.

'Just go, Jake,' she said. 'Before either of us says something we can never take back.'

'I have a right to be with him.'

Her fists clenched, perfect red talons digging into pale white flesh, ready to unleash another tirade. And then, as exhaustion flickered in her eyes, she took a step back.

'You have no rights, Jake. You and Tom never married.'

He recoiled. 'How does that matter?'

'Please, stop fighting me on this.' Her voice grew hoarse and raspy. 'My brother told me he needed a break from you.'

A tightness gripped his throat.

'Tom would never—'

'You're too much for anyone.' Rona folded her arms. 'He wanted one night to himself, Jake, and you refused to give him that.'

The walls around blurred and swirled. The windows became distorted funhouse mirrors.

'We agreed. He said... I never—'

'He wouldn't have been on that road if it wasn't for you.' She spoke to the floor, her words no longer flung in his face. 'My brother would be alive.'

Jake backed away. 'I'm going. No need for fuss.'

But he didn't leave. Instead, he sat on the far side of a still-overwhelmed A&E department. *Tom wanted a break.* How come Jake, who prided himself on reading people, on knowing when to step in... how did he not pick up that? And what sort of break? From him? From their life together?

A permanent break?

Still, he couldn't leave Tom here. Alone. With strangers. He wouldn't walk away and act as if he didn't care. Like none of this mattered. When it mattered too much.

Vending machine. Bunched-up tissue. Antiseptic gel. Angry man. Coffee spill.

Armrest. Phone. The ring he forgot he was wearing. Leg.

Phone. Door swishing. Another phone.

Stale sweat. Cheap perfume.

He called Tom's voicemail. Sweet and low, the man he loved spoke with the smallest of lisps and a whisper of a stutter. Jake told himself Rona *had* got it all wrong. Tom wasn't dead. He was caught in three lanes of slow-moving traffic, or queuing for coffee in a service station with patchy 5G. That he'd call any minute.

Every part of him chose that moment to ache.

Doubt took root. What if Tom had stayed in Bristol because he needed space? And what if Tom was drinking again? In secret. What if all their late-night talks, all the moments when Tom insisted he was happy... what if those had been well-crafted lies to protect Jake from a truth he couldn't handle?

A pair of sensible flat shoes appeared in his downcast field of vision. Without looking up, he knew it must be a nurse, likely at the end of her tether, running on fumes and forced to insist he leave.

'I need a minute,' he said. 'That's allowed, right? This area is public. I have rights.'

It was the nurse from before. The one who'd shown concern.

'Who are you here for?' she said.

'My partner. Tom. Tom Carter.'

A detached, professional expression softened.

'Come with me, please.'

```
INT. CITY HOSPITAL - NIGHT
A side room, with no windows, just a
flat hospital bed on which a body
lies, unsupported by pillows, covered
by a white cotton sheet. There are
monitoring machines, all turned off.
```

The room was too hot, too bright, and Jake's eyes stayed fixed on the still form lying on the bed. A thin white sheet covered most of Tom's body, but the outline of his frame was unmistakable. His once vibrant, expressive face had found rest, his dark hair messy in the way it always got after a long day. Tom, who'd always seemed a billion times larger than life, was now so small.

'Was Rona lying?' Jake whispered. 'You wanted a break?'

He reached out, his fingers trembling as they traced the contours of Tom's cold hand, visible beneath the sheet.

'You didn't need to rush back. I know what I said, but it didn't matter.'

He slid from an orange plastic chair to perch on the narrow bed and rested his head on the pillow, eyes shut, trying to imagine they were back home. In their bedroom, with the low hum of traffic from outside, and their neighbour's TV set blaring through too-thin walls.

A faint beep broke the silence, coming from the pocket of his shabby denim jacket, and he fumbled for his phone. A new message notification blinked. He opened it, his breath catching.

RONA STAPLES

You need to be out of the flat tomorrow.

INT. 16 HAVERCROFT LANE – DAY
The home where JAKE grew up. A cosy
living room with floral wallpaper and
efficient but unfashionable furniture.
Sunlight streams through lace
curtains.

Mums always said the right words. That had been why, first thing on Monday morning, Jake had boarded a bus out of town. The journey was long and slow, detouring through most every faceless housing estate going, but an hour later, he had walked up Havercroft Lane, past houses that never seemed to change. Houses where he'd gone for his tea after playing out. Others he would cross the road to avoid because a bully lurked in one of the bedrooms. 25 years had passed since kissing his mum goodbye and leaving for college. The only difference came in the number of cars parked on the drives or up on narrow grass verges.

Even though it was early, Jake knew he'd be welcome. His mum would sit him down, put the kettle on, and find a way to fix everything that was wrong. Like when he was six, and she'd rub dock leaves on nettle stings.

'Go through,' she'd said. 'I'm just making a cuppa.'

In the kitchen, she arranged the best china cups on the best china saucers, and the tea was loose leaf.

'Are you expecting a state visit?' Jake said, and his mum nodded for him to push the kitchen door shut.

'We saw Dr Morgan,' she whispered. 'He's arranged an occupational therapist.'

Jake's already broken heart splintered more. 'Did things change?'

She smiled. 'It's nothing to worry about, Jakey. They do this as a precaution. Dr Morgan took his blood pressure and heart rate. Made sure he remembered his own name and where we live. Your dad passed with flying colours.'

'It's not got any worse?'

It being early-onset Alzheimer's disease. She looked away. Far too quickly.

'Twice last week he lost the car keys,' she said. 'But who can remember everything? I keep forgetting where I put my phone...'

Her voice trailed off, and Jake felt obliged to prompt for more. 'But?'

'He got into a mess about when his brother was next coming to visit.'

Jake stiffened. Uncle Bob had died during lockdown. Of leukaemia.

'How's that girl you used to give a lift to college?' His mum did what she always did when things turned awkward. She changed the subject.

'If you mean Emma, she's still married to Chris. Still working twelve-hour shifts in geriatric care.'

'Such a pretty girl. But nice with it. She didn't realise the effect she had on men.'

He couldn't leave it any longer. 'Tom died.'

He might as well have said it would rain. His mum nodded, picked up the teapot and strainer, and poured.

'Did you hear what I said?' Jake tried not to sound annoyed. 'There was an accident on the motorway. Just outside West Bromwich. The other driver didn't have a scratch on him.'

She stopped what she was doing. 'When did this happen?'

'Friday. There was at conference thing. He was driving back from Bristol.'

'Why didn't you call me?'

His default setting had been to find a way to cope. To tell nobody. And then he'd weakened. Emma had been devastated and turned up on his doorstep within the hour. Fred followed, along with Stu. Jake had spent Sunday on Emma's sofa, watched the twins play Fortnite.

'The police think he might have been drinking,' he said. 'There'll be a post-mortem.'

His mum chewed her bottom lip, filing away information. Adding each detail to an index card and putting them into little wooden drawers. Just as she did back when she worked at the university library.

'I'm so sorry, love.' She reached out to touch his arm. Which was a big deal. They'd never been a tactile family. 'Tom was like a son to us.'

Jake stared down at his hands. It all still felt like a nightmare. His mother let out a heavy sigh.

'He always made us laugh, didn't he? Remember that Christmas when he bought your dad that cap and we all said it made him look like Elmer Fudd...'

Jake didn't dare look up. He'd shatter into a million pieces.

'Funny thing, your dad's been asking after him. Keeps talking about those custard tarts he used to bring us off the market.'

A warmth seeped into his chest. 'I thought he wasn't keen on them.'

'You know how he acts,' she said with a sniff. 'One minute they're too sweet, the next he's sneaking down in the middle of the night to finish them.'

She pulled out a chair, slumped down, and stared at him, punch-drunk. 'You need to let yourself grieve, love. Don't hold it in for our sakes.'

From the other room, his dad called out, his voice high-pitched, almost frantic.

His mum didn't stir, just tapped the table.

'Hold your horses,' she said. 'The cavalry's on a break.'

Jake glanced towards the hallway door. 'He sounds upset.'

'When I get there he won't remember why he wanted me.'

'Should I go?'

His mum pushed back her chair. 'Best I tell him you're here. Prepare the ground.'

Something about her words raised new fears. Was his dad slipping further away? Had the cruellest of conditions decided to step up its attack?

'Some days are good, some are bad,' she said. 'Today isn't the best.'

```
INT. BÄCKEREI BRETZEL - DAY
SUPER: '23 JULY 2024'
A charming, intimate 'Austrian style'
cake and coffee house, nestled within
a bustling arcade, popular with a
diverse mix of patrons.
```

Emma was waiting in their regular café. As Jake pushed open the heavy wooden door, a gentle chime sounded. The transition from a bustling Victorian arcade to the hushed chatter and occasional hiss of the vintage espresso machine was immediate and comforting.

He'd found the place by chance after lockdown ended. A lorry had hit a bridge near Snow Hill station, cancelling all trains in and out of Birmingham. He'd gone in search of coffee and discovered this hidden gem.

Emma stood up, pulling him close, and he breathed in her perfume. Warm and floral. 'Has there been any more news?'

Jake shook his head. 'I called, and they said something about a toxicology report. But I'm not family…'

'Rona won't leave you out.' Emma waved for him to sit. 'As soon as she knows anything—'

'She wants me gone from the flat.'

He saw her jaw tighten, her fingers wrapped around her coffee mug with a grip that turned her knuckles white. 'She can't just do that.'

'My name isn't on the deeds; she can do what she likes.'

Emma leaned forward, her eyes locked on his. 'When Mum died, probate was a nightmare, but that's actually a good thing.'

A sting took hold behind his eyes. 'How is anything about Tom dying good?'

She reached out and squeezed his hand, her touch firm, grounding him. 'That's not what I meant. Rona can't sell the flat until she gets probate. I suppose you never got around to writing wills?'

He didn't look up. 'It always felt like something old people do.'

'OK, that means Tom passed away intestate. Probate is going to take six months minimum. She can't throw you out of your home.'

Jake forced a smile, for Emma's sake. She was doing her level best to make him think positively. 'What if I don't want to live there without him?'

'Not long term, no. But for now. What is it they say? When something big happens... like this. Make no big decisions for at least a year.'

'I presume whoever they are, they have access to enough money for the deposit on a flat of their own?'

'You could rent somewhere.'

He nodded. 'I thought of moving back home. Mum's struggling with Dad, and it might help.'

Even as Emma forced a smile, Jake saw the anger pulse. 'I swear, if I ever see her...'

'None of this is helping.' Jake wanted to curl into a ball and wait until the bad stuff went away. *He'd caused this, couldn't she see?* 'I just want to move on.'

Still shaking, her hand reached for a spoon to stir already half-finished coffee. 'Families can be the worst.'

He glanced over to the counter, past the huge glass display case loaded high with pretzels and pastries. Tom had loved coming here and called the place Carb Heaven. Jake had always envied how he could work his way through a slab of double-iced fudge cake and never get fat. He wasn't a gym bunny. He didn't jog. Tom had been one of those annoying people who could eat whatever he wanted whenever he wanted.

'I don't get what to do,' he said. 'What if she tries to stop me going to the funeral?'

Emma's eyes grew wide. 'You're giving her too much power. Funerals are public events. My nan used to go to them all the time. She even took sandwiches. Her and her mates treated it like a day out.'

He found himself smiling. 'I haven't told Lucy yet.'

'She'll fall apart.'

Lucy had been closer to Tom than any of their other friends. They'd hit it off big style. He'd only held off because she was up to her eyeballs in wedding admin. A holiday fling had turned into a whirlwind romance. She was marrying her Canadian boyfriend in October.

'She called me first thing,' Emma said. 'To announce she wants actual diamonds sewn into her veil.'

Jake was grateful for his friend's tactful subject swerve. 'You told her diamonds cost actual money, right?'

Emma held up surrender hands. 'Bridezilla strikes again.'

Jake's phone beeped. A message from his mum. 'Dad's locked himself in the shed. She wants to know if I know where he keeps his toolkit.'

She rested her chin on her upturned palm. 'OK, so maybe it wouldn't be the worst idea to take a few weeks out and let your mother cook for you. If she ever mentions making her jam sponge pudding, count me in.'

He thought it through. A few weeks sounded less like forever. Less like giving up.

'You didn't cause the accident, Jake,' Emma said. 'Don't let Rona force you into anything.'

```
EXT. WESTON SUPER MARE - DAY
SUPER: '27 JULY 2018'
A sweltering summer day in a bustling
British seaside town. The beach is
crowded with sunbathers and families,
colourful umbrellas dot the landscape.
In the distance, food vans serve
typical beach fare, their aromas
wafting on the breeze.
```

On the radio, newsreaders spoke about how temperatures that day might top 40 degrees. Tom had driven them to Weston Super Mare in his air-conditioned company car, and the second they parked up and Jake opened the door, the heat hit like an oven blast. The air was thick and heavy, layered with smells from vans serving popcorn and candyfloss.

They'd found an empty bit of beach and sat side by side under a Bowers Estate Agency golf umbrella, sharing a bottle of lukewarm Lidl Cola. Tom's fingers played with a strand of Jake's hair.

'Do you ever wonder how you might die?' he'd asked, his tone contemplative.

Jake had shifted to stare at his boyfriend of three months. 'Is there something you need to tell me?'

Tom's eyes narrowed, crinkling his brow. 'When Mum died, it made me think about how I'd never made anything of myself.'

Jake had stayed quiet.

'It bugs me that I won't ever have kids,' Tom said. 'I reckon I'd make a brilliant dad.'

They'd had this conversation before. Jake didn't hate kids. He was godfather to his best friend's twin boys and loved them to bits, but playing happy families had always been something other people did.

'Gay people can adopt,' he said, ignoring how his insides contracted at the thought. 'Perhaps one day we could look into what's involved.'

Even as he spoke, he had his fingers crossed that one day never dawned.

Tom leaned in. 'I love you.'

Jake's chest tightened. For once, he hadn't been the first to say it. He leaned in and kissed Tom, pouring everything into the meeting of their lips.

'And I love you too.'

INT. JAKE AND TOM'S FLAT – DAY
SUPER: '23 JULY 2024'

A forgotten load of laundry smelled of must, three days abandoned in their cheap tumble dryer. Jake sorted clothes into two piles: *Mine* and *His*. He folded Tom's shirts with precise, robotic movements, smoothing out each wrinkle.

The last time Tom had worn this, he'd been on his way to AA. Their twice-weekly routine had become so normal, Jake hadn't even looked up from his phone as the front door closed. Should he tell Tom's group? Would they worry when he stopped turning up, think he'd started drinking again?

What if that was what happened? What if that was why he...

Jake sorted socks into matching pairs.

He sat on the bedroom floor, grabbing a towel Tom had used the day before he drove to Bristol. Jake buried his face in the rough fibres, breathing in a man who no longer was.

Tears flowed. He rocked back and forth, his breathing ragged.

A cup lurked under the bed, out of vacuum cleaner range. Tom's idea of tidying up meant shoving mess out of sight, stuffing drawers until they wouldn't close. A folded leaflet caught Jake's eye—the antifascist march they'd planned to attend. The media buzzed with stories about the far-right's sudden rise, Tommy Robinson barking hate from a Cypriot sun lounger.

Guilt churned. Tom had lived for this stuff, raging about the 'Vote Reform UK' posters next door. Jake shared his anger, but never his fire. The thought of marching through London with a placard had filled him with dread.

He'd march anywhere now, just to have Tom back.

'I'm sorry,' his whisper cracked. 'You know I cared though, right?'

He scanned the room—half-folded laundry, drawers spilling Tom's things. Everything held a memory. Behind each cupboard door, a landmine lurked. Their sanctuary had become a maze of grief.

In the freezer, he found lasagne for one and pierced the film lid. He'd kill for a glass of wine, but there was none in the flat, and he couldn't face the corner shop. The guy behind the counter would ask after Tom, all friendly concern. He'd have to lie, say everything was fine.

Except Tom wasn't fine. Tom wasn't anything at all.

Work had been good about the time off, but he was sick of living in this bubble while life went on. The Customer Service inbox would still be there tomorrow, stuffed with complaints about dirty bathrooms and bedbugs. Time to go back, prove he could still pass for human.

He'd fake it until it felt real.

INT. JAKE AND TOM'S FLAT – DAY
SUPER: '24 JULY 2024'

He'd had better days. After a sleepless night on his side of the bed, Jake had got dressed and caught a bus into town. Like always, he didn't get a seat. Like always, he'd struggled to get off because nobody wanted to move, and he'd almost missed his stop.

The security guard at Horizon Seeking Holidays didn't look up when he said good morning. So far, so normal. The bit where his world tilted came when he typed his password into his computer and an on-screen message flashed up to say he'd been locked out. He'd called the IT support desk, and two minutes later, Milly from HR had appeared and asked if they could have a quick chat.

'I understand how difficult things must be,' she'd said, sharing a sympathetic smile. 'So if you could follow me.'

Jake had sat opposite Milly and his line manager, Simon, in a tiny meeting room and listened as they told him how sorry they both were to hear about Tom. Milly had quoted an article she'd read just that morning about the stages of grief and assured him it was fine if he wanted to cry. Jake had told them both that he was fine and just wanted to keep busy. That had been the point where Milly's smile tightened.

'The team here want to offer maximum support,' she'd said. 'So we've jiggled the rotas to allow you to take ten days' compassionate leave.'

'But I don't want...'

'It would help departmental budgets if you could take this out of your annual leave.'

Jake had just nodded.

'We're also able to offer you unpaid leave on this occasion. Obviously, it's not policy, but if it would help...'

'So I'm being told to go home. Told to rest and get better. But you'd rather not pay me while that happens?'

There was an awkward silence. Milly's smile froze.

'You would retain all other benefits,' she said. 'You should take advantage, Jake. Use your staff discount and book a last-minute holiday. Get some sun on your face.'

'Am I looking pale or something?'

She didn't answer. Simon just nodded.

The room had been too small to flounce with any hint of drama. Instead, he'd thanked them both for being so incredibly understanding.

```
EXT. 'RAVENSWOOD' - DAY
A large house set back from the road.
A brass nameplate reveals the house to
be named 'Ravenswood'. Two recent
model SUVs are parked on a gravel
driveway. One red, one black. There is
a small, artificial lawn, unnaturally
green.
```

Rona lived in an imposing Edwardian townhouse in Edgbaston, one of Birmingham's most affluent suburbs. It didn't have a number; it had a name—Ravenswood—a nod to Edgar Allan Poe. Her husband was something to do with a satellite wing of some US megachurch. Jake had always thought it dodgy. Tom insisted they were good people. Deep down.

Signs attached to each lamp post advertised Neighbourhood Watch. Ring doorbells recorded every move. Jake had chosen not to call ahead, figuring he should just turn up if he wanted to appeal to this rumoured better side. He'd knocked twice before someone appeared on the other side of frosted glass.

Rona's husband, Harry, answered the door, tall and lean, with eyes that never stopped darting, transmitting concern. 'Jake. What brings you here?'

'I want to talk to Rona.' He tried to keep his tone calm and measured. 'Is she in?'

In the hallway, shoes were scattered, a child's drawing lay abandoned on the floor, unopened letters teetered on a marble side table. A faint whiff of stale milk lingered. Harry offered a closed-mouth smile and muttered something about it being the school holidays, adding that the church was running a playgroup.

He nodded towards where a coat hung from a half-open door. 'Rona is through there.'

Jake stepped into the living room, where Tom's sister perched on the edge of a bottle-green velvet couch, her posture rigid. She wore a simple grey cardigan over a striped, blue top and baggy jeans.

'What do you want?' Her voice was tired, lacking its usual bite.

She'd lost Tom too; he had to allow for that. 'I came to talk. About funeral arrangements.'

Rona's face flashed anger and exhaustion. 'Matters are in hand.'

'I'll help with the planning. Tom had friends—'

'We've taken a decision to restrict the funeral to immediate family.'

Jake had expected this and had words ready. 'I'm not asking to give a eulogy or anything. But we were together for six years. I loved him. His friends loved him. We all deserve to grieve.'

Her eyes narrowed into sharp slits. 'You swooped in and stole my brother when he was at his lowest ebb. He was engaged to Amelia. They'd just lost their baby.'

He wanted to scream. This all-too-simple version of Tom's life got trotted out too often. Tom had been engaged to Amelia, but only because he'd got drunk and somehow ended up in bed with her in the middle of what he called his questioning period. Amelia had miscarried six months in. Things took a turn, and Tom accepted their relationship was over. It wasn't the cleanest or kindest of breaks. Rocks were flung, but Jake wasn't a part of that. He'd met Tom five weeks after the engagement ended.

Harry appeared at the sitting room door. 'Rona, darling, perhaps we should all sit down and—'

She shifted around to stare through the window, fixing her

gaze on something outside. 'I want him out. Out of Tom's flat. Out of our lives.'

How come Rona, a woman whose approval he never sought, still had it in her to make him feel inferior? Tom had never defended his sister, saying she was the way she was because she always got whatever she asked for as a kid, and anyone who dared refuse endured wailing sulks and public meltdowns.

'I know you're hurting,' Jake said. 'But so am I.'

Rona's composure crumbled. 'You don't know how hurt feels. You have no idea what you suffocating my dear brother has done to our family. To me.'

For one startling moment, he saw beyond her anger to the pain beneath.

'All I'm asking for is closure.' A lump formed in his throat. No matter what, he wouldn't cry in front of this woman. She wasn't going to get to see how she'd made him hurt, how much more misery she'd added to an already unstable stack of sadness.

Rona got to her feet and walked over to the doors that led out into the garden.

'I've been polite,' she said, without looking around. 'I've listened. Now I'd very much appreciate it if you'd return the honour and leave.'

His hand in his pocket found a photograph. One he'd brought along, intending it as a peace offering. A picture of Rona and Tom together in Cannon Hill Park, taken years before he'd known either of them. His fingers folded the picture in two, then into four, then his fist balled around it.

'I'll see myself out,' he said. 'You have my phone number.'

INT. JAKE AND TOM'S FLAT - DAY

Two days had passed since Jake tried and failed to appeal to

Rona's basic human decency. But he was coping. The woman he'd spoken to at Citizen's Advice confirmed what Emma found online: Rona couldn't just turn up, tell him to leave, and change the locks.

Saturday had started out wrong. Tom and Jake always had a lie-in at the weekend, then Tom would do the big shop while Jake cleaned the flat. Evenings were spent on a rota—either chez Emma and Chris, Fred and Stu, or in their flat. Lucy never hosted because she lived in a show home, and her nerves weren't up to red wine being anywhere near her cream sofa. Tonight, Emma was hosting. Chris had bought a gas barbecue the size of a small car and wanted to show it off. Jake had claimed a headache.

Still wearing yesterday's shirt and a pair of Tom's jogging pants, he'd avoided his neighbours by waiting until he was sure everyone was out before hurrying downstairs to grab the morning's post. Back within four walls, he threw out the junk mail and set aside a bill from Tom's dentist. He'd pay online. That just left a letter addressed to him, stamped *Private* and postmarked Birmingham; the neat-and-tidy typeface behind a plastic window suggested bad news. He set it down, filled the kettle, and made tea.

Jake scouted around for laundry, gathering discarded socks and used-once tea towels. He sprayed the bath and spent ten minutes scrubbing at a soap stain, before mopping the grey-tiled floor and squirting half a bottle of Domestos around the toilet bowl. He hunted high and low for a feather duster Tom had bought as a joke Christmas present and used it to rid the flat of every cobweb. He fluffed cushions on the sofa and fanned magazines on the coffee table.

And then he read the letter.

His heart had hoped for the best.

His heart was disappointed.

Nigel Harrington of Harrington, Thorne, and Partners was acting on behalf of Mrs Rona Staples, sister of the late Thomas Carter.

The letter used simple words, the kind used to explain to a child that their favourite pet had gone to live on a farm. Tom had died intestate. This meant he hadn't made a will. With his mother deceased and his father missing, presumed dead, this made Rona next of kin—the rightful heir to Tom's estate, and that included their flat. The letter acknowledged this as a difficult time but stressed a need to address matters. It made no mention of probate, serving up the future as a fait accompli.

He'd jumped up, pacing the room, trying to stay calm. How could she do that? To him. To the man her brother had loved. Their combined life lay scattered throughout that flat in cupboards, drawers, boxes, and bags. He reached for a framed photograph, taken on the beach at Weston Super Mare on the day Tom had first said he loved him.

'Dear Mr Harrington,' Jake dictated his reply to Rona's solicitor, holding the photograph close to his chest. 'Thank you for your recent letter. Please convey my best wishes to Rona Staples and let her know she can go fuck herself.'

He needed company and turned on the TV.

Far-right mobs had clashed with anti-racist demonstrations. Jake's hand hovered over the channel button. Tom would have been glued to this, ranting about the dangers of extremism. But without him, Jake felt adrift in a world that seemed so much larger and more threatening.

Jake texted Emma. He'd spent too much time alone.

INT. EMMA AND CHRIS'S HOUSE - DAY
A modern family home, equipped with
modern, flatpack furniture, and high-
end items of home decor.

When Lucy answered the door, she pulled him into a hug. He'd struggled free, handed her the bottle of red he'd bought en route, and assured her he was doing just fine.

'Where are the kids?' he asked, noticing a lack of screaming from the garden. Annie Lennox was playing on networked Sonos speakers: *Walking on Broken Glass*.

Lucy shrugged. 'Sleeping over with a neighbour. I thought you weren't coming.'

'Popped a pill, and... ta-dah.' He tried for jazz hands.

He followed her out into the garden, where Fred and Emma greeted him like those faithful dogs you see on YouTube videos greeting super-buff marines returning from war zones. He was handed a beer and told to sit. They had questions.

Emma, Lucy, and Fred formed a semicircle around Jake, their faces a mix of concern and curiosity as he ran through the contents of Rona's solicitor's letter.

'If she's lawyered up, you need to do the same,' Emma said.

'They're snakes,' Lucy agreed. 'You should talk to the one my father uses.'

Fred, ever the problem-solver, sat up straighter in his chair. 'Stu knows a brilliant lawyer. I'll have him text you a number.'

Jake stared at the ground, cradling a can of Heineken. The stubble on his chin spoke of days without shaving. 'Do you think it might be easier to move out and mail her the keys?'

'Mate, are you joking?'

'It's just a bunch of rooms. I can't be there without Tom. It's too full of memories.'

Fred shook his head, and Jake could sense that it wasn't in

disagreement. 'If you let the Wicked Witch of the West have her way, she'll sell the flat and move on. And all those memories just disappear.'

Jake swallowed. 'That won't happen.'

'It might.' Fred reached for his hand. 'Why would you even risk that?'

'Grub's up.' Chris had been toiling over his barbecue, flipping burgers, posing like an Ibiza DJ. 'Form an orderly queue.'

Emma glanced around. 'Insist it's the best you ever had. And not at all as if some heavy-handed pillock added too much salt to the minced beef.'

In the garden, the twins sat in folding chairs, staring at screens, radiating irritation.

'Their friends have gone ice skating,' Emma explained. 'We're officially ruining their lives.'

Chris presented Jake with what looked like a lump of spent charcoal in a bread roll. He wandered over to where Fred sat watching a blackbird hammer all hell out of what used to be a snail.

'Rona will come around,' Fred said. 'Right now, she's in pain. Call her in a few days and suggest meeting up. Somewhere neutral.'

He snorted. 'Like Switzerland. Perhaps at a place where you book a room to end your life. She'd pay decent money to shut me up.'

Fred's smile burned lukewarm. 'I was thinking a branch of Costa, but you do you.'

Jake looked over to where Lucy had cornered Emma and was paging through photos on her phone. She'd thrown herself into wedding planning to the point it had become her sole topic of conversation—one they'd all agreed to endure on a strict rota. Fred revealed that yesterday she'd called him seventeen times. Her fancy London florist struck out sourcing Himalayan blue poppies.

'Am I turning into her?' Jake said.

Fred grinned. 'You've always had child-bearing hips, but otherwise, I think you're OK.'

'Am I becoming a stuck record. Are you guys taking it in turns to let me talk about Tom?'

'For fuck's sake, man, you lost the most important thing in your life. It's not the same at all. Grief isn't linear. You don't work through it in a few days and then you're cool.' He stashed his half-eaten burger behind a wooden planter. 'Grief creeps up and jumps out when you least expect it. When Stu's sister died, his brother tried to cut everyone out of the will. That solicitor I mentioned... he's good, Jake. He sorted everything.'

'Was he... expensive?' Jake hated having to ask, but Stu had once hired a helicopter and flown Fred to a private island for dinner. On a random Tuesday.

'Let us worry about the money side of things.'

'Don't treat me like a charity case.'

'That's not what I'm saying, but the guy works for Stu all the time. He'll cut you a deal.'

Jake took a swig of beer. 'There's so much noise right now. All I want is for everyone to stop talking and let me catch up.'

Fred pulled out his mobile. The very latest iPhone in a shiny black rubber case. 'OK, hear me out on this. And again, this isn't charity. But I got talking to the head of merch at Harvey Nicks and he told me about this place...'

'Do they offer unlimited diazepam?'

'They serve lentils. And homemade rhubarb wine. It's a silent retreat.'

Jake raised an eyebrow. 'Not one of those happy-clappy places where they hand around the talking stick, and make you hug trees?'

'Do you want to hear more, or...'

'Sorry, ignore me. That's the non-linear grief speaking.'

'Serenity Retreat is in Clent, so not a million miles away. You can get a taxi. The Harvey Nicks guy said it changed his life.'

'For the better?'

'OK, it's had a few shitty reviews. He reckons the owners have upset the neighbours, so they need more customers and improved ratings. Hence the low-cost, one-time offers.'

'I'd score a free room for saying the place is brilliant. Isn't that fraud?'

Fred groaned to himself. 'I'm telling you about a free holiday, and you're finding fault.'

Emma came to sit on the ground. 'You two look to be plotting something. If it involves gagging Lucy and having her left in a field to find her own way home, can I be in on it?'

'What was it this time?' Jake asked.

'She wants all the bridal party to wear pink. Blancmange pink. Because she's seen it in one of her bloody magazines and it looked *oh so incredible.*'

Fred handed Jake his phone. 'This is the place.'

He squinted at a stock photo of a serene lake at sunset, overlaid with a slogan about finding your inner peace. The Serenity Retreat promised holistic healing and mindful living.

'The chef used to work for Gordon Ramsay,' Fred said with a small grin. 'So at least the lentils will be cooked right.'

Jake scrolled further. 'Are you sure it's legit? The website is sort of basic.'

Fred raised his eyebrows. 'Places like this don't need flashy graphics. Besides, I read the reviews—most of them are good. You'll always get one moaning Mary saying it caused their slipped disc.'

Jake mumbled an apology, rubbing the back of his neck.

Fred waved it off. 'No stress, mate. Just trying to help.'

Emma shifted closer. 'When was the last time you got a proper night's sleep, Jakey? I mean, a solid eight hours?'

He opened his mouth, then closed it, realising he couldn't remember. The days had blended into one enormous blob of guilt and misery. A memory surfaced, of Tom laughing in the kitchen, flour on his nose, trying to bake a birthday cake. His chest tightened.

'I don't know what to do,' he said. 'It's like I'm drowning.'

Fred rested a hand on Jake's shoulder, his voice steady and sincere. 'This retreat might not be a magic fix, but it's a place to breathe and rest. And you deserve that.'

He dared himself to look at the website again. *Silence is Golden,* it said across the photograph of a middle-aged woman in skin-tight lycra, her smile beatific.

The other good thing about silence was he might get a break from the guilt that still roared in his ears.

INT. JAKE AND TOM'S FLAT – NIGHT

Save for the glow of Jake's laptop screen, the flat was shrouded in darkness. Jake sat on the sofa, the leather creaking with each movement. The silence had become oppressive, broken only by the soft hum of the refrigerator and the occasional creak of settling pipes. Tom being nowhere had made him show up everywhere. His favourite mug sat washed-up on the drainer, waiting for him to ask for tea. The book he'd been reading was hidden behind a cushion. A bundled pair of socks waited to be picked up from the bathroom floor.

Jake had got home just before midnight, taken a shower, and then changed into an old T-shirt. When he rummaged under the bed for slippers, he'd pulled out the anti-fascist march leaflet. Perhaps there would be another one soon. Maybe more local. He could go. And prove Tom wrong. He *was* politically motivated.

His fingers hovered over the laptop keyboard before hitting *enter* on a search page, taking calm, even breaths as the results loaded. A news alert caught his eye: *'Far-right group True North gains traction in Canada.'* Jake's thumb hovered over the link, and he found himself thinking of Lucy. Her new man lived near Toronto. The report detailed a targeted shooting in Markham, a suburban area, home to Southeast Asian communities. Without Tom's voice in his ear, Jake felt disconnected from the world beyond.

Outside, a car alarm blared, its shrill wail cutting through the night. Jake flinched, his nerves frayed. He rubbed gritty eyes, blinking back tears. More than anything, he wanted to call Rona, to try one more time to make her understand. But it was late. And she'd just spew venom and blame.

'I'm trying,' he whispered to nobody. 'I'm doing my best here.'

Nervous as all hell, he reached for his phone. He couldn't stay in the flat for one more night. The bed was too empty. Everything was too empty.

No matter the time, he knew his mum would pick up the phone. The line rang twice before her sleepy voice answered.

'Jake, love. Is everything alright?'

'Mum, I think I need to come home for a bit. Just until I figure things out.'

He could picture her sitting up in bed, half-awake, his father snoring next to her.

'Of course, love,' she said. 'Your room's always here for you.'

A weight lifted as his mind then drifted to Fred's offer of the silent retreat. The idea of being in a place where he wouldn't have to explain or justify this all-consuming grief. Maybe there, in the quiet, he could make sense of this chaos in his head.

'I need to go somewhere first for a few days,' he said, 'but is it OK if I bring my stuff over tomorrow?'

'I'm doing a roast.' Her voice was warm with love and relief. 'Just make sure you arrive hungry.'

After making a promise to bring a bottle of wine, he sank back into the plush sofa, his gaze fixated on the intricate patterns of the ceiling. The thought of leaving this flat—their shared space—weighed heavy on his mind. But for the first time, a glimmer of hope peeked through the cracks in his heart.

INT. 16 HAVERCROFT LANE – DAY

Pale morning light filtered through faded *Star Wars* curtains. Jake lay on a too-small bed, both feet dangling off the edge, staring up at the ceiling where gold and silver stars had long since lost their ability to glow in the dark.

From downstairs, the sound of the television blared. His mother clattered pans. His dad called to her to come see something.

Jake remembered being eighteen, ready to spread his wings and fly the nest for university. He recalled packing a borrowed holdall with all the things he would need in halls, along with all the little extras his mother had added in—toothpaste, a towel, antibacterial cream for his runaway acne. How he missed that version of himself: an innocent about to have his heart broken by a succession of men, before finding one he could love.

Emma sent a checking-in text.

EMMA HOPE

Here when you need me 🩶

He started a reply. Hit delete. Started another, and made do with a thumbs up.

His mum knocked. 'We're having sausage sandwiches for breakfast, love. Do you still prefer brown sauce?'

'Yeah, please. I'll be down in a minute.'

The floorboards creaked as she made her way back downstairs. Jake glanced in the dressing table mirror. God, but he looked old.

EXT. 16 HAVERCROFT LANE - DAY
A quiet suburban residential street,
with cars parked bumper-to-bumper.

Another grey day dawned in a summer of miserable grey days. The news had only added to the sense of gloom, with reports of more unrest—this time in Leicester and Stoke. The cancer taking hold of the country was getting closer.

Across the road, Mr Sudhindra mowed his lawn, raising a hand in greeting.

'The old sod never misses a trick,' Jake's mum muttered, before waving back. 'He'll have told everyone about you moving back by lunchtime.'

Mr and Mrs Sudhindra had a reputation for gossip. And yet you never saw them together. Like the figures on an old-fashioned clock, when one stepped out of their house, the other went in.

Jake picked up his bag, shading his eyes. The taxi was late.

'Are you sure you've packed enough underwear?' His mum fussed, adjusting the collar of his shirt for the umpteenth time. 'And don't forget to call us when you get there.'

He managed a small smile. 'I'm going to a silent retreat, not joining the foreign legion. They might not even allow phone calls.'

She glanced at his dad, who cleared his throat, shifting from foot to foot. 'Son, I know I'm not great with... words and feelings and all that. But I'm proud of you for doing this. For trying to... you know.'

'Thanks, Dad,' Jake said, surprised at the lump that formed in his throat. 'And even if I can't call you, I'll text.'

His mum launched into another round of last-minute instructions, bag checks, and worries—did he have tissues? Did he want a normal toothbrush in case there was nowhere to charge his electric one? Was he certain she couldn't make him a sandwich for the journey?

The journey was eight miles as even the most misguided crow might fly. He was sure he'd survive without food.

He knelt to check the zipper on a side pocket of the bag. It was where he'd put a letter written in the small hours, addressed to Rona and Harry Staples. He still wasn't sure if he'd ever get around to sending it. Maybe after the retreat, when he'd had time to clear his head.

His phone buzzed—a text from Fred. Just two hearts. Animated. Breathing.

A car pulled up outside. It was time to go, and Jake couldn't swallow how heavy the sorrow became.

'I will be OK,' he said, more to himself than to his mum and dad.

A sleek black car pulled up, out of place among a street of family sedans and silver SUVs.

'Your chariot awaits, love,' his mum's voice wavered.

Jake hesitated, looking around at the street where he'd grown up, at the houses where he'd called on friends. What he wouldn't give for a time machine.

'Go on, son,' his dad whispered. 'It'll all still be here when you get back.'

He nodded. Because it would be.

Hugs were exchanged, promises to call were made, and before he knew it, Jake was settling into the back seat. As the taxi pulled away, his parents grew smaller through the rear window—his mum waving, his dad's arm around her shoulders. The image blurred as tears took over.

Was this a huge mistake? Or the best idea ever? Would it be all yoga and wheatgrass smoothies, or would he find the peace he craved? Perhaps he might even make a friend. The place must surely be a magnet for broken souls.

He pulled out his phone, needing a distraction, anything to numb his thoughts. BBC News drummed a constant beat of doom and gloom. *The Guardian* carried a checklist of what to do first should the 'three-minute warning' sound—the gist of it being shag anyone and everyone. A breaking news story exposed far-right activities in a US megachurch.

Jake tapped on the headline and frowned. The name of the church was familiar. *Too* familiar.

The Covenant Light Fellowship claimed to stand for faith, unity, prosperity, and traditional values. These values seemed to revolve around the burning of books and tearing down anything that didn't fit with their rigid worldview.

There was a photograph of a building Jake knew, because he'd been there once with Tom. To anyone else, it was a detached Edwardian villa, set back from a leafy, tree-lined road. To Jake, it was home to Rona Staples. The woman who blamed him for everything.

A chill ran down his spine.

He refreshed the screen, and the story updated. A video clip showed Rona's lanky husband, his face like a slapped arse, shaking hands with a prominent American evangelical leader, the connection unmistakable.

FADE TO BLACK

vicky

FADE IN
INT. BIRMINGHAM OFFICE - DAY
SUPER: '31 JULY 2024'
VICKY sits at a glass desk, staring at
her computer screen. Birmingham City
Centre high-rises line up on the other
side of the floor-to-ceiling windows.

A faint hum from the air-conditioning filled the pristine office. Even though Vicky liked to keep her door closed, she could still make out the eager chatter from the communal kitchen, where her presence was required at 11AM.

The door remained shut not because she was working on state secrets or because she needed to focus. Vicky just didn't see herself as a people person. She showed up, did her job, often burning the midnight oil, but when her chores were over, she vanished. Vicky was never one for *Friday Night Drinks* at the nearest bar serving bottomless jugs of something sweet and toxic. She drew a line: Victoria Harper, Senior Partner at

Walker, Haynes & Dobson, was efficient and precise. Vicky Harper, fumbling and stumbling her way through life, was someone else entirely.

At two minutes after eleven, there was a knock. Someone she sort of recognised smiled, apologised for interrupting, but reminded her she'd agreed to say a few words to mark a 60th birthday. Vicky was, after all, the senior partner in family and property law.

'Gosh,' she said, blinking in mock surprise and checking a watch she shouldn't have bought because it cost a month's wages, but all the senior partners seemed to have one, so she'd put it on a card. 'Is it that time already?'

Over five and a bit years, she had perfected the charade: smiling on cue, nodding at the right moments, ensuring people believed she knew the names of everyone working on the 23rd floor.

She adjusted her silk scarf, a sartorial quirk born from a lifetime of hiding. 'Let me just hit send on this email, and I'm all yours.'

```
INT. WALKER, HAYNES & DOBSON - DAY
A sleek, modern communal kitchen.
Stainless steel appliances, marble
countertops, and large windows show-
casing the cityscape.
```

Vicky plastered on a smile as she stepped into the kitchen area, her stomach twisting at the sight of small-talking colleagues gathered around an oversized cake. Her self-curated Ice Queen reputation meant she could make do with nodded greetings and avoid the casual chit-chat.

'Right then.' She clapped for attention, wondering if that made her look and sound like a frazzled geography teacher shepherding kids on a school field trip. 'As a senior partner, it falls to me to say a few words about our birthday girl.'

Everyone stopped talking, as if she'd called for fingers on lips.

'Carol is a true superstar.' She prayed that was the right name.

A voice chimed in, '25 years with us.'

'Indeed.' Vicky nodded. 'A quarter-century of dedication. That's remarkable, isn't it? An absolute grafter.'

She paused, hoping that someone might chime in to support her over-egged statement. No such luck. Ten pairs of eyes locked onto hers.

'Carol...' She scanned the kitchen area, short on inspiration. 'Carol is like that... ficus plant.' Heads turned. 'That lovely green plant is always present, always... growing. Figuratively speaking. Just like how Carol's knowledge branches out into all areas of our practice.'

Vicky winced. She was rambling, talking absolute crap. Carol was a ficus. Was that the best she could manage? She had a law degree. Three times a week, she argued for often morally bankrupt people to win sole possession of a house, hamster, or child. Words were supposed to be her superpower.

'Let's raise our glasses... or coffee cups to Carol. Here's to another 25 years. Or however long you plan to stay with us. Because, I mean, that would be fifty years, wouldn't it? And I don't know how old you are, but...'

She trailed off as the cake appeared, contemplating whether to break her rule about keeping work and life separate. Maybe she didn't always have to be the partner in the glass box.

Two associates gossiped by the water cooler.

'Did you see the new guy in Corporate Strategy?' one said. 'He's a technical wizard. I heard Tarquin say he's going to revolutionise how we handle data.'

She made a mental note to keep an eye out for this addition to the team, though she doubted their paths would cross much.

'I wouldn't say no to him handling my data,' the other one said.

They both laughed.

Was that kind of friendship too much to want? Vicky wondered, then looked away. She'd been staring, consumed by wonder, wishing she had someone like that in her life. There was Jenny at the Outreach Centre where she volunteered once a week. Pleasant company, but not someone she truly knew. Vicky had lived in Birmingham for almost five years keeping everyone at arm's length.

Sick of trying to fit in, she made a beeline for her big glass desk in her little glass box. The money was good. She might make named partner next year.

Stick to the plan, Vicky. Keep your eye on the prize.

Quitting had never even been an option. Vicky would be paying a mortgage long after retirement after winning a fierce bidding war for a high-rise unit in what her estate agent had called a "sought-after" building. *Sought-after* being code for eye-watering service charges. A senior partner should own a yacht, not be facing a bill to strip and replace illegal cladding.

The confused kid from Brixton had dreamed of something different, something bigger. Something more beautiful.

```
INT. KELLETT ROAD - NIGHT
SUPER: '2002'
Brixton, London. A small, cluttered
bedroom with band posters on the
walls, a single bed, worn carpet.
```

The faint pounding of reggae music drifted through an open window, mingling with the distant thrum of traffic from Coldharbour Lane. Inside a modest terraced house, family photos lined the narrow hallway—glimpses of summer holidays and proud school moments.

Upstairs, behind a closed bedroom door, a Black teenage boy stood before a mirror. On his wall, he'd pinned posters of powerful women—athletes, politicians, activists. His fingers trembled, brushing against the curls of a shoulder-length wig, its texture picked to mimic his natural hair.

She was still trapped. Still hiding.

A sharp rat-a-tat caused him to startle.

'Vic?' His sister's voice carried a note of impatience. 'You gonna hurry? Dinner is ready.'

The boy removed the hairpiece, tucking it away in a drawer beneath socks before squaring his shoulders and turning to face the door.

'Coming,' he called out, his voice a touch higher than usual.

As he reached for the handle, he paused, casting a last, longing glance at a now-empty mirror. One day he would be her.

INT. VICKY'S OFFICE – DAY
SUPER: '31 JULY 2024'

A stack of files demanded Vicky's attention: a property tycoon trying to hide assets from his third wife, a celebrity chef embroiled in a bitter custody battle over three pedigree dogs, and a footballer desperate to keep an affair with her agent a secret from the tabloids.

She had thought that becoming a lawyer would be like being a superhero. She'd end crime, lock up all the bad guys, bring justice to town, and parade it through every dodgy office, shop, pub, and café. The truth turned out a little different. Law firms, political parties, corporations—they intertwined in a complex dance of power and influence. The stakes stayed high, and the lines between right and wrong often blurred.

She reached for her phone to call one of her oldest clients—Gerald Penrose, better known to viewers of the BBC's *One Show* as The Scambuster. He had demanded an air-tight prenup after hearing his daughter was marrying a man she'd met on holiday in Canada. His key concern was protecting the family home. Aldeburgh was a Grade I-listed manor house, surrounded by fields just south of Birmingham, and a recent valuation came in at six million.

'Lucy sees the good in everyone,' he'd told Vicky. 'Men take one look and see pound signs.'

When Vicky met Canadian Colin online, he struck her as standoffish. He'd insisted on sharing the screen with his mother —a woman exuding the icy charm of a blend between Anna Wintour and Cruella de Vil. The mere mention of a prenup caused her eyes to narrow, but not one word passed her lips during the twenty-minute call. Even through the pixelated Zoom display, Vicky could see how Colin had inherited his mother's prominent ears, though his had turned the colour of overripe tomatoes.

Every time Vicky spoke—which was all the time—he did this nervous thing where he pushed his glasses up then immediately adjusted his laptop screen, as if somehow that might minimise her presence.

Vicky had only ever once managed to actually speak to Lucy and struggled to understand how someone who'd sounded so full of life might fall for a gangly, awkward mummy's boy.

A pop-up message flashed on her laptop screen. She was two minutes late for the weekly partners' meeting.

```
INT. WALKER, HAYNES & DOBSON - DAY
A large, glass-walled conference room
with a view of Birmingham's skyline.
VICKY sits at a long mahogany table
with other partners.
```

Malcolm Sanderson tapped his pen on the table, demanding order for the weekly partners' meeting. Vicky was seated as far away from Malcolm as it was possible to get, a strategic choice born from experience of his wandering hands at office parties. Despite thinning, greasy grey hair and a paunch, Malcolm considered himself God's gift.

'Shall we run through our high-profile cases?' He turned to his right and signalled for Tarquin Walker to begin.

Vicky tuned out the boys' club. They used words like *wonga* and *bang to rights*. She was the only woman in the room and the only one who hadn't spent the eighties screwing over her best friends in the name of cool, hard cash. And then the *haw-haw* stopped. When she glanced up, she realised they were waiting for her to say something.

Willing herself not to let on that she'd been miles away, Vicky painted on a smile.

'I'm focused on the Penrose prenup this week,' she said, knowing the mere mention of The Scambuster would have them sitting up and paying attention. Gerald had become a hero to men of a certain age. 'My client is concerned about protecting significant assets from his daughter's new fiancé. And having met him online—'

Malcolm guffawed, cutting her off mid-flow. 'Classic Penrose. Knows how to handle the female of the species.'

Vicky, remembering the struggles that had earned her a seat at the top table, felt obliged to hold her tongue, though she was dying inside. 'My role is to draft an agreement that's fair to both parties.'

'Just make sure you don't go soft on the old boy, Vic,' Tarquin chimed in, always insisting on using the name she'd left behind. Not because he knew—he shortened everyone's name to a single syllable, as if he didn't have room in his head for anything more.

Malcolm tidied a pile of papers he'd not so much as glanced at. 'Penrose has had his fair share of favours from the firm. Keep an eye on those billable hours.'

She nodded and stared down at her own notes. Words began to swim. 'I do have several other cases, if you want—'

Tarquin rose to his feet. 'Don't know about the rest of you rum buggers, but I have a lunch date with a pretty little filly. As much fun as this has been, I can't waste my time listening to you lot waving around your collective dicks.'

As he left, his hand lingered on Vicky's shoulder, managing the smallest of squeezes. Her jaw clenched, but still she smiled.

```
INT. LONDON COCKTAIL BAR - NIGHT
SUPER: 'AUGUST 2021'
An ultra-chic cocktail bar in the
heart of Soho. Exposed brick walls
contrast with sleek, modern furnish-
ings. Low-hanging Edison bulbs cast a
warm glow over intimate booths.
```

Ice clinked as the indistinct murmur of shiny, happy people filled the low-lit bar. Vicky traced the condensation running down her cocktail glass.

'I'm old school, Miss Harper.' Tarquin Walker had clicked his fingers to signal for refills. She hadn't even touched her drink. 'I have to ask, why a pretty face like yours chooses to waste her time helping spongers and freeloaders? You're slumming it in that dingy little law centre. I'm offering you a chance to make something of yourself, earn real money. Mix with the people who matter.'

Vicky clenched the fingers of one hand, day-old bright red acrylics digging into her palm. The Brixton Community Legal Aid Centre had become her life. Although the pay was crap, she knew that her work made a difference. The big-city law firms had swallowed up everyone else from her year. People she once thought of as slackers were spending their days helping the already rich get richer. And word was out: the centre was likely to suffer a funding cut. She needed a Plan B.

Tarquin Walker was, in fact, Plan C. The less said about B, the better.

'Wouldn't working for a big firm mean selling my soul?' she asked, making the question sound like a tease, even though she was deadly serious.

'I have to disagree with how you characterise working for a major practice.' He fixed her with bright button eyes. 'You would be amplifying your impact. Imagine the resources at your fingertips. The reach. Why settle for a single note when you could be up front, conducting the entire orchestra?'

She'd already met with two named partners at big-city practices, but Tarquin Walker was different. For one thing, the job on offer would mean shifting her life out of London. But Birmingham wasn't the other side of the world.

'I need a few days to think through the practicalities,' she told him.

Unlike the other two men who'd wined and dined her on their company cards, Tarquin hadn't been staring at her tits. He didn't make veiled suggestions they go somewhere private. Tarquin Walker talked as if he actually wanted her to work for him.

'I suppose it's the thought of leaving London behind,' he'd said, raising an eyebrow, and for the first time, his smile appeared genuine. 'And that, I'm afraid, Miss Harper, is the one thing beyond my control. Birmingham is our home. You would be expected to relocate.'

Vicky had been living in a rented room, little bigger than a walk-in wardrobe, with her best mate from college Mia. And that had been fine at first. Fun even. But Mia had begun moving in different circles.

'Change is good,' she said without thinking. 'I've lived here all my life. Who's to say Birmingham isn't my city?'

Walker laughed. 'Perhaps you should come for a little visit before making any further sweeping statements.'

'Would I have scope to take on pro bono work?' she asked.

He all but spat out his Old Fashioned. 'Goodness me, no. Why would you bother with that? In our world, we move mountains, not pebbles.'

She managed a small, humourless laugh. 'What a poetic metaphor, Mr Walker.'

He snorted. 'I prefer my friends to call me Tarquin.'

Vicky knew right then that she would never be his friend, nor would she ever use his first name. Who calls their kid Tarquin, anyway? Entitled, middle-class white people, that's who. Walker sat back, giving her space, allowing her a chance to get up and leave. What he didn't know was she'd already decided.

'When will you need my answer?'

He shrugged. 'The offer stays on the table for ten days, but after that, I'll recast my line. We need someone in role by September.'

It was July, and London had been in the middle of a heatwave. She loved walking home after work, past cafés and bars where drinkers spilled onto street corners. Windows stayed open. Music played. Post-pandemic, free of masks, people smiled again. And it had only served to make her realise just how lonely she'd let herself get.

Moving to Birmingham would mean jumping from a sinking ship.

'I'll take the job,' she said.

'Just like that?'

Vicky smiled. 'Just like that.'

```
INT. LGBTQ+ OUTREACH CENTRE - DAY
SUPER: '31 JULY 2024'
A modest, worn-but-welcoming space
that's seen better days. Mismatched
furniture fills the main area, with
faded posters promoting inclusivity
and support services lining the walls.
Fluorescent lights flicker overhead,
casting a harsh glow on the scuffed
linoleum floor.
```

Vicky rubbed dry eyes, her head banging from yet another twelve-hour day of dealing with well-heeled clients convinced that throwing money at any problem would make it disappear.

The sharp scent of cheap disinfectant mingled with the earthy aroma of fair-trade coffee from an ancient machine bolted to a charity shop table. Vicky shared a rickety desk with Jenny, the closest thing she had to a friend. Four and a bit years in Birmingham, and the only constant in her life was the lonely echo of overpriced designer heels clicking through an empty flat. She'd tried speed dating and pottery classes, but neither yielded much. She ate pasta with a man whose name she kept forgetting and spent a sweaty afternoon on a climbing wall with another who had their lives planned out in unsettling detail—

and a pink ashtray that resembled something Grayson Perry might flog to the British Museum to keep him in fags. Friends remained elusive.

Jenny was a tireless volunteer who lived on her nerves and energy drinks. Tonight she wore a baggy *My Body My Choice* T-shirt and cargo shorts.

'We're screwed.' She looked up from an ancient laptop balanced on her knees. 'Might as well hang up the closed sign.'

Vicky put down the case file she'd been studying. 'Show me the email.'

Jenny handed her the laptop. 'Don't be fooled by the bit about hoping to continue working together. They're letting this place to a chain that runs gastropubs.'

The email was addressed to Jenny and came from the head of the community micro-fund they'd sourced after Birmingham City Council declared bankruptcy. Jenny fiddled with a friendship bangle.

Vicky read the last paragraph twice more, to be sure she hadn't misunderstood.

'It says here that they'll continue to pay whatever they can to support the centre,' she said. 'That's good, isn't it?'

Jenny held out a handwritten note from their landlord, citing the cost-of-living crisis and soaring fuel bills. Vicky's eyes fixed on a huge number at the bottom of the page. 'He can't just double the rent. Any increase must be reasonable and in line with market rates. I'll draft a reply.'

'We've had a fair run. What's the point fighting?'

In her heart, Vicky knew Jenny was right. She could try quoting equality legislation. She could appeal to their landlord's better nature, but when push came to shove, they'd survived for years on a peppercorn rent, thanks to council funding. The owners were well within their rights to hoick it up.

What the centre needed was a reliable benefactor. Someone with money to spare.

An idea landed.

'I might be able to fix this.' Vicky crossed her fingers under the desk. 'One of my clients... He's rich and...'

Was she aiming too high? Penrose was a teddy bear of a man, but cut-throat with it. She didn't intend to ask him for cash; rather, she would mine his knowledge of where household name investors buried their bodies. Vicky knew he'd share the names of anyone on the council who could loosen tight purse strings.

INT. VICKY'S OFFICE – DAY
SUPER: '1 AUGUST 2024'

As Vicky sank into her office chair, the leather creaked, cool against her back, and she let out a noise somewhere between a sigh and a shameful groan. Her phone blinked with a missed call. And a message. She hit play.

'Vicky Harper.' Whoever it was sounded to be using some sort of voice-altering device. 'Stop sticking your pretty little nose where it's not needed.'

Her breath caught. She'd seen people get this kind of threat in films and TV shows, but surely low-rent criminals had moved on from trying to scare people by impersonating a Dalek. And where was she sticking her nose, anyway? If the plan was to threaten someone, think it through. Be specific. She played it again.

Great. Just what she needed.

Though honestly, with what she'd been handling lately, it could be anyone. Walker, Haynes & Dobson's latest marketing brainwave had made sure of that. Some bright spark in Brand Strategy and Growth had launched an online campaign aimed at victims of intimidation, inviting them to "reclaim their peace of mind." The linked website offered clear information on legal options, which meant she'd moved from juggling cases of men hiding assets from ex-wives to pit bull custody battles. Not that she was a snob. She'd been brought up to know the value of money. But there had been two in-office fist fights in the past month alone.

Her mobile vibrated, snapping her into the here and now. It was Penrose, returning her call. She needed to pull herself together.

'Harper, I received your email.' Traffic sounds suggested he was outside. 'When you say you're looking for people in the market for an ethical investment, am I to take it you want me to introduce you to grimy underworld gangsters?'

She took a sip of water. 'It's easier if I come see you.'

'Can this wait? I'm on my way to board a train.'

'When are you back?'

'Tuesday.'

It was Thursday. Could she bottle this up for five whole days? What choice did she have? 'Right, fine. Can I book you for first thing when you get back?'

'What? Sorry. You'll have to speak up, Harper. Did you say you're under attack?'

She might as well be. 'I'll bring a draft of the prenup.'

'Jolly good show, Harper.' The sound muffled, and he seemed to be talking to someone. 'Does this mean you've spoken to my daughter?'

'She's called. A few times.'

'But have you spoken to her?'

Vicky hesitated, choosing her words with care. 'I've attempted to reach out to Lucy, but she seems... reluctant to discuss the prenup.'

Penrose snorted. 'Lucy has always been headstrong. But this

isn't only about protecting my assets, Harper. It's about safeguarding her future.'

Vicky tried to ignore a familiar twinge of discomfort. She understood his concerns but couldn't shake the feeling that there was more to this story. She took a breath—should she mention Canadian Colin's mother? 'When I talked to the fiancé—'

'Harper.' Penrose cut her off, his tone sharpening. 'I've been in this game a long time and seen decent people taken advantage of. I won't let that happen to Lucy. Don't worry about the logistics. I have friends in high places. One call from me, and doors will open. Or close, if need be.'

Vicky bit back her retort. She knew better than to argue with a client, especially one as savvy as Gerald Penrose.

'I understand,' she said. 'I'll do my best to draft a fair and comprehensive agreement.'

She turned to stare out across the city centre. It had been a rare blue sky morning, bringing everyone out in crop tops and T-shirts. Men with pale white legs wore shorts. She ought to be outside, breathing in the summer, not locked away in an air-conditioned box.

'Tuesday morning,' Penrose said. 'And after you've proven to me I'm not paying good money for nothing, I'll treat you to lunch. You always seem as if you could use a hot meal inside you. Young girls these days are all skin and bone.'

Anyone else might have taken offence, but Vicky knew he meant well. And she had lost weight. Not intentionally, but just the other day she dared herself to fit into a beloved pair of jeans long since consigned to her "never again" pile. And she'd done up the buttons. With room to spare. Sleepless nights swapped for solo sessions at the company gym were starting to pay dividends.

A click ended the call, and her laptop pinged with a notification of new content on the Walker, Haynes & Dobson intranet. Had Don Haynes finally announced his retirement? Was the worst-kept secret out?

It was an email from Emmaleigh, leader of the Inclusive Culture and Transformation Team. She was invited to join them on the company float in Birmingham's upcoming Pride parade. Vicky got this all the time. Being Black and trans, she ticked two boxes on the must-have form. The sender had requested a read receipt. She hit *deny*.

She scrolled through her morning emails, drawn to a last-minute offer from someone no longer able to take up their place at a silent retreat.

Three nights away from everyone and everything. Space to breathe. Space to think. A space where she could avoid having to talk to anyone. All for three hundred quid. Three nights to decide how to decline Emmaleigh's offer. Without telling her to go fuck herself.

```
INT. LONDON STUDIO FLAT - NIGHT
SUPER: 'JUNE 2021'
A cramped but smart flat. Everything
is in one room, with two single beds
partitioned by a double wardrobe set
into an alcove. The kitchen-diner is
along the far wall. There's a futon
sofa under the single window. A door
leads to a small bathroom.
```

Vicky sat cross-legged on the floor, surrounded by stacks of papers from the Legal Aid Centre. She absently twirled a lock of hair that was overdue for a cut around her finger. The door burst open, and Mia breezed in, her designer handbag swinging.

'Hi honey, I'm home,' she said, kicking off her beloved Louboutins.

Vicky offered a tired smile. 'How was it? Did you slay any dragons?'

Mia flopped onto their lumpy folded futon. 'Man, it was brutal. The partners had us prepping for a massive merger.' She glanced at Vicky's work spread out across the floor. 'Which good fight are you taking on now, mate?'

'Budget cuts. The council—'

Mia stretched and yawned, cutting her off. 'Did I dream it, or did we leave wine unfinished last night?' She was up and over by the fridge in seconds, pulling out a re-corked bottle. 'You in?'

Vicky didn't want to drink. She needed a clear head, but saying no would make her boring in her flatmate's eyes. 'Sure... whatevs.'

Mia squeezed two glasses of leftover wine, topping them up with soda water.

'A spritz, innit?' she said, handing one to Vicky.

For all of ten seconds, Mia stayed silent. It had to be a personal best.

'So...' she said, reheating a discussion they'd had plenty of times already. 'You made up your mind about this weekend?'

It was Pride. London's turn to transform into a vibrant display of love, acceptance, and equality. For three spectacular days, rainbow flags would fly from Trafalgar Square to Soho, as over a million people marched and partied.

'I might be too busy,' Vicky said, a hint of wariness in her voice.

'Fabric is having their big queer night on Saturday. We have to go.'

She hesitated. 'I don't know, Mia. Clubs aren't really my scene.'

'Enough with the old lady act, bud,' Mia wheedled. 'You work too damn hard. Live a little.'

Vicky sighed, looking down at her papers. 'People are counting on me.'

Mia's voice softened. 'You get that you don't need anyone's permission to celebrate who you are. Being trans, being Black, being a kick-ass lawyer – it's all part of you. You've got to stop hiding yourself away.'

She met her friend's gaze, a small smile playing on her lips. 'I know. I just... I don't feel like I have to make a big deal out of it, you know?'

Mia nodded, understanding. 'Fair enough. But the offer stands if you change your mind.' She stood, rummaging in her bag for her wallet. 'I'm getting takeout. You in for pizza?'

Mia was always paying for pizza. For wine. For just about everything. Would it kill her to kick back and have fun? Just this once.

'Sure,' she said. 'But I'm paying half. And no anchovies. They make me heave.'

'And wine?'

'One bottle.' She knew that Mia would return with two. 'I have to read all this shit tonight.'

```
INT. VICKY'S FLAT - NIGHT
SUPER: '1 AUGUST 2024'
A sleek, minimalist apartment with
panoramic city views, located in the
high-rise Manbury House. The space is
immaculately furnished with high-end
pieces, though the pristine environ-
ment betrays a certain loneliness—more
showcase than home. In the living
room, a cream sofa anchors the space,
```

adorned with carefully arranged cush-
ions. An upcycled console table sits
near the entrance, often catching keys
and daily detritus. The entire flat
radiates expensive taste and careful
curation—everything in its place,
nothing out of order.

An eager estate agent, smack-bang in the middle of a vicious acne breakout, had boasted about Manbury House having an "active" residents' association. He'd called it a selling point before trying—and failing—to open a rusted-shut window.

Vicky should have read between his shiny-suited, over-hair-gelled lines and understood that "active" was just another way of saying "fucking annoying."

Within two weeks of moving in, she'd been invited for drinks and nibbles at the penthouse flat and cajoled into giving free legal advice for a planning application. When the plans fell through, Vicky had become persona non grata.

She sort of preferred it that way.

After tossing her keys onto an upcycled console table, she stepped out of her painful but essential-for-the-job shoes and padded into the living room, calling to Alexa to lower the blinds. True to form, Alexa turned on a random lamp. Too exhausted to care, Vicky fell into her cream sofa, building a wall of cushions for her head, then stretched, flinching at the cracking sound her neck made.

The first thing she always did was turn on the TV. She'd grown up in a house where there was noise from dawn until dusk. Her mother turned the radio on before breakfast and sang along.

Jenny messaged again, but Vicky was running on fumes, and the centre would have to wait. For once, whatever had sprung a leak, fallen off, fused, or made a funny noise wasn't her concern.

She poured herself a glass of red and sank into the sofa. Wine snobs said to let it breathe for an hour prior to consumption. Who had that kind of time? It had been a gift from a client she'd helped take out a non-molestation order against a partner who'd aimed a fake gun at her precious pet poodle. She'd checked online to see just how grateful her client had been. The bottle had cost 64 quid, making each mouthful worth more than tonight's ready meal: French country chicken with fluffy white rice.

She did have a pretty little nose. Thanks to good genes. It was sweet of the Dalek voice to notice.

INT. KELLETT ROAD – NIGHT
SUPER: '2012'
A cramped living room. Faded floral wallpaper, and way too much furniture.

When her mother rubbed her eyes, it smudged makeup applied with care, revealing a hint of discoloration.

'A cupboard door,' she'd told anyone who asked. 'You know how it is. Sometimes I don't look where I'm going.'

Vic knew better. He'd listened to the fight, heard the sickening punch and the cry of pain. It made him more certain that leaving the family home was the right move.

'You no have to go today, you hear?' his mother said. 'Is getting late. Dark. The street isn't safe this time a-night.'

She stopped short of saying *for someone like you*. But Vic heard it anyway.

His outfit gave little away: black leggings and DM boots with dirty white laces, a heavy felt jacket, hair hidden beneath a cap.

He could be a man. He could be a woman.

'That university is just a half hour upon the Tube,' she said. 'You don't need for squandering money upon no lodging. And who this friend you want to stay with?'

Why did she have to ask? She'd met Vic's new roommate twice. Mia wasn't someone you forgot—a whirlwind of energy and colour, her hair a riot of purple and blue braids, her nails long, each finger painted a different shade.

'Mum, we've been through this.' He hauled a bag into the narrow hall. 'I'm doing this. For me.'

When the back door slammed, they both fell quiet. His father appeared, a looming presence, sucking all the air from the room. Bloodshot eyes, tinged with the telltale glaze of one too many tots of rum.

'Wha' gwaan? Boy, you still 'ere?'

The tension ratcheted up, as if someone struck a match in a room full of petrol-soaked rags.

'I'm about telling him it make no sense to be lodging,' his mother said.

Her words were met with a sniff. 'When he walk out, the batty boy don't think about coming back.'

'He's your son.'

Vic pushed past, grabbing his bag and heading for the front door. 'I promised to be there by now.'

'Oh. Ho.' His father rocked on his heels. 'So be it, then? You formed some sort of promise. Nothing like no promise you made the Lord?'

His mother snatched for his arm. 'Please, my boy.'

He released himself, brushed one thumb across her cheek and smiled. 'I'll be safer there, Mum. I can be myself.' He paused, then added in a whisper, 'And maybe... you could be safer too. If I'm not here. Think about it.'

The words hung between them, heavy with unspoken

understanding. Vic didn't want to start another fight or be the reason for one more sleepless night, but he hoped the seed he'd planted might take root.

```
INT. VICKY'S FLAT - DAY
SUPER: '2 AUGUST 2024'
```

Vicky woke to a head full of fuzz, curled up on the sofa, covered by a woollen throw. The TV was still on. Her back ached. She was way too grown-up to be sleeping anywhere but on an extra-firm mattress.

Her phone was ringing. What time was it? Seven o'clock. What day was it... Friday? Shit, she needed to be... Then she remembered sending an email to Tarquin Walker, booking last-minute leave, inventing an ailing relative.

'Ms Harper?' The voice on the other end belonged to a teenage boy. 'This is about your upcoming visit to the Serenity Retreat. We're dealing with a staffing issue which means we might not offer a full programme of activities.'

She spotted two empty wine bottles. What had she been thinking? 'Go on.'

'Our kitchen team are also... taking an extended break.'

The silent retreat website had promised a gastronomic journey courtesy of an award-winning chef using only the finest locally sourced ingredients.

'OK, so thanks for letting me know.' She was on her feet, limping to the kitchen for water. 'You are serving food, though?'

The awkward pause lasted a second too long. 'There will be a full catering service available throughout your stay.'

'And it's still no talking?'

To be fair, the "silent" part had been what attracted her. The idea of switching off her phone on arrival and not having to make small talk with strangers sounded like heaven. Who cared about sumptuous breakfast buffets and exquisite fine dining? She'd be happy with crisps and a sandwich.

'Serenity Retreat remains committed to holistic healing.'

'Yeah, but nobody's allowed to speak?'

She was sure she heard a gulp, and the sound of someone leafing through papers, trying to quote the company line. 'Guests may converse, but only by mutual consent, and any such interaction must occur away from communal areas.'

This was enough. 'Bang on. I'll see you around lunchtime.'

She needed coffee.

CONTINUOUS

The pre-booked taxi was late. Vicky planned to leave a stinging review—not because she enjoyed wielding power, but because she'd spent the morning fielding emails and calls from Emmaleigh.

'It's going to be so am-a-zing, Victoria. And you'd get to be with your people.'

'My people?'

'And we're doing this thing with traditional foods—think samosas and jerk chicken. But obvs totally veggie, right. Or are you vegan? Can your people tolerate lactose?'

She'd hung up on her twice, but the texts and emails didn't stop.

The lousy summer had become headline news, but after days of cloud and drizzle, the sun put in an appearance.

Assuming the good weather wouldn't last, Vicky had packed for comfort. Her Longchamp Le Pliage Cuir travel bag held yoga pants, breathable tops, flip-flops, and a lightweight sweater. She tossed in two granola bars pilfered from the office kitchen, a company-branded water bottle, an unread novel about an abusive Hollywood director, and a baseball cap.

She unplugged her laptop and hid it under a sofa cushion. She'd take her phone—not because she wanted to stay in touch with work or irritate the living hell out of Emmaleigh by marking every text as read without responding, but because she'd made a promise to Jenny to sort the centre funding problem.

She needed Penrose to come through.

INT. BLACK PRIUS - DAY
Immaculate leather and polished wood
interior. The driver, in dark
sunglasses, glances at the GPS. The
engine purrs.

Vicky's heels rested on plush carpet, her manicured fingers tapping against her phone screen. Already, she mourned the loss of reliable 5G. The car's leather interior creaked as she shifted, the faint scent of pine air freshener mingling with the driver's aftershave. Her mind wandered, conjuring up images of the retreat. The website had gone big on stock photography; it could be a total dump.

She gave herself a pep talk.

Just for once, Victoria Harper, try to see the good in people. Not everything has to be a shit show.

The car slowed, turning off the main road and down a narrow, winding lane, beneath a canopy of branches creating dappled shadows.

Relax. Give in to the moment. Live in the moment. Enjoy the moment.

Who was she kidding? Thanks to Emmaleigh, and countless shitty clients, she was tense as hell, and three days of silence wasn't going to fix a thing.

As the GPS showed them nearing their destination, doubt gnawed at her. Should she really be taking time off when the centre needed her?

'It's just down this lane.' The driver's gruff voice broke the silence.

She peered ahead, seeking any sign of civilisation.

Serenity Retreat sat at the end of an overgrown path, barely visible through a tangle of brambles. Its walls were a dreary grey, the windows smeared. It was nothing like she'd imagined, yet somehow exactly what she'd expected.

A shit show.

```
INT. SERENITY RETREAT - DAY
A once-grand Victorian country house.
The faded grandeur of a bygone era
lingers in rich, dark wood panels
lining the walls and ornate patterned
carpets, now worn thin in places.
Antique furniture lines dim corridors,
gathering dust. A musty smell pervades
the air, mingling with the faint scent
of ageing wood and neglect.
```

The first thing that hit Vicky when a young boy unlocked the door to The Gloucester Suite was that the Serenity Retreat had once been super fancy. Sunday supplement stylish. Rich, dark wood panels lined the walls, and the patterned carpet reminded her of school trips to stately homes.

'Are you booked up?' she'd asked the kid leading the way.

He didn't turn around. 'Not these days. Mum blames Covid. Reckons everyone spent that long not being able to talk to their mates, the last thing they want to do is pay someone to stop them doing it again.'

'Do you mind me asking how old you are?'

He stopped outside a pale blue door, where the scratched brass plaque confirmed this to be her home for three nights.

'I'm sixteen next month,' he said. 'And if you need anything during your stay, just ask someone to come and find me.'

'And your name is...?'

'Bryn. Bryn Granger.'

Vicky was to spend the night in a grand four-poster bed with crisp white linens and a carved headboard. That at least made things better. On the dresser, a folded note caught her eye.

She picked it up and read the elegant script.

Welcome to the Serenity Retreat.
We encourage our guests to settle in and reflect in solitude, in silence, until dinner at 7 PM.
Enjoy the peace.

There was no key to lock her bedroom door. This felt like one of those places she'd seen on sleepless nights, watching reruns of *Four in a Bed*. Passive-aggressive bed and breakfast owners took turns staying at each other's establishments, smiling over a full English, only to slate everything about the experience. The biggest whinge was always about rooms without locks. That, and spiders.

Her room most likely had spiders. Old places in the country had hundreds. She imagined at least ten sets of eight eyes watching her every move.

She could go wandering; the kid who seemed to be in charge had said to find him if she had questions. But the polite-but-firm note had suggested otherwise. This was a silent retreat. She needed to chill.

An antique clock on an ornate stone mantelpiece indicated it wasn't even three o'clock. There were four hours to kill before dinner.

Her stomach demanded food, and she rummaged through her bag, wishing she'd ignored her inner voice that had insisted this would be a chance to break bad eating habits. Vicky craved Monster Munch and Toffee Crisp.

Perhaps there was a minibar loaded with overpriced bottles of wine and a giant Toblerone. What she wouldn't give for a Toblerone. Or a massive Kit Kat, the kind that made your gums bleed. She opened and closed every cupboard door before accepting that the Serenity Retreat was not that kind of place.

Bedsprings creaked as she tried to get comfortable, her fingers tracing the delicate embroidery on the faded covers. Through the large windows, she spotted someone wandering around the neglected garden—a man, in his early forties. Well-dressed but weary, walking like a dark cloud hovered over him. Vicky found herself staring, watching his slow, deliberate steps, wondering about his story, about what had brought him to this place of silence and solitude. As if sensing her gaze, he paused and looked up toward her window. Before their eyes could meet, she jumped back, self-conscious, hoping she hadn't already broken some sort of rule.

And how did she get into the garden, anyway? A walk might shake off the city and all the stress—which was, after all, why she was here.

That, and a Toblerone.

INT. SERENITY RETREAT - NIGHT
Two long wooden tables dominate an
austere room. Places are set with
mismatched glasses and cutlery. Torn
kitchen roll, folded in four, serves

as napkins. The dining room, like the rest of the retreat, suggests an establishment clinging to pretensions of grandeur while operating on a shoe-string budget.

Vicky had decided to dress for dinner, feeling it was the thing to do in such an upmarket setting. She'd chosen a tailored Stella McCartney black midi and a McQueen silk-chiffon scarf in a muted floral print. Lambskin ballerina flats complemented her diamond stud earrings and a hammered silver bracelet.

A handful of guests were already seated: an older man with an expensive watch peeking out from under his bobbled blue cashmere cardigan, a younger woman in yoga pants, and the man she'd seen earlier, now wearing a rumpled pale pink Oxford shirt.

Choosing a seat that allowed for a quick escape, Vicky settled in as Bryn emerged from the kitchen, balancing trays of microwaved ready meals.

Her suspicions about "teething troubles" were confirmed as she was served a plate of congealed sweet and sour pork with overdone rice.

The man from the garden smirked in her direction, mouthing the word *prison* as he poked at what should have been a nourishing and delicious home-cooked meal. Vicky bit back the urge to laugh. She couldn't be red-carded for rule-breaking during dinner on her first night. But there was something in his expression—something disarming, as if he were offering an escape route.

He gave a subtle nod towards the door. Against every one of her usual instincts, Vicky stood.

```
EXT. SERENITY RETREAT - NIGHT
The grounds, which might have once
been meticulously maintained gardens,
have surrendered to wilderness. The
grey stone walls are weathered and
stained, windows smeared with grime.
Beyond the house, neglected gardens
stretch into overgrown wilderness. A
solitary stone bench sits near a tiny,
glimmering pond. In the distance, a
Hollywood-style Winnebago, parked up
on bricks, serves as the owners' resi-
dence. A thick power cable snakes
through the trees, connecting it to
the main house.
```

The cool evening air was a relief. Vicky leaned against the stone wall, pulling a vape from her pocket. Smoking and vaping were forbidden anywhere at the retreat, but after food like that, she figured she was owed at least one broken rule.

The rumpled pink-shirt guy appeared, smoothing down his dark, messy hair. There was something endearingly awkward about his primary school teacher-on-casual-Friday vibe that made her lower her guard, just a fraction. His eyes widened at the sight of her vape, and his expression shifted from surprise to conspiratorial approval. He mimicked taking a drag, grinning when she shrugged in a *sue me* gesture.

'We can't all be saints,' she whispered.

He tilted his head toward the garden path, nodding for her to follow. Vicky was far from naïve; she walked nighttime Birmingham streets with keys clamped between her fingers, 999 pre-dialled on her phone. But this stranger's openness felt different —something about the way he couldn't quite meet her eyes, how he seemed more uncomfortable in his skin than she was in hers. He wasn't trying to impress anyone. So, she took a breath and followed, already cursing herself for ruining her favourite pair of ballet pumps.

The path widened, revealing a small lawn, a solitary stone bench, and a tiny, glimmering pond.

'I think this is family-only,' the guy whispered, glancing around. 'Pretty sure they live in that.' He pointed toward a battered Hollywood-style Winnebago, parked up on bricks, a thick cable running through the trees towards the main house. There were no lights inside.

'You seem to know your way around,' Vicky said.

'I've been here since Monday.' He made it sound like court-imposed house arrest.

'Monday?' She couldn't hide her disbelief. 'How come you haven't succumbed to malnutrition?'

His wide, genuine grin caught her off guard. 'Started out fine. They bribed some students from a catering college. It all kicked off two nights back. They vanished, and the microwave took over.'

Vicky looked around. 'OK, don't call me a stickler for rules, but you do know we don't need to whisper. If this part of the garden belongs to the owners, then it's no longer communal. We can do what the hell we want.'

His eyes lit up, impressed. 'What are you, a lawyer or something?'

'I wish I could say *or something*.' She managed a smile. 'I'm Vicky.'

'Jake.' He nodded for her to sit. 'If you reach into the hedge, there's a cool bag.'

She did as he suggested, feeling ridiculous as her hand fumbled through damp leaves, before pulling out a bright blue cooler bag. When she opened it, a tiny laugh escaped. Jake had stashed two cans of beer and a bag of Mars Fun Size.

'Emergency rations.' His cheeks turned a shade of pink. 'If I have to do one more guided meditation about being a tree reaching for the sun, or write another letter to my inner child...' He trailed off with a grimace.

Vicky met his gaze, and for the first time in what felt like forever, the barrier between her and the rest of the world softened.

'Good thinking,' she said, popping the ring pull on a can of Carling.

'There really are way too many wankers in this world,' he said, a smile forming. 'And at least half of them are booked in here.'

They toasted the night.

For a while, they didn't speak, just stared into the darkness, taking occasional sips of beer and exchanging shy smiles. It was like a bad first date. Jake broke the silence.

'What brings you here?'

She shrugged, not sure how much she was ready to share. He was, after all, a stranger—a stranger with beer and choco-late, but still someone she didn't know to trust. 'Last-minute deal. Company message board. Seemed too good to be true. Turns out my instincts were spot on. What about you?'

'My friends figured this would improve my mental health.' Jake pulled a crumpled pack of cigarettes from his pocket. 'I don't actually smoke, but cool people do, so I bought these to use as an icebreaker.'

Vicky turned so she could see him better. He was about her age, and take away the thrown-together, off-duty burnout look —not bad looking.

'You brought an icebreaker to a silent retreat. Dude, the clue is in the name.'

Still, she took one, not entirely sure how long it had been since she last smoked an actual cigarette. Something about this time and this place and this stranger made it seem like the best idea ever.

'I don't actually have a lighter,' Jake admitted.

'No drama.' She reached for her vape. 'This thing has a coil we can use.'

Jake's eyes widened. 'It's like drinking warm beer with Bear Grylls.'

He watched as she fiddled with the device, before losing an acrylic nail to the cause.

'What am I even doing?' she said, throwing back her head and groaning. 'I'm not fifteen, trying to sneak a crafty fag behind the bins by the shops.'

Jake pushed his cigarette back into the crumpled packet. 'Perhaps this is a sign from above. Smoking bad. Vaping good.'

The silence returned. Vicky flicked on her vape, offering him a puff, but he waved it away.

'My friends would be so proud.' His tone shifted. 'Actually, they'd probably stage another intervention.'

She studied his profile in the dim light. Something in his vulnerability made her want to understand more. She took a sip of beer, wondering if she was ready to ask, ready to share. The night air wrapped around them like a blanket, and somewhere in the distance, an owl called out.

'So,' she said as her vape battery signalled it was running low, 'want to tell me about that intervention?'

CONTINUOUS

Jake was midway through justifying the existence of Marie Kondo when twigs snapped in the darkness. Vicky tensed, but he just grinned.

'That'll be the ice butler,' he said.

She recognised the gangly teenager who emerged from the shadows, all elbows and Adam's apple. It was the kid who'd checked her in and shown her to that spider-filled room without a lock. He held up a clear plastic bag of ice cubes. Bryn.

'Had to wait for Mum to finish her evening meditation circle.' He rolled his eyes. 'See you've made a friend at last.'

Jake handled introductions, then handed Bryn a tenner.

'You're paying a child to keep you in ice?' she asked.

'I'm nearly sixteen,' Bryn sounded hurt. 'If this was Austria, I could vote and buy beer.'

'Talking of beer,' Jake intervened, 'I'm out, so the ice is surplus to requirements.'

Bryn stared at the cool bag. 'You do realise there's no refunds, yeah?'

Vicky shuffled around and fixed him with the kind of smile she usually reserved for obstinate judges refusing her client access to what had once been the family home. 'You do realise I'm a lawyer, yeah?'

'Technically, you're also a trespasser. This area isn't open to guests.' Bryn tucked the tenner into his back pocket. 'I could turn a blind eye... but one good deed deserves another.'

She folded her arms. 'I'm like the Royal Family. I never carry cash.'

'I was thinking more about how I could fix your current situation,' Bryn nodded at the cool bag. 'I know where Mum keeps the car keys. There's a Londis literally ten minutes up the road.'

'OK, but taking a vehicle without permission is known as stealing, and neither of us would be insured to drive.'

'I've got my provisional; all it needs is someone with a full licence in the passenger seat.'

Vicky glanced at Jake, who was no help. He just shrugged. 'Still no.'

'Fair enough.' Bryn dropped the bag of ice into the cool bag. 'Guess I'll have to find other ways to fund my gap year. Maybe write a blog about life at a silent retreat. All the things people get up to after dark.'

She stared. 'Are you actually trying to threaten us?'

'Just spitballing ideas.' Bryn's smile became cherubic. 'The Londis guy never cards anyone after nine because he's too busy watching porn on his phone.'

Vicky found herself laughing. 'You're quite terrifying, you know that?'

'I prefer entrepreneurial.' He turned as if to go. 'So, who's for a road trip?'

INT. WHITE FIAT 500 – NIGHT

'It's quite roomy,' Bryn said as Vicky folded herself into the back seat of what felt like a toy car. 'Mum says it's deceptively spacious.'

'Your mum's never had to sit behind you, has she?' Jake twisted to look back at her. 'You OK there?'

'Living my best life.' She watched Bryn adjust the mirrors with excessive care. 'Just to be clear—this is officially the stupidest thing I've ever done.'

Bryn pulled at his seatbelt. 'Including paying three hundred quid for a silent retreat?'

'OK, second stupidest.'

The car hip-hopped down the potholed dirt track leading to the main road. Bryn drove like a driving instructor's dream student. Six checks at each junction. Both hands on the wheel. Mirror-signal-manoeuvre for everything, even on the empty farm tracks.

'You're actually not terrible at this,' Vicky admitted.

'Got to be good at something.' He grinned at her in the rear-view. 'Can't all be lawyers.'

The Londis looked abandoned. Windows shuttered, sign dark, the tiny car park deserted with an overflowing skip in one corner.

'I think we might be out of luck, mate,' Jake said.

Bryn signalled and turned in. 'Everybody thinks it's shut. Porno John hates customers.'

Inside, the shelves sagged with multipacks of crisps and value beans. A handwritten sign declared, "Hot Food Till Late," though the hot cabinet was empty save for a fossilised sausage roll. Behind the counter, a ham-faced man with greasy hair didn't look up from his phone.

As Jake grabbed a six-pack, Vicky checked the limited selection of magazines. She'd need something to fill the next two days. Inside Soap or The Angling Times? A stack of newspapers caught her eye, with a headline shouting about some local church's far-right links.

'You good to go?' Jake was done shopping. Along with the beer, he'd grabbed a bottle of Czar's Delight vodka and a family pack of Mini Cheddars.

'Yeah.' She opted for Inside Soap. Fictional drama had to be better than actual fishing. 'Though I'm questioning every life choice that's led to this moment.'

'Four quid for the magazine,' the man behind the counter mumbled, thumb still scrolling. 'And I didn't see who was driving that Dinky Toy parked in the disabled space.'

Bryn beamed. 'Cheers, John.'

INT. SERENITY RETREAT – DAY
SUPER: '3 AUGUST 2024'

The Meditation Suite resembles a run-down school hall with blue gym mats.

Vicky woke with a headache that could only come from drinking dodgy Polish vodka. She chugged water, dressed for comfort, and made her way down to breakfast, hoping to run into her new best friend, Jake.

Something about sleeping in a strange bed in a house rigged up for hospitality—not to mention the drums playing inside her skull—had left her craving a full English. The only option was muesli, served with long-life milk. Her empty stomach growled.

A photocopied sheet pinned to a whiteboard detailed the day's optional activities. She could go for a walk around the overgrown garden or meditate. Having already explored everything the garden had to offer, she opted to sit cross-legged, clear her head of every thought, and hope that, at some point in the next two hours, her vision might return to normal.

The compulsory meditation robes—shapeless, unflattering, and made from a stiff, unyielding fabric—were a drab shade of beige. The sleeves were too long, and the hems uneven, like the baggy clothes she'd once worn while trying to hide her true self.

In the complete silence, Vicky found herself fixated on the wheezing of an older woman with an obvious wig and far too many rings. The woman tried and failed to sit cross-legged on the mats until Bryn came to her rescue, dragging over a rickety wooden chair.

Vicky wanted to clear her mind, but that odd voicemail lived rent-free in her head.

It shouldn't matter. She'd put up with worse—from her own father. So why did this, what could very well be a prank call, bother her so much? Maybe it was the anonymity, the sheer cowardice. Or the timing. They'd caught her at a low point:

overworked, under-loved, hoping to make named partner but knowing the title would likely go to someone far less capable and far more male. And white.

A bell chimed, signalling the end of their meditation hour, and Bryn hauled open the heavy double doors. Fellow meditators grunted and groaned as they stumbled and swayed, joints clicking. At least one of them broke wind.

INT. VICKY'S ROOM – DAY

Someone had knocked—to service her room. Hauling herself from a pile of pillows, Vicky plastered on her sweetest smile and opened the door.

'Oh,' she whispered, surprised to find Jake standing there in last night's chinos and a cream button-up, sleeves rolled to his forearms.

'I'm going to try yoga,' he said. 'You up for that?'

Vicky's heart soared. Maybe she'd been wrong about the joys of silence.

'Is there a house-imposed dress code? Because the meditation robes were… a choice.'

'I think it's a come-as-you-are deal.'

Again, she caught a glimpse of Jake's dark cloud, a weight that seemed to follow him everywhere. He put on a front of casual cheer, but she sensed a hidden story.

'Just an idea,' she ventured, careful with her words. They were still strangers, after all. Strangers who'd shared far too much Londis vodka and talked shite for hours, but strangers all the same. 'But have you ever done yoga before?'

'Once, during lockdown,' he admitted. 'I tried following Joe Wicks.'

She smirked. 'Yeah, but actual yoga can be brutal. It's not all tinkling bells, green tea, and downward dogs. I've been to classes where the instructor thinks she failed if nobody throws up in the buckets provided.'

'That's vivid.' His smile turned crooked. 'Do you have something better in mind?'

'I need cake,' she said, glancing conspiratorially down the hall, conscious they were already breaking every Serenity Retreat rule. 'And when I say cake, I mean lots of cake. All the cake in the world.'

```
INT. THE VILLAGE BAKERY - DAY
Brick facade and flower-adorned
windows. Inside, the shelves are
loaded with cakes and loaves. Staff
serve amid low chatter and clinking
teacups.
```

Vicky had gone less than a day without decent coffee, yet she downed her first double espresso in one go, like a junkie getting a fix. She let out an audible groan of pleasure.

Jake eyed her from across the table. 'Do I need to call your sponsor? Do you have a problem with caffeine?'

'I hate all that clean-living shit,' she said, almost defensively. 'Honestly, I don't know what possessed me to book a weekend out here, not talking to anyone, acting like I've taken vows.'

'So the voicemail wasn't the reason?' he asked.

Vicky froze. They'd drunk a lot last night, but she prided herself on an ability to separate drunk Vicky from sober Victoria. Had she let something slip? Had she shared how she was tired of having nobody in her life except Jenny and super-needy Emmaleigh? Had she mentioned the anonymous Dalek threat?

'The message we all got,' Jake clarified, 'the one about respecting the silence and staying out of the family areas? You were going to sue someone for implying you'd broken the rules.'

She let herself breathe again. 'Oh, yeah. That was the drink talking. I say crazy shit when my brain disengages.'

Jake fell silent, a hint of something unspoken in his expression.

'You all right?' she asked. 'I mean, your friends must've had a reason for suggesting this whole retreat intervention.'

He looked up at the ceiling. 'What's that thing they say on dating sites? It's complicated.'

Vicky rested her chin on her hand, nodding. 'Life just is.'

Jake exhaled, his voice softening. 'My partner... he died. It was recent. Sudden.'

She shifted, genuinely moved. 'I'm sorry. Losing someone close... it's a bit shit, isn't it?'

Jake nodded, chewed his lower lip, and then seemed to decide to continue. 'Tom was an alcoholic. I knew, all our friends knew, but he didn't want just anyone finding out. Especially his workmates. He was an estate agent, so they were all wankers.'

Vicky smiled. 'Seriously, Jake. Try working with lawyers.'

'At those corporate events, he'd call ahead or talk to whoever ran the bar to serve him cranberry juice in a wine glass. We were doing great. He'd been going to meetings, had his two-year chip...' Jake's voice wavered as he wiped his eyes, staring down at the table. 'Then the accident happened... they're ordering toxicology reports. They think he might've been drinking.'

'The accident?' Vicky asked.

'He'd been to a sales training day. In Bristol. They said it was quick... that he wouldn't have known what was happening.'

Her mouth went dry, and she suddenly regretted the coffee.

She regretted last night, drinking so much, acting like it was nothing.

'His sister blames me. She says I pushed him to drive back that day,' Jake's voice cracked. 'She wants me out of the flat we shared.'

'Does she own it?'

'It was in Tom's name. We never got around to putting my name on the deeds.'

'You know,' she began, picking her words carefully, 'if you and Tom were partners for a while, you could have what's called a beneficial interest in the property. It's not straightforward, but you'd need proof you contributed—bills, receipts, things like that...'

Jake looked up, his eyes rimmed red. 'Her solicitor said I could negotiate how long I needed to move my stuff out.'

'Well, the law is the law. Document everything. Payments, photos, letters... anything showing you were a couple living together.' Vicky leaned back. 'Do you know the solicitor? I might know them.'

'Harrington, I think. Can't remember his first name.'

Surely not Nigel Harrington. Life couldn't be that cruel. She remembered her interview with him all too well—a memory she'd tried to bury.

'So... do you know him?' Jake asked.

She shook her head. 'We breed like rats. But I can ask around.'

Vicky waved down the server to pay, but as she reached into her bag, her phone lit up with a missed call from an overseas number she didn't recognise—and a new message:

+1 (800) 555-0135

Pretty little noses break

Jake was talking, saying something, but his voice faded. Her vision blurred, and her heart hammered in her chest.

'You OK?' Jake said. 'I probably couldn't afford your rates anyway.'

'Sorry. What did you ask me?'

'It's just... I need a solicitor. Since you already gave me great advice, I wondered if...'

His eyes were still red. The message was still there.

She pushed back her chair with a clatter and bolted for the door, her heels clicking against the pavement as she stumbled towards the bus stop. A bus pulled up just as she reached it. The destination read *Train Station*.

INT. VICKY'S FLAT – NIGHT

Vicky had showered. She'd changed her clothes, called the Serenity Retreat, and told Bryn the same lie she'd told Tarquin Walker: the same ailing relative had been rushed into intensive care. He'd negotiated cancellation charges better suited to a five-star hotel, but she'd agreed. After finding clean bedsheets, Vicky had wiped down every surface.

Still, she didn't feel right.

Was she being watched? Had someone been in and hidden a device? She could go crazy and start ripping things apart, digging into walls, unscrewing bulbs and plugs. But to what end? The Dalek voice, whoever sent that text message—they wanted her this way.

Vicky turned to logic, sitting down with a pad of paper and a pencil and working through actual names of actual people holding actual grudges.

Troy was too obvious. Their breakup was messy, sure, but they'd run into each other three months ago, and he'd insisted on talking. He'd moved up north, rising through the ranks at a

Manchester law firm, before headhunters came calling. Sharing a bottle of wine had been strange, like old friends catching up. He'd offered his number, but she'd declined.

Her phone buzzed.

'Harper,' she answered, clipped.

'About bloody time.' The booming voice belonged to Gerald Penrose. 'Your office voicemail fobbed me off with some nonsense about you being on holiday. And I said to myself that had to be wrong, because I happen to be relying on you to make sure Malcolm the fucking Mountie doesn't fleece my idiot daughter.'

Vicky flinched. 'I was away. I'm back now.'

'Have you talked sense into Lucy?'

Vicky pinched the bridge of her nose. 'I've left messages, but she's not returning my calls. Perhaps if you—'

'There's something else, Harper. This fiancé's mother... people tell me she's friends with questionable politicians. And yes, I do know how you ladies often have to cuddle up to the odd frog to find your prince, but this is different.'

Ignoring off-the-clock misogyny, she played along. 'Define different.'

'Nothing concrete, but I've heard whispers about a group called True North. Keep an ear out, will you?'

'Mr Penrose. I will try, but—'

'Harper, I don't need excuses. If you're not up to the job, I'll find someone who is.'

Vicky bit back an overwhelming urge to tell Gerald Penrose to go to hell, that she had other things to worry about. That it was the weekend. But professional pride won over.

'I will reach out to her,' she said. 'First thing Monday morning.'

He allowed her a sigh, the smallest of admissions that he might understand just how hard it was to tie Lucy Penrose down to anything, least of all a prenup she'd already made clear she had no intention of signing.

'My daughter thinks I'm trying to interfere,' he said. 'And perhaps I am, but come on, Harper, she hardly knows the man, and yet she's willing to love, honour, and obey. And don't get me started on the mother.'

Vicky stayed quiet.

'You know how I work, Harper. Half the time a tip-off is a bluff, but Patricia Macluskey's name keeps cropping up. People I've come to trust tell me she's mixed up with the kind of people setting fire to hotels housing migrants in this country.'

'But she's in Canada.'

'The far-right doesn't actually give a flying fig about borders. "Stop the boats" is just another version of what I used to see outside lodging houses in London—no blacks, no Irish. Their grubby, racist fingers find their way into all kinds of pies.' He paused. 'True North, Harper. Keep an ear out, will you?'

'Obviously, I'll carry out due diligence, but the woman's a college principal, and people like that tend to be... liberal.'

'I trust nobody, Harper. And that, in case you were wondering, includes you.'

A shiver moved down her spine. 'You've investigated me?'

'Whatever possessed you to pay over the odds for a lease-hold property is beyond me. You realise the freeholder can screw you for every penny you haven't got.'

Her mouth had gone dry. From somewhere outside, a group of boys passed by, their voices raised.

'I don't work for MI5,' he said, as if she'd asked out loud what else he knew. 'Although I do have contacts. If I find myself needing more on young Colin Macluskey, it won't take more than one call.'

Her heart hammered. 'You can do that sort of thing?'

He stayed silent.

'I mean, if you needed to investigate something. If somebody had received a voicemail or a text message...'

There was a long silence.

'This someone, Harper. It wouldn't be you?'

Vicky crossed her fingers. 'I need to ask a favour.'

The line crackled. 'Go ahead.'

INT. BÄCKEREI BRETZEL – DAY
SUPER: '5 AUGUST 2024'

She'd never been in the cute, funky café where Jake had suggested meeting up. On the way across town, Vicky had stopped at a pop-up gallery and bought a vanilla-scented candle, hoping this might work as an apology for bolting without warning. She'd arrived ten minutes early and ordered a coffee, adding a pastry on account of breakfast being a protein bar in the office gym. Half an hour later, Jake burst through the Bakkerei door, shiny with sweat, full of apologies, and slumped onto the chair opposite.

'I got waylaid,' he said. 'My friend was trying on frocks for her wedding. Things turned ugly fast.'

She grinned. 'There was me thinking you were getting your own back.'

His mouth formed a confused smile. 'For what? Anyone would think I've never been dumped in a cake shop before.'

He ordered a pitcher of iced tea and fanned himself with the menu, catching Vicky up on the past few days. He'd been to Citizens Advice, and they'd explained how probate works, how he could stay in the flat, at least for now.

Vicky pursed her lips. 'You do know I'm an expert in family and property law? Why Citizens Advice?'

Jake ducked his eyes. 'After what happened, I figured...'

'That was just me being me,' she said. 'I had shit to sort.'

He topped up his tumbler of tea. 'And it's sorted now?'

'Let's say I have matters under control.' She put down her coffee cup and reached under the table for her impromptu gift. 'I got you a little something. To say sorry.'

He pulled open the silky black ribbon on the white bag and peered inside. 'This is from that new gallery shop, right? The one that runs a credit check before letting anyone in. You must be incredibly sorry.'

Vicky took a slow, deliberate breath. 'I'm also running light on friends, and given someone has taken to sending me nasty little letters, I could do with one.'

As she poured out her story—the mysterious messages, how she'd made promises to save the gay centre based on calling in a favour—Jake's expression shifted from concern to disbelief and then to understanding. When she was done, he let out a low whistle. 'And I thought I had problems.'

The corner of her mouth twitched. Letting in this guy had been a good move. She should try this whole being normal thing more often. 'It's why I'm not a people person, as a rule.'

'Can I hear the voicemail?'

She fished out her phone. 'They called my office line, so I recorded it.'

The couple at the next table paused mid-conversation to eavesdrop, then quickly looked away when she flashed them her don't-fuck-with-me eyes.

'You mentioned your client base has changed,' Jake said. 'You don't think this is someone—'

She shook her head. 'I'm a senior partner. Most of the Legal Aid stuff gets farmed out to associates.'

'Have you upset anyone lately?' He grinned. 'Beyond those nice ladies at the next table.'

Her eyes rolled. 'More than I can list on the fingers of both hands. Upsetting people comes with the territory. I'd have ignored it if they hadn't texted my personal phone. I've spent years dealing with crap like this. Every time I tell someone I'm trans, I wonder if they plan on using it against me.'

'You're out. If they went to your boss, what difference would it make?'

She turned away. He was right, and she knew in her heart there was nothing to fear. 'There was a guy. I got him all wrong. He'd acted like none of it mattered, kept telling me I was the same person he fell for. And then came the questions. When did I know I wasn't born into the right body? Was I sure? Did I ever think I might want to change back?'

Vicky pinched the bridge of her nose. Her shoulders heaved.

Jake nodded. 'I sort of had all that with Mum. I mean, she's cool now, but when she first found my *Men's Health* stash hidden under the bed, she freaked and wrote me a letter, asking me to dispose of them and reconsider my choices. Put it in an envelope and everything. Slipped it under my door while I was at school.'

She all but spat out her coffee. 'You white dudes do things differently. My mum yelled and screamed and tried to pray the devil out.'

For one long minute, the two of them sat in silence.

'Pretty little nose...' Jake peered at the text message. 'It's old school. Who talks like that?'

She froze. Who did she know who prided themselves on being old school, who talked about pretty little fillies, rum buggers, and dick waving? Was Tarquin Walker behind this? Was her boss trying to warn her off running for named partner?

'I just remembered something,' she said, grabbing her phone and dropping it into her bag.

Jake sat back and folded his arms. 'So I'm dumped again?'

'The candle was really expensive. That has to buy me another free pass, right?'

He grinned. 'Next time, we're having lunch, and you're paying.'

```
INT. GERALD'S OFFICE - DAY
The reception area of Penrose Finan-
cial Services is unmanned. A patterned
carpet complements a dark wooden desk
and a single bookcase, loaded with
leather-bound volumes.
```

Vicky knew better than to barge in without first ringing the front desk, hotel-style bell. If Tarquin Walker was old school, Gerald Penrose was the architect who built the school and ensured each brick met his exacting standards.

Ten minutes passed, and she pondered trying the bell once more. There was a chance her most exacting client might be out and about—just like there was a chance Nigel Farage might 'fess up to being in it for the money. She could set clocks by Penrose's predictable routine.

Five more minutes.

She considered texting, just in case. He'd once delivered a six-minute lecture—timed to the second—for her 'egregious overuse' of the bell.

Another minute passed. Then thirty-six seconds more before the double doors slid open, and the man himself appeared: tall and slender in a tailored grey pinstripe suit, with a receding hairline and a groomed moustache. Vicky ignored the urge to leap to her feet and curtsey.

'I'm going to assume you're here to tell me my daughter has signed the prenup,' he said, peering over half-moon glasses.

'Not yet, but I wondered if you maybe had five minutes. I need a steer on something.'

Penrose drew in a breath, pausing long enough to survey the lobby as if checking for any hint of her having moved a book or touched the dusty vase of fake flowers.

'Four minutes,' he said, his voice a not-at-all-quiet verdict as he waved over at a battered honey-brown leather armchair arranged to face his polished mahogany desk.

'If this isn't about the work for which I am recompensing you in a manner that many might consider handsome, would you mind explaining your unannounced presence?' He poured water from a glass pitcher into a small tumbler. Vicky wasn't offered a drink. 'I presume this is to do with your ethical investment?'

'Actually, it's another favour.'

His shoulders slumped, like a disappointed parent handed a rubbish school report. 'You have heard the expression *quid pro quo*, one assumes?'

Her phone pinged with an office round-robin complaining about the state of the ladies' toilets on her floor.

'How well do you know Tarquin Walker?'

'The man's a dinosaur, but he knows his stuff. What's happened? Did he touch up one of the typing pool?'

Penrose knew full well there was no such thing as a typing pool; he was winding her up.

'I think he's trying to block my run for senior partner,' she said.

He took off his glasses before leaning back in his chair. 'Why the devil would the man want to do that? It pains me to provide feedback in this way, but you're good at your job. As a rule.'

She nodded and forced a smile. 'I've been getting messages.'

After playing the voicemail and showing him the text, she switched her phone to silent.

'Walker wouldn't know how to do that technical thing with his voice,' Penrose said. 'And if I'm being completely honest, I do wonder if it's within his skill set to send an SMS.'

'So you don't think it was him?'

'You've clearly annoyed someone else. Someone other than me.'

He opened a drawer in his desk and pulled out a pale green folder. She spotted her name in his lazy, leaning scrawl on a sticky note. She was in for a dressing down.

'It's quite convenient to have you here, Harper,' he said, pushing the folder across his desk. 'For one thing, you've saved me the cost of feeding you up, for another, it gives me a chance to speak of something that concerns me. Something I might not be at ease discussing in a more public space.'

The folder contained printouts of emails, news reports, and a photocopied letter. She recognised a headline from some-where: COVENANT LIGHT FELLOWSHIP UNDER INVESTIGATION.

'Is this for one of your Scambuster investigations?'

Penrose turned around to stare through a window. 'It's possibly connected to my daughter, Harper. I fear she might have got herself wrapped up in something rather sinister.'

INT. VICKY'S OFFICE – DAY

Vicky spread Penrose's documents across her desk, moving aside a half-empty protein shake. Sunlight blazed, the afternoon heat turning her glass box into a greenhouse despite the rattle of air-conditioning. She'd cancelled her three o'clock—some trophy wife trying to hide a Porsche from her soon-to-be ex—to focus on this.

The whole thing was absurd. As fearsome as she'd been on that one conference call, Lucy's future mother-in-law was no far-right sleeper agent. Patricia Macluskey ran a local Facebook group and posted about her book club.

But Penrose didn't do conspiracy theories. He was a forensic investigator, dealing in facts, figures, and due diligence. He'd once delayed a million-pound deal over one missing receipt from 1987.

Her fingers drummed against the desk. The thing about Lucy was she'd never had to think about protecting herself. Never woken up to find her bank account drained by someone who'd sworn eternal love. Never had slow-given trust shattered by a single betrayal.

'Must be nice,' she muttered, pulling up Lucy's latest email. Another breezy brush-off about the prenup. Something about love being about faith, not legal documents.

Faith. Right.

She opened YouTube, following a link in Penrose's notes about True North protests. He was sure he'd spotted Patricia in the crowds. Grainy footage showed a crowd outside a community centre. Her cursor hovered over the pause button as a face appeared in the background. The woman was about the right age, had similar bone structure, but it was no smoking gun.

She typed out an email, choosing her words carefully:

VICTORIA HARPER

Quality poor, could be coincidence. Lucy still avoiding prenup discussion. Will keep pushing.

Her finger hesitated over 'send'. Was she failing her favourite client by not taking this seriously enough?

Now to let Emmaleigh down gently by claiming she needed to tend to a sick relative and wouldn't be around for Birmingham Pride. She'd invent the relative—a second cousin or something. No point tempting fate.

Her phone buzzed.

That same, strange US number that texted before. She let it ring out.

INT. BÄCKEREI BRETZEL – DAY
SUPER: '7 AUGUST 2024'

'The shop was all out of vanilla candles.' Vicky slid into the chair opposite Jake. 'How about you get to pick a pastry, and I pay?'

Jake glanced over at the huge glass display case by the till. 'Even the apple strudel? That's practically the same price as gold in this place.'

'We can share one. Call it a celebration.'

When Vicky had called Jenny to tell her Penrose had talked Meridian Estates into lending a helping hand with Outreach Centre finances, the news was met with stunned silence before Jenny began shrieking and screaming and then crying with relief. Just a week ago, she'd been drafting goodbye letters to service users, working out who she could refer where. Trust Gerald to know someone with deep pockets and planning permission problems. Meridian's CEO was apparently "delighted to demonstrate his commitment to the diverse communities of Birmingham." Vicky could almost hear the PR team crafting that press release.

'Any more mystery callers?' Jake said as he returned with what looked like enough apple strudel to feed six.

She shrugged. 'Radio silence. I figured it's like when you start getting scam calls about your broadband password being compromised. Hang up enough times and they move on to the next gullible twat.'

Jake's fork paused halfway to his mouth. 'You know how you told me I should have come to you, and not go running to Citizens Advice to deal with Rona?' Vicky nodded. 'I might need to take you up on the offer. Her solicitor has taken to sending threatening letters.'

'Which firm?'

'Not sure, but he's called Nigel Harrington. I know this is a bit like when someone hears you're from Birmingham and asks if you've ever met their brother Kevin, but does that ring any bells?'

The name hit like a slap. Harrington. She'd hoped him long since out of her life. But what good would it do to tell Jake what an absolute arse the man could be? She forced her expression to stay neutral.

'I'll do whatever I can to help.' Vicky stirred her coffee. 'To be honest, probate is a cakewalk compared to trying to tie down someone who refuses to sign a prenup.'

'Speaking of lawyers being a pain,' Jake said between mouthfuls, 'my friend Lucy won't shut up about one who keeps chasing her about some contract.'

Vicky put down her fork. 'Lucy as in Lucy Penrose?'

'You know her?'

'Lucy Penrose is the daughter of my most important client. The man who helped save the Outreach Centre. The one who also thinks his daughter is marrying into a far-right sleeper cell.'

Jake snorted. 'Colin's a nerd. He's about as far-right as a *Guardian* reader at a Corbyn rally.'

Vicky sat back and folded her arms. All this time she'd been communicating with a client who refused to return calls, when all she needed to do was play the friendship card. Maybe she should become more of a people person. The finishing line appeared up ahead. 'If I help you shut down Rona, you have to get Lucy to sign the prenup.'

Jake was done with the strudel. All that remained were slithers of pastry and two lonely sultanas. 'Deal. But you do understand she's certifiable?'

INT. VICKY'S FLAT – DAY
SUPER: '15 AUGUST 2024'

Vicky glanced in the hallway mirror. A black suit would be too formal for today's meeting. Jake had clued her up. In every photo he'd shown her, Lucy Penrose was cutesy Boho chic. In her bedroom, she quick-changed, opting for tailored trousers and a cashmere sweater.

Her phone buzzed with a news alert. More riots. More government promises to jail those responsible. She'd been about to hit delete when she read the name of a man whipping up online hate. Al Whitmore. Head of a Canadian far-right group called True North.

Should she call Penrose?

The decision was made when he called her.

'I've been doing a little more digging,' he said. 'Wouldn't mind eyes on what I turned up.'

Vicky had the chance to say no. That her area of law was strictly family and property. She'd finished work on the prenup, and an invoice would follow.

'These people,' he said. 'They're dangerous. Not to me. Not to my daughter. They're coming for you and your friend Jake. And this is our chance to stop them.'

Vicky set her phone to silent and dropped it into her bag. For now, she was done with wicked people doing bad things.

FADE TO BLACK

lucy

FADE IN
INT. GERALD'S OFFICE — DAY
SUPER: '6 AUGUST 2024'

Lucy Penrose ached to rearrange the gilt-framed photographs lined up on her father's desk. He'd positioned them so that the one of her with an arm around Colin was obscured, hiding her fiancé's face behind a sepia-toned shot of her parents' wedding day. She could just make out the edge of Colin's blue polo shirt, and remembered the way he'd stooped to fit in frame, those kind brown eyes squinting through thick-framed glasses. Her mother's face beamed out from another photo, frozen forever at 35. Lucy touched the frame, remembering how that same smile used to appear at her bedroom door each morning, and how it vanished when she was fourteen.

'Careful with that,' her father said, returning from the tiny office kitchen bearing an ornate silver tea tray. Two blue china cups and a small plate of Rich Tea biscuits—exactly as her mother would have arranged them. 'The frame is rather old and delicate. Your mother bagged it in France, after haggling for hours over a bottle of wine with the chap in charge of a brocante.'

Lucy glanced up, catching a familiar wistfulness in his eyes before his media-ready face took back over. The same smile that appeared on breakfast television and *The One Show*. Gerald Penrose was The Scambuster—defender of the underdog, writer of a bestselling book.

She smoothed her floral sundress—a designer piece that had eaten half a month's salary from her "creative consultancy" work, but worth it if it meant he might actually notice her for once. They needed to talk.

Lucy was 29, old enough to know her own mind and decide who she wanted to marry. Old enough to know that Colin's steady presence, his unwavering attention, filled a void that had been growing since that morning she'd woken up motherless, since every time her father chose his career over parent-teacher meetings and school plays.

'Did you have to ask for Mother's hand in marriage?' she said, settling into a battered leather armchair. 'Did your father-in-law demand a prenup?'

He checked his phone while pouring tea, and she caught how his eyes flickered to his computer screen. His attention was divided. There was always something more important than her wedding. At least Colin answered her calls, remembered the little details she shared, made her feel like she mattered. The ring on her finger represented something real—someone who saw her, who chose her, who put her first.

Surely he could see how Colin Macluskey, Assistant Head of Regulatory Compliance at the Royal Bank of Canada, was a good catch. They had so much in common. Think of all the hours they could spend discussing insider hacks for users of Excel. Her dating track record was poor. There had been Gary, who ghosted her after three months. Then François, who only wanted a visa. And Si, who'd slept with her exactly twice before deciding they "should see other people." Lucy had a type all right—men who built castles in the air, then left her standing in the rubble. Men who found the footie/their mate/their ex more important than her. Colin was different. Real. He didn't need to fill silences with bluster or lies.

Her father sniffed and passed her a cup of tea, milky pale with two sugars. 'The prenup is non-negotiable, Lucy. I'm very much with Mahatma Gandhi on this—the future depends on what you do today.'

'Colin doesn't think Kev will be allowed to fly soon after surgery,' she said, deciding to change the subject. 'And that's thrown a spanner in the works.'

'Surgery?' Gerald took a sip of tea. 'I thought the clumsy sod ended up in a cast after behaving like a teenager.'

Kev Macluskey—Colin's brother and best man—had shattered his leg in six places attempting a complex skateboarding move. After three days in hospital, he was sent home with metal rods and screws supporting the fracture. And an eight-week no-fly order.

'It's more than a few broken bones,' Lucy said. 'He could be out of action for months, and there's no way I can reschedule.'

Lucy had pulled off a coup securing an ultra-exclusive, members-only venue for her wedding. The Cube had featured in *Brides Magazine.* Twice.

'Perhaps this is all some kind of sign.' Her father raised his eyes towards the heavens. 'From one of those pagan gods you like to worship.'

She bit her tongue. How could she expect someone closed to other cultures to understand Feng Shui, Hygge, or Vastu Shastra? Last summer he'd been her grumbling partner at a

Japanese design exhibition. In his booming voice, he'd told her —and just about everyone within a ten-mile radius—how an internal zen garden would only encourage mice.

She was determined not to let him wind her up again. 'How viable would it be to book Colin's brother onto a sea crossing?'

'Entirely,' Gerald replied, reaching for a biscuit. 'But don't expect me to foot the bill.'

He'd been finding ways to cut corners on her big day ever since she'd pointed out how tradition dictated the bride's family cough up for most every expense.

Her lips pursed. 'Sometimes I think you say things to wind me up.'

Gerald pulled his butter-wouldn't-melt face. 'Can't you ask one of your friends to step in and thank the bridesmaids for putting up with being made to dress like something served up at a kid's tea party?'

Pink had proven a hard sell, with maid-of-honour Emma already threatening rebellion, but Lucy was determined to pull off the Reese Witherspoon look, even if her budget didn't run to a Monique Lhuillier wedding gown.

She looked away, burning with frustration. 'I did a tarot reading this morning, and the cards believe unexpected change will lead to positive outcomes.'

'Well,' her father peered at his computer screen, 'if the cards said it.'

Lucy's oven-ready temper had been looking for an excuse to boil over. 'Why don't I put you down as undecided on the RSVP list? If you're doing nothing special on the day, drop in. I'll text details.'

He stayed silent for all of two seconds. 'When I was your age, people didn't get married in a glorified discotheque.'

He was using olde-worlde words to get a rise out of her, and she wouldn't let him win.

'There's a waiting list to get on the waiting list for The Cube. Why would I want to drag my friends to a musty church with a leaky roof when they can bask in unrivalled views of the city skyline?'

He went to eat a second biscuit, then seemed to think better of it. 'I'm sure it will be... banging, darling.'

Lucy's face was on fire. He'd wound her up again. Just like always. 'There's no way I'm changing anything now. People have RSVP'd.'

Her father's jaw twitched. 'Seriously, Lucy, would it be so very awful to delay your nuptials? Use the time to learn more about the boy.'

The suggestion lit an angry flame. 'What exactly do you have against Colin?'

He turned to gaze through windows looking out onto the canal basin. She sensed him picking over words, trying to find the least bad way to answer.

'How much do you know about the Macluskey family?' he said. 'As far as I can tell, the father retired and mows the occasional lawn for neighbours, and the mother—'

'You've carried out background checks?' Another furious wave crashed.

'Due diligence, darling. I wouldn't expect any of my clients to go into a situation blind.'

Lucy huffed tears. 'But I'm not one of your clients, am I? I'm your daughter.'

He leaned forward. 'Patricia Macluskey may have taken part in events that give rise for concern.'

Lucy balanced her cup on the edge of his desk. 'You were master of ceremonies at the Tobacco Manufacturers' Awards.'

'Fifteen years ago, Lucy. And my presenting work helped pay for your education.'

'Colin's mother is a respectable pillar of the local community. She's a college principal, for God's sake.'

He nodded but didn't speak, just did that thing where he exhaled through his nose with his lips pursed tight.

'OK, so what is she supposed to have done?' Lucy said.

He shook his head. 'You're right, darling. I should keep out of your affairs.'

'Tell me.'

His eyes glanced first at his computer screen, then back at her. 'Have you heard of True North?'

She thought for a minute, then shrugged. 'As in points of the compass?'

'True North is a Canadian political movement that your in-laws appear to support.'

'Like you supported UKIP?'

He blushed. 'I've apologised for that a hundred times over. I was wrong. You were right. I'm 63 years old, darling. Everyone my age has had at least one major lapse in judgement.'

Lucy got to her feet and picked up her bag. 'Sometimes, there's no talking to you.'

'I only want you to be one hundred per cent sure, darling. Marriage is a huge undertaking, and I know you young people see it as a simple piece of paper. Something to tear up and dispose of when it no longer works, but there's much more to consider.'

'We're in love.' Her voice quavered. 'Isn't that enough for you?'

He looked away, staring once more through a window.

'Colin seems like a good man.' Her father's voice grew quiet. 'But a decision like this should be made with both your heart and your head.'

```
EXT. NIAGARA CITY CRUISES DOCK,
NIAGARA FALLS, ONTARIO - DAY
SUPER: '15 SEPTEMBER 2023'
A winding line of eager tourists wait
to board the next boat heading under
the falls. The warm, sunny day is
punctuated by spray from the
waterfall.
```

The mist rose in great billowing clouds, turning everything dreamlike and soft. Lucy adjusted her yellow poncho as the queue shuffled forwards. Behind her, a German couple muttered about the wait. But she didn't mind. The wait meant she had more time to steal glances at the tall guy up ahead, all elbows and awkward angles.

He turned, caught her looking, and his ears went pink. There was something endearing about how he hunched his shoulders, as though trying to fold his gangly frame into a smaller space. His glasses fogged, made worse when he wiped them with the corner of his poncho.

Lucy excused herself through a family between them and offered him a tissue.

'This will be less... squeaky.'

'Thanks.' His voice was soft, careful, with that distinctive Canadian lilt that made everything sound like a question. 'I, uh, probably look sort of dumb right now?'

'We're all wearing banana-yellow bin bags.' Lucy shared a genuine smile. I think you're safe.'

He laughed, and something inside Lucy shifted, clicked into place. Behind her, Fiona was going on about the perfect Insta moment, but the world narrowed to this man and the way a smile transformed his whole face.

'I'm Colin,' he said, cleaning his glasses properly now. His eyes, when they emerged from the fog, were kind. The warm brown of coffee with just a splash of cream.

'Lucy.' The queue moved again, and she stumbled, bumping his shoulder. 'Sorry, I—'

'No, I'm sorry, I—'

They both laughed, and there it was again, that feeling of rightness.

The falls roared louder as they neared the boat, the spray painting rainbows. Lucy's heart did something complicated in her chest, like it was trying to learn a new dance step.

'You're here with friends?' Colin asked, nodding towards Fiona and the others.

'Yeah, doing the whole North America thing. You?'

'Just me.' He shrugged, those shoulders rising and falling. 'Needed to... I don't know, find something.'

'And did you? Find it?'

The queue moved, and this time they stayed in step. Their ponchos rustled, yellow against yellow, and Lucy thought of those nature documentaries where two awkward birds perform a mating dance.

Colin looked at her then, really looked, and grinned. She couldn't help but notice, the guy had perfect teeth.

'You know what?' he said. 'I think I might have.'

```
INT. HAUTE CAKES BAKERY - DAY
SUPER: '9 AUGUST 2024'
A stark, white unwelcoming space with
cold white lights and framed artwork
and harsh lighting.
```

The lobby of Haute Cakes Bakery was a study in sterility, a million miles from the welcoming atmosphere Lucy had envisioned. A scent of industrial cleaning products lingered in the air, and bright, overhead lighting cast unforgiving shadows, amplifying the coldness of a polished marble floor. Everything about the place appeared to be designed to strip away any sense of warmth or joy, as though cakes and baking were a serious business. A science.

But Haute Cakes had come with recommendations from a recent wealthy client. And Lucy wanted them to create her wedding cake. This bakery wasn't a place where you rocked up and asked to sample whatever they'd just cooked. There was no website, and the phone number remained a guarded secret. You either knew Haute Cakes existed, or you didn't.

'Are you sure this is the right place?' Emma had said. 'It's a bit school science lab.'

Lucy responded with a stiff nod. The front-of-house manager could be watching on a hidden camera. During a getting-to-know-you call, Marmolite Godalming had apologised for the somewhat strict rules. There were to be no phones, cameras, or other recording devices. Anyone present at the tasting would be required to sign a non-disclosure agreement.

'Is this supposed to be art?' Fred pointed to a framed white canvas featuring a single oversized crumb.

Emma leaned in to read the brass plaque. '*Existential Void Number Seven.* Apparently, it captures the fleeting nature of modern ennui.'

Lucy nodded, like this meant something. 'I know it seems a bit much, but their creations are legendary.'

Fred sniffed. 'I can't smell anything cooking, and I should do, right?'

A white door set into the bare wall burst open, and out swept a woman with a mad scientist's gleam in her eyes, flour dusting her hair. Arched eyebrows framed a pale, pointy face that seemed perpetually on the verge of announcing a breakthrough.

'Marmolite?' Lucy forced a professional smile—all teeth, no lips.

The sprite of a woman bounced on her toes, conducting an invisible orchestra. 'You're my two o'clock? Brilliant. I've perfected a new molecular gastronomy technique involving centrifuged mango and atomised champagne. The results are quite revolutionary.'

Lucy reached out a hand, and Marmolite pirouetted backwards.

'Sorry, no touching—I'm in the middle of an experiment with bacterial cultures. For the sourdough, you understand. Each batch has its own personality. Like tiny pets.'

She beamed at them as if expecting shared enthusiasm.

'I don't eat processed sugar,' Fred said, tapping his flat stomach. 'So I'm more along for the visuals.'

Marmolite inhaled, her nostrils flaring. 'Your plus one is already installed in the tasting suite.'

Lucy felt herself relax. Jake had come after all. She'd been certain he'd find some reason not to join them.

'My wedding is an important occasion,' she said. 'We're being featured in *Brides Magazine.*'

Marmolite squinted. 'I'm afraid, I don't...'

Emma intervened. 'I've just worked two nights wiping the bums of people who no longer know their own names. I've stopped a woman in her 70s from climbing through a third-floor window and another in her 80s from having a great big shit in the middle of a corridor, so while I appreciate making a cake is an achievement, could you show me where this tasting suite is? I need to sit down.'

Marmolite held up her hands, stepping away like Emma might be infectious. She shooed them towards the open door, calling after them that she was going to the office to print off copies of the NDA.

```
INT. TASTING SUITE - DAY
A cramped, white room with one
mirrored wall, containing a long table
and four brass chairs. The space feels
more like an interrogation room than a
place to sample wedding cakes. The
lighting is deliberately stark and
unforgiving, emphasising the "scien-
tific" approach to baking.
```

Jake was installed on one of the uncomfortable-looking chairs arranged around a pine table. His hair lacked its usual sheen, his chin sprouted three days of stubble, and when Lucy leaned in for a kiss, he radiated must and stale sweat.

'You didn't need to come,' she said, pulling out the chair next to him.

He shrugged. 'I've taken extended leave. My head isn't ready to tell Gloria from Derby she can't have a full refund because she caught impetigo from a water fountain in St Mark's Square.'

'And they're OK with that?'

'It's not like they can force me to work. I've just lost Tom. It's...' His voice cracked, and he looked away, sniffing. Lucy wished she hadn't asked such a stupid question.

'Today will be fun,' she said, resisting the urge to hug someone who appeared set to shatter. 'We get to eat loads of cake.'

He nodded without meeting her eyes. 'Working there was only ever supposed to be a stopgap. I've been thinking about... doing something else.'

'Whatever it is, you know we'll have your back.' She meant it, even as alarm bells rang. Was this grief talking?

'I'm 42.' His voice had a new edge. 'In ten years, I'll be in my fifties, and nobody wants to employ a guy in his fifties. If I'm going to make anything of my life, it has to be now.'

Marmolite pirouetted around them, distributing paperwork and pens with the intensity of a scientist documenting a breakthrough. Only when she'd secured signatures from everyone did she signal across the room for the first cake.

'What sort of something else?' Lucy said. 'Like uni or moving to the Outer Hebrides to breed sheep?'

Jake's face flushed pink under his stubble. 'I always wanted to act. There was a thing in *The Guardian* about a woman who landed her first role at 62. Morgan Freeman was 50 when he made *Driving Miss Daisy*.'

She glanced up to see Marmolite hopping on the spot. 'Time for the debut creation.'

A young boy in chef whites positioned a huge orange plate on the table with the precision of a lab assistant.

Fred was first to speak. 'You think a clue might help here?'

Marmolite vibrated with unhidden glee. 'What you see before you is Experiment 247B. A precise blend of sultanas, currants, dates, and figs, calibrated to exactly 27.3% moisture content. The crumb density has been calculated using advanced algorithms, and we've aged it for six months in a temperature-controlled chamber to allow the molecular structure to achieve perfect harmony.'

The four of them peered at four oversized crumbs. Lucy caught her friends exchanging looks and knew what they were thinking. Who the fuck ages cake? If there's a slice left after two or three days, you dip it in tea and eat it in the bath like a normal person.

Emma reached for a delicate gold tasting fork. 'Do we just... dig in?'

The boy-assistant nodded but maintained his respectful silence.

Lucy winced. The acclaimed confection tasted like cardboard fished from a dirty puddle and dipped in Sunny Delight.

'We've infused it with our signature brandy reduction—exactly 42.7 millilitres per cubic centimetre of cake,' Marmolite said, scribbling in a notebook produced from nowhere.

Jake lunged for his water bottle.

Lucy needed to move things along. 'Traditional is always a great way to start, but perhaps we might try something more... experimental?'

The silent assistant cleared away the plate, returning moments later with four precisely measured spheres of pink foam.

'Behold, Formula R-L7.' Marmolite's eyes sparkled. 'A rosewater and lychee mousse achieved through reverse spherification. The sponge molecules have been infused with pure Moroccan rosewater at exactly 31 degrees Celsius, then layered with pureed lychee compound and mascarpone with a pH balance of 6.2.'

Emma's nose wrinkled. 'I'm not nuts about lychees.'

Lucy helped herself. The flavour reminded her of a perfume favoured by the woman who'd lived next door when she was growing up. A woman her auntie Kath had called loose and blousy.

'It's an acquired molecular structure,' Marmolite conceded. 'But Lord Reginald Blackwood's taste receptors responded most favourably.'

Lucy was thrown. If a Lord appreciated these molecular experiments, was she missing something? The Cube had featured in *Vogue*—twice. Her dress was being made by a designer who'd worked with actual celebrities. The cake had to be perfect. Everything had to be perfect, or people might start asking questions she couldn't answer. Like why she was rushing to marry a man she'd known for less than a year.

A different assistant appeared with a third oversized platter. This one offered four precisely cut slivers of pale sponge cake, each topped with what looked like a plastic raspberry.

'Presenting Experiment VB-432.' Marmolite was all but dancing. 'A classic vanilla bean structure enhanced through sonic wavelength manipulation, topped with citrus acid molecules reconstructed at a quantum level.'

Whatever it was, this creation actually tasted of cake. Granted, it reminded her of the Mr Kipling French Fancies Auntie Kath brought round on Fridays, but it wasn't awful. Emma looked impressed. Fred hadn't resorted to napkin-spitting. She turned to Jake for the deciding vote.

'It's the only one that tastes vaguely edible,' he said.

She leaned back. 'We have a winner.'

Marmolite consulted her notebook. 'Fascinating result. I'll add you to our laboratory waiting list. We're currently running experiments through to next June.'

Lucy stared. 'But my wedding is in October.'

'Our molecular gastronomy schedule is quite precise.' Marmolite twirled. 'We're currently engineering confections for three duchesses and someone who had a speaking part in *Bridgerton*.'

Lucy's stomach clenched. Those were people who belonged in this world of luxury and privilege. People who wouldn't have to justify their choices to anyone. People whose fathers would be proud to walk them down the aisle instead of investigating their fiancé's family political leanings.

'My father is The Scambuster,' she heard herself say, hating how she still reached for his name like a shield. Just like she had at school when the other girls questioned why he never showed up for parents' evening.

Marmolite's eyebrows performed an elaborate dance. 'Is

that some sort of chemical compound? We don't use artificial ingredients.'

Lucy's head threatened explosion. 'I don't care if you're baking for Meghan fucking Markle. I need a cake by October.'

'Oh dear.' Marmolite's lips tightened, her fingers tapped against the table. 'I'm afraid the laws of culinary physics won't allow it. The molecular structures require time to achieve harmony.'

The gloves were off. 'What molecular structures? We're talking about a basic cake. An overgrown Victoria Sandwich with jam and a shed load of icing sugar, not something that might win a Nobel prize. Do you understand basic customer service?'

Jake had one arm, Fred the other. Lucy had gone full.

'This isn't over,' she yelled. 'Everyone will hear about this excuse for a junior school science lab masquerading as a high-end bakery. Lord Blackwood, my bloody arse.'

The lab assistants appeared to reset the testing area, and Marmolite disappeared through another secret door.

'Fuck them,' Lucy said, blood pumping. 'Fuck their experimental cakes. I'll find someone better. And when I do, I'll tell *Brides Magazine* exactly what kind of idiots are running this place.'

They were alone.

She blinked back angry tears. It wasn't about the cake, not really. It was about proving she could create something perfect, something even her father couldn't pick fault with. Colin was steady, reliable, safe—everything her mother would have wanted for her. So why did it feel like she was still that fourteen-year-old girl, trying to win her father's attention?

INT. LUCY'S FLAT – NIGHT

The cake-tasting debacle faded from Lucy's mind when she arrived home to find a beautiful pink box, tied up with wide silver ribbons, waiting with the building concierge. Her dress designer had worked magic and sent over the veil they'd agreed would add the necessary magic to her bridal gown.

Lucy had always thought veils very old-fashioned, until she'd tried one on. The sense of being hidden from the world until the last moment had captured her heart. Jean-Claude had insisted he be permitted to start work at once.

'You will see it and be *accablée.*'

She lifted it from the matching pink tissue. Even in jeans and a T-shirt, it was fantastic. She was indeed completely *accablée.* Stunned. She would have the wedding she'd dreamed of since her ten-year-old self dressed Barbie in begged, borrowed, and found scraps of lace and tulle for her big day in a cardboard box church with Ken, who'd made far less effort and wore denim cut-offs.

Her phone jiggled. Colin's mother was on WhatsApp. Even Patricia Macluskey couldn't ruin this moment.

'Hi there,' she said, not bothering to remove the veil.

Patricia's face loomed, unsmiling, stern, her highlighted blonde bob arranged with geometric precision. She sat ramrod straight, calling from her office, judging by the plain blouse and a string of pale pink pearls.

'Whatever are you wearing?' she said. 'Do you keep bees?'

'It's my wedding veil. The designer sent it over for me to try on.'

'I do hope you haven't paid the charlatan. It's revolting.'

Lucy yanked it off, her good mood ruined. 'How can I help you, Patricia?'

'I'd prefer it if you call me Mrs Macluskey for now.' Her ice-cold eyes didn't blink.

'I trust this is a suitable juncture?' Patricia spoke in a tone that would freeze magma. 'I want to make certain we're clear before we proceed. Colin must remain unaware of this communication.'

Lucy mimed zipping her lips and hated herself one bit more. It met with a short, sharp nod.

'Marriage is a commitment, Miss Penrose. And it's crucial to ensure both parties understand the implications.'

Oh Jesus. Was this some sort of birds-and-bees-style talk? Had Colin told her about Lucy's mother dying when she was fourteen? Did Patricia think she didn't know how sex worked?

'I want to make sure both you and my oldest boy are certain about marriage, given the considerable differences both in your ages and backgrounds. I wish to explore shared values.'

A cold sweat broke out in the small of Lucy's back. She twisted her engagement ring. What did Patricia mean by values? Did Colin forget to tell her he was a Jehovah's Witness? Should she profess admiration for the music of Prince and Ja Rule?

'Go on.' Her voice came out hoarse, her fingers clutching the phone so tight she expected the screen to crack.

Patricia's mouth twitched. 'It's crucial to understand that marriage extends beyond the bride and groom. This union, should it proceed, will bring together families and traditions. As Colin's mother, it is my responsibility to verify that everyone involved is clear on their role.'

Lucy swallowed, even though her tongue had somehow glued itself to her front teeth. 'I went to taste wedding cake today.'

Why did she need to tell her that?

A transatlantic sigh conveyed boredom. 'You've only ever experienced Toronto as a visitor. What you might not grasp is that life here has a unique rhythm. It's important to understand that not everyone may be receptive to someone from outside the community. And I mention this out of genuine concern.'

'I appreciate your concern, but—'

'It's essential to be prepared for potential challenges and to consider your readiness for change before such a life-altering event goes ahead.'

She thought back to the last time Colin left for a flight to Toronto. How, just like always, he'd done all he could to talk her out of joining him. And now she got it. He was scared of his mother. But she'd be over three thousand miles away.

'I appreciate your concern.' Lucy channelled her inner zen. She'd have this out with Colin later. 'But we are committed to each other. And very much in love.'

This earned her one more sigh. And another non-smile.

'We need to discuss matters with my other son.' Patricia used the tone frustrated teachers fell back on at the exclusive girls' school Lucy had attended from the age of twelve. A place where she'd ached to escape and be just like everyone else. 'Kevin's accident has already made full family attendance problematic.'

Lucy had looked into Kev delivering his speech long-distance. She'd found a firm online that would print life-size cardboard cut-outs of anyone you wanted. They left space for the face. If Colin framed his iPad just right, it could work.

'By far your simplest option overall would be to relocate the ceremony,' Patricia said. 'I can pull strings and arrange the most perfect of halls, and Kevin will still get to wow everyone with his witty but erudite speech.'

Lucy had met Colin's younger brother once. He'd farted and laughed about the smell. Witty was a push. Erudite, impossible.

'Everything is booked. I mailed the invitations,' she said. 'But thank you for such a generous offer.'

Patricia shook her head. Her hair didn't move. 'This is far from a generous offer. It's what is going to happen.'

Lucy wanted to end the call. And block Patricia. Hell would freeze over, melt, and freeze again before she got married in Canada. For one thing, her father would refuse to fly. After a heart scare and a stent, he'd been advised against transatlantic travel. Much as he could be an interfering busybody, she wouldn't tie the knot without him.

'OK, but—'

Lucy was talking to a blank screen. Patricia had gone, leaving her staring at her phone, waiting for it to burst into flames.

Her hands shook with anger as she tried Colin. He needed to stand up to his awful mother. The woman had no right to bulldoze her way in and change everything.

His cheery voicemail greeting played.

Furious and frustrated, she ended the call, walked to her kitchen, stared at an "anytime is wine o'clock" fridge magnet, and poured herself a generous glass of Cabernet.

INT. LUCY'S FLAT - NIGHT
SUPER: 'ONE MONTH EARLIER'

Would hiding Colin's passport be breaking the law? There was that bit printed in the front about allowing the bearer to pass freely, without let or hindrance. But would she be arrested? And if that were to happen, Colin would surely take her side. He'd view her accidentally dropping it into the waste disposal unit as *un crime passionnel*. The Canadian embassy would need days, weeks even, to arrange a replacement, meaning they'd get to spend more time together.

'The Uber is still nine minutes away,' Colin called through from the living room. He'd been pacing and checking his phone.

'Traffic is a nightmare in this part of town,' she replied. 'You'll soon learn, when they say five minutes, multiply it by four.'

He poked his head around the kitchen doorway, and Lucy froze. 'I thought I put my passport in my bumbag, but it's not there.'

The first place he checked was under the bed.

'Found it,' Lucy said, opening and closing a nightstand drawer.

Colin looked up, his glasses halfway down his nose. 'How did it get in there?'

'Maybe I tidied it away without thinking.' He'd never buy that. Lucy employed someone to dust and hoover twice a week. Truth be told, she wasn't totally sure she knew where the cleaning supplies lived.

He took it from her, getting to his feet as the intercom buzzed.

'You really do have to go today?' she said, hoping for a last-minute reprieve. 'You've not met any of my friends. Or my father. Couldn't you stay for the weekend?'

The whole point of his visit had been so she could parade her lovely new man in front of friends. She envied Emma, whose three sisters had grilled Chris for hours before giving him their blessing. And Stu, who'd won over not just Fred's parents but six exacting first cousins before being deemed worthy.

'My ticket is non-refundable,' Colin said, running a hand through his always messy hair, 'and Mom is expecting me.'

The guy was 35.

'Is she throwing a party or something?' Lucy hated how

that sounded. 'What I mean is, do you need to rush off... like today?'

'She's doing a thing.'

Lucy wanted to ask, but Colin had been oddly elusive when talking about his parents. All she knew was his father retired after 50 years working in a public library and his mother was the principal of a Toronto college. And very scary, judging by the photos he'd shown her.

An idea formed.

'I'll push back appointments and come too,' she said. 'Spend a few days getting to know my future in-laws.'

Colin shared a warm smile, revealing perfect Canadian teeth. 'We've got the rest of our lives to get to know people.'

'OK, so I'll stay here then. On my own.'

His grin wavered for a split second. 'I'm not saying don't come.'

She grabbed her phone and tapped at the screen. There were seats on the same flight, but only in business class, and surge pricing would have made it cheaper to charter a private jet.

She clicked for details of other flights.

'I could get a train to Glasgow; there's a cheap ticket here going via Dubai and New York. I'd be there within a day.'

He leaned in to kiss her cheek. 'We'll talk online every day. Just you wait and see, Lucy-loo. Time will fly.'

She put down her phone. 'Unlike me.'

EXT. VICTORIA SQUARE - DAY

SUPER: '10 AUGUST 2024'

A grand civic space surrounded by imposing Victorian architecture. The square is dominated by the classical facade of the Council House, its

columned entrance and ornate clock
tower ("Big Brum") presiding over the
plaza below. Stone steps often serve
as impromptu seating for office
workers and shoppers.

After a sleepless night, thanks to Patricia Macluskey channelling Norma Bates, Lucy woke knowing she needed to find a way to tell Colin he needed to grow a backbone and stand up to her. At 2 AM, as she sipped chamomile tea in her dressing gown, Lucy had tried to see things from Patricia's point of view. Her son was getting married. Her other son was supposed to be the best man. Colin had glowed with pride as he shared photographs of nieces and nephews, stoked to be involved. If Kev couldn't fly, would that mean they had to stay home too? Lucy had no nieces or nephews, or sisters or brothers. The family guest list was just her and her father.

A father who was always rushing off to another meeting or bragging about his latest scam-busting crusade. But who'd somehow made time to take against her fiancé. Couldn't he see how this awkward, genuine man made her feel real? Made her feel cherished? Sure, the sex wasn't fireworks, but Colin was there. Present. If he promised an 8 PM Zoom, the call came at 8 PM exactly—not a minute early, not a second late. Love came in different shapes and shades. What they had might not be blazing passion, but it was love all the same. Real love.

What if Patricia refused to budge on the Canada wedding? She needed her father there. In a moment of weakness, she'd even checked flights, hoping to minimise his time in the air. The doctor who inserted his stent had been clear: no long-haul air travel. But with a stopover in Iceland, the longest leg would be six hours—doable, according to her online search. Chatrooms were full of people taking far longer trips without issue.

She needed input from her friends. And thanks to a Groupon booking at a new city centre spa, she'd get to sound them out. If the subject didn't come up during a morning of primping and pampering, she'd whisk them somewhere lovely for lunch, ply them with fizz, and list her concerns.

As she and Emma walked down the stone steps leading into the top end of New Street, they passed a froufrou bakery.

'We should treat ourselves,' Emma said. 'The twins ate all the eggs, so I missed breakfast.'

Lucy refused to risk the smallest of glances at a window display loaded with calorific temptation. 'Jean-Claude needs me to lose eight kilos before my wedding day.'

'OK, what's the plan? Have a leg amputated?'

'I'm on target,' she managed between gritted teeth. 'Seven and a half to go.'

'Given we're spending the morning locked in a steam box, you'll sweat it off.'

Lucy had spotted Fred getting out of a black cab, just as her phone rattled with a text from La Petite Mort Spa.

'Too late,' she said, relieved to move past the eat-me window. 'We're already running behind schedule.'

```
INT. LA PETIT MORT SPA - DAY
A place that to the untrained eye
could be an old-school hair salon,
beamed in from the 1980s. The decor is
white with red 'Bowie' style flashes.
Six framed photographs of different
women with colour variations on the
same asymmetrical bob line one wall.
```

La Petite Mort was a disappointment from the second they stepped through the door. Harsh lighting bathed everything in a sterile glow. A cheap scented candle tried and failed to mask the stench of perming fluid from the adjoining hair salon. A bored-looking receptionist glanced up from scrolling through her phone.

'Do you have a booking?'

Lucy took control. 'Penrose. Party of four.'

The girl peered past her. 'I only see three people.'

Jake had confirmed when first invited but then went quiet. Lucy wondered if he'd checked the place out online and gone into hiding.

'Someone else is joining us later.'

The receptionist picked up what looked like a Fisher-Price walkie-talkie.

'Gwen,' she yelled into the scuffed black plastic box. 'I've got your ten o'clock spa party.'

Crackles carried a distorted voice.

'Was that "send them through," or "has that stain not come out"?'

Another crackle. More words.

The girl put down the walkie-talkie and forced out a smile. 'It's cash only. If you wouldn't all mind taking a seat. I'll arrange complimentary cucumber water?'

```
INT. TREATMENT ROOM - DAY
A cramped, candle-lit space with
scuffed, peeling walls. Sheets hang
over shelves.
```

Emma, bless her, did her best to keep everyone's spirits from plunging into deep, dark holes. But a stockroom was a stockroom, even if someone had hung low-thread-count flat sheets over modular steel shelving, sprayed scent, and furnished the bare concrete floor with beanbags.

'The website made it look so lovely.' Lucy kept her lower lip from wobbling. 'I shouldn't have paid up front.'

'We'll make the most of it,' Emma said. 'What matters is the company, not the surroundings.'

All three of them chose that moment to glance around. All three of them focused on a poster advertising half-price highlights throughout August. From the other side of the door, the constant hum of hairdryers did little to drown out a local radio station DJ reading out the traffic news.

Fred yelped. 'Did anyone else see that?' He pointed towards a far corner, shrouded in darkness, home to one gigantic dust ball. 'Have they got mice?'

Lucy was every kind of mortified. And sorry.

'This was meant to be a treat,' she said. 'My way of saying thank you for all your support. I'm aware I might have been a little bit... demanding.'

Fred snorted. 'You made Joan Crawford look like Mother Teresa.'

Emma shushed him. 'Stop blaming yourself. Weddings are stressful. No one expects you to be perfect.'

'I *have* to be.' Lucy heard how she was whining. 'Patricia Macluskey thinks I'm not good enough for her son.'

Fred was on his feet, kicking at the dust ball. 'It's not mice. But it might still be alive.' He turned around. 'You do know you're marrying Colin, not his mother?'

Confession time. 'She wants to move the wedding to Toronto.'

Emma's eyebrows shot up. 'Toronto? As in... Canada? When were you planning to tell us?'

Lucy sank into one of the beanbags, the fabric sighing. 'I don't know. When I'd figured out how to handle it? When I'd worked out how to tell my father's solicitor where to shove her bloody prenup. When Colin develops a spine. It's just... a lot.'

Fred crouched down, his expression softening. 'Listen, we'll back you. Even if you have to face off with the dragon queen of Toronto.'

Emma reached over to squeeze Lucy's hand. 'You and Colin are all that matters.'

She nodded. 'I get that. It's just...'

The door to the stockroom opened. The girl from before was holding three towels. 'Time for your sensual massage experience.'

The three of them exchanged looks.

Emma stood, determined. 'We won't need those. What we *will* need is a full refund.'

'You'll have to ask Terry,' the girl said.

Fred leaned in to read the receptionist's name badge.

'Chanterelle,' he said, 'my friends and I do not wish to spend one more minute in this vermin-infested hellhole you advertise as a day spa. I am a lawyer, and I'm already considering a minimum of six trading standards breaches. Please don't make me add extorting money with malice to the list.'

INT. BÄCKEREI BRETZEL – DAY

The three friends laughed. Lucy did yet another impersonation of Fred at his self-righteous best.

'Please don't make me add extorting money with malices to the list.'

He glared. 'Do I sound that camp?'

Emma patted his hand. 'Your performance was most impressive, my love. But yeah, camp as fuck.'

Lucy's high peaked and slumped in short order. 'That was a disaster,' she said. 'I can't tell you how sorry I am.'

The café door chime sounded. Jake's raised eyebrows suggested he'd like to know why he'd received a text saying the promised spa morning had been cancelled. Despite a warning shake of the head from Fred, he demanded the full story, and when Lucy was done venting, he grinned.

'You could at least agree with me,' she said. 'It was a total rip-off.'

'I can't remember when I last got to smile for real,' he said. 'I wish I'd been there when this one pretended he was a lawyer.'

'I was brilliant.' Fred glowed with pride. 'I've seen every episode of *The Good Wife.*'

'Oddly enough, I met a lawyer at that silent retreat. If you ever need someone—'

Lucy sat up straighter. 'I'm already dealing with the one my father employed to protect the family silver from seizure by my husband-to-be. I deem the phrase prenup to be banished from the English language.'

Jake smiled again. 'Funny story...'

She cut him off. 'Victoria Harper is a total nightmare. And she acts like I'm some spoiled rich girl.'

He was staring. 'What are the chances of there being two Victoria Harpers who work in family law in the same city?'

'You've met her?' Lucy sat bolt upright. 'Then you know.'

'Actually,' Jake said, 'Vicky's pretty decent. She's helped me work out what I need to do with my life.'

'Of course you'd take her side.' Lucy stirred her coffee with unnecessary force. 'Everyone thinks I don't know my own mind.'

He shifted in his seat. 'Vicky suggested... fuck, I might as well tell you...'

Fred raised an eyebrow. 'Why do I sense incoming drama?'

'Tom used to love open-mic nights, and we once dared each other to get up and give it a go. I found a stand-up comedy course at the Outreach Centre that sounds brilliant. Six weeks, with a showcase at the end.' He pulled out his phone, scrolling to show them the details. 'I've signed up.'

The silence lasted three seconds too long. Fred and Emma's faces were frozen in identical rictus grins.

'That's...' Emma began.

'Fabulous.' Lucy cut in, her voice forced bright with enthusiasm. 'You've always been funny. Remember that time at my birthday when you did that impression of my father trying to pronounce "focaccia"?'

'You think?' Jake looked up from his phone. 'It's just, after everything, I thought maybe I'd try something different. Get out of my comfort zone.'

'Different is good.' Lucy nodded, daring the others to disagree. 'And if you need someone to try out material, we're all here for you.'

Emma chimed in with support. 'You can make anyone laugh.'

'Why not?' Fred agreed. 'Tom would approve.'

Lucy had an idea. 'You could be Colin's best man.'

Everyone fell silent. Jake broke first. 'Isn't his brother doing that?'

She explained about his stupid skateboarding accident, the broken leg, the multiple fractures, the eight-week no-fly ban.

'I'm in,' Jake said. 'Right now, I need life goals.'

A weight lifted from her shoulders. Patricia Macluskey could indeed go fuck herself. She'd sorted the best man problem. There was no need to relocate the wedding to Canada. 'You'd be digging me out of a huge hole.'

Jake held out a hand to shake on the deal. 'Consider your big day my first paid gig.'

Lucy grimaced and he laughed.

'OK, this one's on the house. Mates rates.'

```
INT. PETIT BOURGEOIS DRESS SHOP - DAY
SUPER: '12 AUGUST 2024'
A narrow, dimmed boutique. The focal
point is a curtained fitting area with
a plush, deep-red velvet curtain.
Spotlights illuminate an ornate
pedestal, where a dreamlike wedding
gown, luxurious yet imposing, awaits.
```

Lucy had chosen not to infer anything from the fact Jean-Claude had texted first thing to apologise. He couldn't make her dress fitting but would leave her in *des mains compétentes* of Sandrine. Just because Sandrine hated Lucy, and the feeling was mutual, it didn't mean the fitting would be a write-off. And anyway, she'd have Emma as support if things turned ugly.

A subtle perfume misted as they entered the shop. Jean-Claude was a classic maximalist. Gilt-framed mirrors adorned every wall, a crystal chandelier hung above a plush velvet chaise lounge. Mannequins posed in elaborate gowns, glittering accessories twinkled in the light from strategically placed spotlights.

Sandrine materialised, as always wearing a tailored black suit, the fabric skimming her willowy silhouette. Impeccably coiffed ash-blonde hair framed sharp cheekbones, while kohl-rimmed eyes regarded Lucy with cool appraisal. A Hermès scarf knotted with practiced nonchalance adorned her swan-like neck, and her manicured fingers bore a single statement ring.

'Mademoiselle.' She tapped her delicate antique gold watch. 'Vous êtes en retard.'

They were indeed late. But only by ten minutes.

Sandrine gestured towards a curtained area. 'Je vous en prie. Do not keep a wonderful creation waiting.'

The thing was, Sandrine wasn't actually French. Lucy had gone to school with her when she was plain old Sandra Watson.

The first girl in their year to get fingered behind the bins by a boy now serving time for fencing stolen sports kit. But, if the dress lived up to the sketches and the veil, she'd set all this to one side and play along. So much about planning a wedding was theatre, after all.

Sandrine flicked a button, and a curtain opened. There, on a pedestal in the centre, stood Jean-Claude's creation. Layers of embroidered pink silk and lace cascaded to the floor. Delicate beading winked like stars, picked out by overhead lights.

'Lucy.' Emma waved a hand in front of her face. 'Are you OK?'

She was more than OK—Lucy was breathless. She circled the podium, reaching out to trail her fingers over intricate detailing.

Sandrine was waiting. 'Vous voulez l'essayer?'

Lucy slipped into the dimly lit changing room and stepped out of her jeans and T-shirt. A second assistant appeared and helped her into the exquisite gown. And Lucy caught sight of herself. It was all going to be OK. Sod Marmolite and her GCSE chemistry; if the dress was right, the cake didn't matter.

The girl began doing up a long zip running up the side of the gown. Halfway, she stopped and called for Sandrine, who whipped aside the modesty curtain and gasped.

'Mais madame a pris du poids.'

Emma intervened. 'You look wonderful, Luce.'

She dared herself a glance in the nearest mirror. Despite four weeks of Monjouro-induced light-headedness, acute indigestion, and raging diarrhoea, the dress accentuated her every curve and contour. And not in a good way.

'Perhaps if you hold in your stomach?' Sandrine suggested, her grin equal parts evil and smug.

Lucy wanted to cry but wouldn't let Sandrine win. 'The

problem here, Sandra, is that Jean-Claude must have used the wrong measurements.'

She swallowed bile. Her eyes stung. The structured bodice squeezed her chest, and the full skirt overwhelmed her frame. This was meant to be a fairytale wedding gown. The tarnished copper buttons were supposed to be gold. And, when she looked closer, the stitching appeared uneven. Lucy had envisioned herself gliding down the aisle, turning heads—not stomachs.

Sandrine clapped her bony hands. 'Mais c'est splendide. Une princesse.'

Sarcastic cow.

Lucy shifted. Her mother's absence hit like a physical blow. She should be here, fussing over the dress, offering words of reassurance. Telling Sandra Watson to go to hell.

'It just... isn't right,' she choked.

Sandrine's eyes narrowed in judgement. 'Mais pourquoi?'

'Get Jean-Claude. Now.' Lucy fumbled with the horrid copper buttons, her vision blurring. 'On the phone.'

Sandrine scuttled away. Emma smiled reassurance. 'The dress is still stunning, Luce.'

'I look like a low-rent drag queen. Colin will run screaming, confirming to perfect Patricia that I'm unfit to marry her precious son.'

Emma fiddled with the folds. 'You don't think you're seeing something we're not?'

Sandrine returned, unsmiling. 'Jean-Claude is *nondisponible*... unavailable, but he says the design matches your specifications.'

'I'm a VIP client, for God's sake. This isn't good enough.'

She shrugged, peak fake-Gallic, and Lucy hauled the dress over her head, sending it flying into a pink pile of lace and tulle.

'My bank will cancel payment,' she said, hating how red her cheeks had become. 'Emma, please arrange an Uber.'

'Mademoiselle, please.' Sandrine was trying for sympathy, but failed to hide her sick pleasure. 'The dress matches—'

Lucy had pulled on her jeans, shrugged into her top, and was heading for the door, pulling on her shoes. 'Stuff your specifications up your fake French bumhole.'

INT: LUCY'S FLAT – DAY

Lucy cleared her throat and swallowed, not wanting Colin to hear she'd been crying. 2PM in Birmingham meant the start of a Toronto working day. Time for the conversation she'd avoided for too long.

After one ring, his smiling face filled the screen, dimples deepening. 'Well, well, look who's calling. Everything OK, Lucy-loo?'

Just hearing his voice caused a small smile to tug at her lips. 'Hey there, you. I'm OK. So busy with the wedding, though.'

'More problems with the cake lady?'

Lucy swallowed. Her mouth was already dry. 'The dress fitting was a disaster, but there's something I needed to ask you.'

'Shoot.'

'I spoke to your mother.'

She heard him take a breath. 'What about?'

Remember, he probably loved her. Lucy had to pick her words with care. 'She kept going on about how different things would be after we're married.' Lucy decided she had nothing much to lose. She might as well ask the question bugging her most. 'Does your mother think we're moving to Toronto after the wedding?'

There was a long pause. 'If this is to do with her wanting to move everything here...'

'It's a direct question, Colin.'

Another pause. A heavy sigh. She could picture him fiddling with his glasses, running a hand through bed hair. 'She just never listens.'

A knot formed in Lucy's stomach. 'Is that you telling me it's what she thinks is going to happen, because—'

'Lucy-loo, quit with the worrying. Mom is Mom, and she likes to think she's getting her way. The best thing is to pretend like she's not even there.'

Lucy grabbed a cushion from the sofa and hugged it to her. She couldn't go through this again. Another man too weak to say no and put her first.

'Can you do that?' she said, her voice a tangled whisper.

'Hey babe.' He sounded concerned. He sounded like her Colin. 'You matter more to me than anything.'

After hanging up, she curled into a ball. Her head throbbed, everything ached. This couldn't be Will Part Two. It just couldn't.

```
EXT: GAS STREET BASIN - NIGHT
SUPER: 'MAY 2022'
A spring evening. People sit outside
bustling restaurants and bars. The
canal is lined with trees just begin-
ning to turn green.
```

This had been where she'd said yes almost one year earlier, when Will Grant got down on one knee and a single violinist played. It felt fitting that this was where it all ended. Will, tall and golden in his cable-knit Ralph Lauren sweater, looked down at her with that familiar mixture of up-himself disdain and faux concern that made her want to slap his smug face.

'You can keep the ring, Luce. Consider it a parting gift.' He actually winked. The moron actually had the fucking nerve to wink. 'Think of it as something to remember me by.'

The diamond—three carats, he'd bragged to everyone at his parents' garden party—burned through her palm. Two years reduced to a 'parting gift' because some trust fund tosser with a yacht needed a crew member. And his mother was all in favour.

'I stood on that fucking platform at Snow Hill for an hour.' Lucy's voice rose above the chatter from café tables laid out for a late spring evening. 'An hour, Will. And you couldn't even be bothered to call. Or text me, because Tarquin or Hugo or whatever bloody stupid name your friend has was "unexpectedly in town."'

A couple of teenage girls nudged each other, pointing at Will. Of course they did. They probably thought he was a model, just like her onetime best friend Fiona had. They'd fallen out over who he fancied. She missed Fiona so much.

'That was ages ago, darling.' He checked his Rolex. 'Look, I've got to run. The yacht leaves Cape Town on Sunday evening, and I'm booked on—'

'I don't care if it's leaving from fucking Narnia.' Lucy yanked the ring off her finger. 'I don't need something to remember you by. I'd rather forget I was ever so stupid.'

The ring bounced off his perfect nose, hit the ground with a musical ping, and rolled. Lucy watched in horror as it dropped through the ornate iron grille of a drain cover.

'Brilliant,' Will said, glancing around, his face turning red. 'Absolutely brilliant. You know that ring cost—'

'More than I earn in a year. Yes, you mentioned that. Several times.' Lucy turned away, refusing to let him see her tears. 'Have fun playing sailor boy.'

She was halfway to the bus before she realised she was crying. And on the bus when she made up her mind she didn't care.

INT. GERALD'S OFFICE – DAY
SUPER: '13 AUGUST 2024'

Lucy had tried to act like her dropping by was just a flying visit as her father looked up from his desk, initial surprise flickering before his regular warm smile took hold.

'My darling daughter. What a pleasant surprise. Tea?'

'I can't stop.' She perched on the edge of a chair, her posture rigid.

On his way to his tiny kitchen area, he stopped. 'I see so little of you these days.'

Her heart clenched. How many times had she been the one saying that? She watched as he ducked into a hidden alcove to fill his silver travel kettle.

'I don't suppose you've had a chance to catch up with Miss Harper?' he said, without turning around.

'That's not why I'm here.'

He switched on the kettle, nodded over at the battered leather armchair, and she sat. For a long moment, she wasn't sure how or what to tell him. On the short walk across town, it had all seemed so clear.

'You've picked up a new client and you need me to check their credit status,' her father guessed. 'Hand over the details, and I'll pull some strings with my contacts.'

'Patricia Macluskey wants us to move to Canada after the wedding.'

The silence felt enormous. She watched as each word found its way into her father's head, his lips hanging on to the smile, his eyes letting go.

'And how do you feel about that?'

Anger flared. 'Is that all you have to say? I tell you I might be moving 3,000 miles away, and you ask me how I feel?'

'It's more like 3,500,' he said, his face flushing. 'You know what I'm like with numbers, darling.'

Words failed to form. Her mouth was dry. She was hurting. This had been his big chance to make up for all those times he sent apology letters to teachers when he couldn't make parents' evenings, when he bought her an expensive dress to say sorry for missing her in the school play. That Christmas Day when she sat with her auntie Kath wearing paper hats and eating cold turkey because he'd been called away to something more important.

'Colin's family have shown more interest in me in the last few months than you have my whole life,' she said. 'How does that make you feel?'

Did she actually say that? Or did the awkward bit only exist in her head? One look at her father, and she knew.

'That's not fair, darling.' He was on his feet, heading her way. Was he going to... he was hugging her. 'Why would you say that?'

CONTINUOUS

Lucy finished her cup of tea. Just like always, it tasted funny. The water in her father's office always came with a tang of Domestos. The milk was UHT.

She sniffed. 'The other day... you told me about Patricia being part of some political group. True something.'

He nodded. 'True North.'

She stared down at the floor. At the worn patterned carpet. The one her mother had picked out. The same carpet they'd had under their dining table, in the sitting room, in their old house. All those years ago. 'Go on...'

'It is better to keep your mouth closed and let people think you are a fool than to open it and remove all doubt.'

Mark Twain. She remembered it from school. Lucy shifted. Part of her wanted to suggest they go for an early lunch. It had been ages since they'd spent any decent time together. Quality time.

She glanced up. 'As the twig is bent, so grows the tree.'

He smiled. 'That private school education I paid for wasn't all wasted then.'

Lucy bit her lip, guilt gnawing. 'Tell me what you found out about Patricia Macluskey.'

EXT. KINGS HEATH – DAY

SUPER: '14 AUGUST 2024'

A bustling suburban high street that maintains its distinct village-like character despite being just a few miles from Birmingham city centre.

Jake had suggested a change of scene for coffee, a place unmarred by memories.

'I need to be somewhere Tom never was,' he'd confessed when they spoke on the phone.

Lucy understood. The city was full of ghosts.

'I know a little bookshop in Kings Heath,' she said. 'Right across from a bakery with pastries to die for.'

Afterwards, they had gone for a walk, arm in arm, and for the smallest of seconds, it felt like before. Before Tom's accident. Before she met Colin.

'Is that place new?' Jake pointed to a florist's shop, tucked between a record store and a vintage clothing boutique. The front window was a riot of summer blooms—yellows, pinks, and purples—with a handwritten sign: *Wedding Specialists*.

```
INT. BLOOMING MARVELLOUS - DAY
A small florist's store, with cool
storage units along one wall, buckets
of blooms along the other. A long
table fills the middle of the store
and there's a doorway leading into a
glass house near the back.
```

As the door opened, they were met with a blast of chilled air. A jumble of ribbons, spools of wire, and half-finished arrangements covered a workbench. Sheets of colourful tissue paper and cellophane rustled in the breeze of a rotating fan.

Lucy glanced around. 'Do you think there's a bell or something?'

'I'll check through there.' Jake nodded towards an open door.

'That's private,' she said, but he'd already slipped through, leaving her no choice but to follow.

A woman with her back to them was speaking on the phone. She looked to be in her mid-fifties, with curly grey hair escaping from a loose bun. A bright floral apron covered her linen dress, and her nails were painted a cheerful yellow. When Jake cleared his throat, she turned around, offering a smile and holding up one finger, indicating she was almost done.

Lucy pretended to be interested in a bucket of roses.

'Sorry about that.' The florist dropped her phone into a pocket. Her voice was warm and inviting. 'What can I do for you today?'

'Himalayan blue poppies,' Jake said. 'Can you get them?'

She shook her head with a rueful smile. 'Stunning, but nigh on impossible to source this year. You're not the first person to ask. Delphiniums are a lovely alternative, or blue hydrangeas. They're much more reliable, and they'll stay beautiful all day.'

Lucy sighed. 'I'm letting everyone down. First the cake, then the dress, now the flowers.' She knew how small and silly this all sounded. 'I'm sorry. None of this is your fault.'

'We should go.' Jake placed a hand on her lower back. 'You have such a lovely shop.'

They were almost at the door when the woman called after them. 'Every girl deserves beautiful things on her wedding day. Let's see what we can do.'

Over tea and lavender-seeded biscuits, Lucy spun a story, veiled in truth. Her father was Gerald Penrose—yes, *that* Gerald Penrose—and the last thing she wanted was to let him down.

'He's such a silly old duck.' She dropped her gaze, awaiting the familiar adoration from another Penrose fan.

The florist folded her arms. 'I'm going to assume I wasn't your first choice for flowers?'

Lucy blushed. 'We were supposed to be using McQueens. *Brides Magazine* sorted it as some sponsorship deal. My father was furious. He said it was sending the wrong message when Birmingham has such wonderful florists.'

She turned away, dabbing her eyes with a tissue Jake had produced on cue from his jacket pocket.

'Dear heart.' His voice was half Noel Coward, half Jasper Carrott. 'Don't let this upset you. McQueens did the flowers for *The Crown*. They're top-notch.'

Lucy risked a glance at the florist, whose expression had tightened. Their impromptu ruse was working. Flower-envy was real. As was teamwork.

'The big London places... all style and no substance, if you ask me. Mass-produced with no soul. Impressive on the telly, perhaps, but up close? Their reputation is as inflated as their prices.'

Lucy hid her smile, sensing victory.

INT. THE HEATH BOOKSHOP - DAY
A cosy, independent bookshop. The
aroma of freshly brewed coffee mingles
in the air. A chalkboard near the door
announces an upcoming author reading.

Lucy carried over two mugs of coffee, and Jake mimed a round of applause. She set them down with a flourish, taking an exaggerated bow. Together, they had played Iris from Blooming Marvellous like a fiddle. The mere mention of McQueens saw her crumble. Now, the Penrose wedding would boast local floral artistry—a feat that had seemed impossible two hours earlier.

She sat down. 'You really should consider going to drama school. I know it costs, but isn't it better to be poor and happy?'

He shook his head. 'Let's see how the rest of my comedy classes go first.'

She was glad he'd brought up the subject. It gave her the chance to offer him a get-out. 'I sort of feel like I steamrollered you into the best man gig. I mean, you don't even know Colin.'

'Are you asking me to step aside?'

Her insides knotted. 'That's the last thing I want.'

An awkward silence threatened. Having thrown herself into planning a whirlwind wedding, she'd neglected the people she loved, breaking the first rule of friendship: showing up. All Jake had needed was someone to listen, and she'd failed. She'd said nothing when he vanished for a week to a silent retreat.

'I'm sorry I haven't been around as much as I should've been,' she said. 'I feel awful about turning into a total bridezilla while you've been dealing with Tom's horrible sister.'

He forced a small smile. 'She's not making things easy.'

'When is the funeral?'

He stared down at the table. 'There are complications.'

Lucy wished she'd stuck to safer topics. The weather, Trump's stance on the death penalty, Polish macroeconomics. 'Fred mentioned a backlog at the coroner's office.'

Jake sniffed. The non-verbal equivalent of a shrug. 'The toxicology reports are inconclusive. Whatever that means.'

She needed something stronger than a cappuccino. Was it too early for vodka? 'But you and Rona... You are speaking?'

A pained expression crossed his face. 'Through her knob-head of a solicitor.'

A pang of guilt twisted in her stomach. 'I'm sorry.' She kept her tone steady. 'That must be awful.'

'Nothing says I've made it in life like moving back into your childhood bedroom in your early forties.'

Lucy winced. 'How's that going?'

'Oh, you know. Mum's fussing, Dad varies between being Dad and threatening to call the police because he thinks I'm an intruder. And then there's my vintage *Star Wars* curtains. All told, it's a total joy.'

Even in his darkest moments, Jake could find a way to make her smile.

'Is it weird of me to say I miss my mother?' Lucy struggled to keep her voice from crumbling. 'I mean, I love my father, but he's not interested in Himalayan blue poppies or lace veils.'

Jake squeezed her hand, but the admission had opened a floodgate of unexpected emotion. Her mother would have known how to fix the dress and where to source flowers. She'd have charmed Marmolite into letting her queue jump for the perfect cake.

'I miss her like I miss Tom,' she said.

Jake reached for his mug. 'Tom would have said something about how you've got the biggest balls going. And obviously, I never knew your mum, but if she was anything like you...'

Lucy held up a hand. It was all too much. 'Can we talk about the weather? Anything but my bloody wedding. Tell me about your comedy teacher.'

Jake's expression stiffened, and he took a long sip of hot chocolate. 'Miranda is intense, but I guess she knows her stuff.'

'I sense a but...'

'The course is not what I was expecting. I suppose I thought learning to do stand-up would be fun.'

'And it isn't?'

He shook his head. 'Every day, around about five-thirty, I get this horrible sick feeling in my gut begging me to find some reason not to go. Like I can't face being told each joke I try is shit. She's acting as if we're all trying out for the Royal Command Performance.'

'It'll come together.' She took a sip of coffee.

Jake squirmed in his seat. 'We've not even started writing jokes. She's got us all bouncing around on the stage, screaming our names into a fake microphone.'

Lucy grimaced. 'You're not going to do that at my wedding, though, right?'

'I promise, if I do, you get full heckle rights.'

Lucy allowed the shift in conversation, sensing he needed it. 'I expect updates.'

'Deal.' A twinkle returned to his eye. 'But only if I can make at least one inappropriate joke in my speech about your father's menopausal fan club.'

'Permission granted. You know he gets sent underwear?'

'What... like old lady pants?'

'It's mostly black and crotchless.'

Jake shuddered. 'Does Colin understand what he's marrying into?'

A stone settled in her gut. She knew right then she needed to set in motion the wheels that would expose quite what she might be walking into.

INT. LUCY'S FLAT – NIGHT

When Lucy's mobile sprang to life with an unexpected call from Colin, her initial reaction was that he had bad news to share. Her mind raced, fearing another Patricia Macluskey-shaped intervention. She sucked in a breath, straightened her shoulders, and answered.

His smiling face came into view.

'Hey, Lucy-loo.' He sounded upbeat. 'Sorry to call this late. Mom said to check in with you on wedding plans. Hope that's cool.'

Lucy all but squealed in horror as the screen split and Patricia appeared, thin lips pursed in a miserable line.

'I felt the need to follow up on our earlier discussion,' she said.

Lucy's heart raced, preparing for confrontation. 'OK...'

'I've reflected at length on how I might have come across to you.' Patricia's sweet-sweet smile was as genuine as a Temu designer candle. 'Things here are unchanged. Kevin remains forbidden from boarding a plane...'

For once, Lucy was ahead of things. 'One of my closest friends has agreed to step in.'

Patricia remained still, unmoving, her expression unreadable. The silence grew suffocating, as if her connection had frozen.

Lucy cracked first. 'Did we lose your mother?'

'I'm here.' Patricia had indeed turned to online stone. 'Would my son be familiar with this so-called friend?'

'I've mentioned him loads. Yeah.' She smiled. At Colin. 'It's Jake.'

'Cool. Right.' Colin was nodding. 'The gay guy.'

'How quaint.' Patricia's voice dripped with disdain. 'A homosexual standing in as *garçon d'honneur*.'

Lucy stared. 'What does that have to do with anything?'

Patricia blinked as if she didn't hear. 'I shall need an online *rendezvous* with your... friend. It's absolutely inconceivable to consider proceeding with the union until that happens.'

'You will meet Jake. At the wedding.'

'That rather brings me to my next point.' Patricia was back to glaring. 'The Macluskey family has important connections here in Toronto. Standards to maintain.'

Unsure where she might be going with this, Lucy chose to nod.

'Each and every day, I'm having to deal with calls from our oldest and dearest friends regretting they cannot attend, citing the inconvenience of travelling to London.'

'Birmingham,' Lucy interjected. 'London is a whole different city.'

Patricia dismissed the correction with a wave. 'My colleagues and compatriots have deep roots and commitments. An overseas ceremony is such a huge ask. Not to mention what sort of message it might send.'

Lucy paused. 'What *sort of message* might it send?'

Patricia leaned forward, her cold eyes narrowed. 'A wedding should find a way to honour traditions and heritage. Our community cares about such things.'

In his half of the screen, Colin's ears turned pink, but he stayed mute.

'This isn't only about location,' Patricia said. 'It's about respecting the Macluskey family roots. Preserving what makes us who we are.'

Lucy's pulse quickened, but she forced a calm tone. 'Like I said... the venue is booked, and the invitations sent.'

Patricia's eyes tried hard for a sympathetic smile, but the effort proved too much. 'What I struggle with is why you're choosing to celebrate your union in a country where you'll no longer be living. I realise we're all part of a global society, but everything involves admin. Your visa status will doubtless be problematic. And moving to Canada, integrating into our way of life, is about more than one big day. Believe me, I have only your best interests in mind.'

Colin wasn't arguing. Patricia might be used to having people bow their heads and say yes to whatever she demanded, but Lucy was a Penrose. Made of stronger stuff.

'First up, thank you for the input, Mrs Macluskey.'

Patricia allowed her a wan smile. 'I felt sure when matters were explained—'

'Nothing will change.'

Patricia's lips pursed. 'I see.' The words sounded marinated in vinegar. 'In which case, I hope everything works out for you.'

Her half of the screen turned dark, and Colin's expanded to fill the void. He did what he always did when faced with any kind of confrontation—he dragged a hand through his messy hair. 'Lucy-loo. I kinda feel like Mom maybe had a point.'

Was he siding with her?

'Moving to Canada?' she said. 'It's one thing to try relocating the wedding day, but your *mom* seems to think I'm about to give up my business, my home, my friends, my father...'

She ran out of words. She ran out of breath.

'Lucy-loo. Think about it—'

She ran out of patience. 'I'm done with this. We'll speak tomorrow.'

As she ended the call, a reminder popped up on screen. Tomorrow morning, she was meeting with Victoria Harper, her father's solicitor. The one charged with putting together the prenup. A document she'd started to think she might consider signing. Only might.

It was ten-fifteen.

Was that too late to ask her father if he'd found out anything dodgy about Patricia Macluskey?

INT. WALKER, HAYNES & DOBSON – DAY
SUPER: '15 AUGUST 2024'

Lucy stepped into an already crowded lift, and as the doors slid closed, she crossed her fingers. A habit she'd never quite managed to quit. A habit she'd inherited from her mother. *Keep your fingers crossed that things turn out just right, and they just might.*

The floor numbers blinked past—3, 4, 5—and she tried to ignore the feeling she was about to betray Colin. On the 23rd floor, as her heels clicked on grey slate tiles, her stomach somersaulted. Abstract art adorned the walls, and the company name was displayed prominently. It was all she could do not to turn and run.

'I'm here to see Victoria Harper,' she told a young woman, dressed in a crisp, starched white shirt tucked into a short, fitted black skirt. 'Lucy Penrose.'

The meeting had been scheduled weeks earlier, and Lucy had never intended to put in an appearance. But last night's

Macluskey three-way had her nerves on edge. She needed advice from a neutral third party.

Her mouth grew dry. Why didn't she grab a bottle of water on the way into town?

'Miss Penrose.'

Lucy startled at hearing her name. She looked up and saw someone even more polished than her LinkedIn profile photograph had suggested. Dressed in a tailored white suit, her father's solicitor exuded a calm, unshakeable authority.

They shook hands, and Lucy followed her into a corner office. Floor-to-ceiling windows offered a panoramic view of the city. Bright, almost sterile, with pale cream walls and devoid of clutter, a glass desk dominated the space, its surface pristine save for a single laptop.

Lucy forced a smile. 'I assume this is where you tell me what I need to sign.'

This met with a signal to sit. 'Mr Penrose is one of my oldest clients. But, I suspect, to you, he's an interfering old busybody who you wish would keep his nose out of things.' Victoria ducked her eyes. 'And in case you wondered, I prefer to be called Vicky.'

'Call me Lucy. And thanks for seeing me. I sort of need advice.'

Vicky perched on the edge of her desk.

'Advice,' she said, her voice softer. 'About the prenup?'

Lucy's eyes darted around, taking in the meticulously organised shelves, a lone succulent on the windowsill—a splash of imperfect green amidst all the sterile white.

She drew a shaky breath. 'It's Patricia—Colin's mother. My father said there's stuff online—'

Vicky interrupted. 'Online can be like the Wild West. If it's something someone said they heard her say or do—'

'He said she was at some sort of rally. For an organisation called True North.'

Vicky frowned. 'The name rings a bell.'

She went around her desk, sat, and turned to her laptop. Lucy saw how Vicky's eyes widened.

'OK, so True North is kind of awful,' she said. 'Have you spoken to your fiancé about your worries?'

'We're sort of not talking.'

Vicky reached into a desk drawer and produced a box of tissues. Pale blue and beautiful. It all but made her want to cry, if only to repay such a lovely gesture.

'Maybe Colin didn't even know about this,' Lucy allowed herself a hollow laugh. 'How do you handle the seating plan for a wedding reception when the mother of the groom is a homophobic racist?'

Vicky leaned back, her fingers drumming a thoughtful rhythm on the glass desk. 'Is Mr Penrose looking into this?'

'He is, but I sort of wonder if he's biased.'

'I have a colleague in Buffalo, and that's not a million miles from Toronto. In our line of work, we tend to spin webs of contacts. If you'd like, I could make discreet enquiries. See if the name sets off alarm bells...'

A spark of hope took hold. 'If I asked you to keep this secret, would that be compromising your relationship with my father?'

'Discreet enquiries,' Vicky said, allowing for the smallest of smiles. 'After all, you're not just marrying Colin. You're joining a family. If a friend of mine were in your position...'

Lucy met her gaze, seeing not her father's intimidating lawyer, but a potential ally.

'Thank you,' she said, meaning it. 'I'd appreciate that more than you know.'

```
INT. CRUMB AND BERRY - DAY
The warm glow of Edison bulbs cast a
golden light. Glass countertops gleamed.
Over tinkling piano music, machines
kneaded dough and mixers whirred.
```

Lucy stared at a chalkboard, unable to get the words to make sense. Her head was a mess.

'What's it to be then, bab?' The guy was smiling, ready to take her order. His name was Ethan—at least, that's what it said on his badge. 'Folk usually have the flat white. The house roast just changed. I'm obliged to inform you it's a dense finish glowing with golden brown sugar notes.'

She glanced around. The place was empty. It was probably closing time. 'Am I able to drink it here, or...'

He nodded. 'You find a table. I'll bring it over.'

She'd rarely bothered exploring this end of town. A few years earlier, it had been buzzing, but then Covid hit, and all the nice bars and cafes shut down.

'How long have you guys been here?' she asked.

'Six months?' He framed it as a question. 'This is only my second day.'

At the far side of the shop, an ornate stand displayed a four-tiered wedding cake that seemed to defy gravity, pearlescent white icing with a cascade of sugar flowers.

'It's something, isn't it?' Ethan's voice cut through her reverie.

She nodded, forcing a smile. 'It's beautiful.'

'Getting married yourself, bab?' He gestured to the ring on her finger.

The question left her reeling. She recovered fast and heard herself say, 'Yes. In October.'

'Congratulations. Who's doing the cake?'

A vision flashed into her head of Marmolite's face as she outlined the Haute Cakes waiting list. 'It's kind of up in the air right now.'

He grinned. 'Want to see our portfolio?'

'Why not?' she said, before she could stop herself.

Lucy's phone buzzed with a text from Colin.

COLIN MACLUSKEY

Everything OK, Lucy-loo? 🤍🤍🤍

Her finger hovered over the reply button, and the world seemed to tilt on its axis.

Ethan returned, placing a leather-bound book in front of her. 'Let's find your perfect cake.'

She looked up at his kind, expectant face, then back at her phone, and decided to let Colin's message go unanswered.

As the young barista launched into an enthusiastic description of what he'd been told were their most popular wedding cakes, she nodded along, her mind a complete mess.

But she couldn't stop. Wouldn't stop. Not until she knew for sure.

Lucy pointed at an elaborate design. 'That's exactly what I want. Can I book in for a tasting?'

Ethan beamed, pulling out an order form. 'My boss is going to freak. Two days in and I booked a cake tasting. When would you like to come in?'

Her phone buzzed again in her bag, but she ignored it, focusing instead on friendly chatter and the comforting aroma of coffee and pastries. The world outside, with all its complications and revelations, could wait. For now, in this bubble of vanilla sugar, Lucy could pretend everything was fine. That she was a bride-to-be, excited about wedding cake.

The denial wouldn't last forever.

Eventually, she'd have to face whatever the truth turned out to be. About the Macluskeys, about Colin, about her future.

But not today.

Not yet.

FADE TO BLACK

jake

FADE IN

INT. 16 HAVERCROFT LANE - DAY

SUPER: '19 AUGUST 2024'

A narrow 'box room' with a single bed.
The posters represent the musical fads
of someone who lived here 20 years
earlier, including a shirtless Sting.
Postcards blue-tacked to a dressing
table mirror include Britney and
Madonna. Silver glow-in-the-dark stars
brighten an otherwise charcoal
ceiling.

Like most mindless trends, bed-rotting landed in the collective consciousness courtesy of TikTok. Bed-rotting required minimal prep; the equipment was easy to find. People reframed duvet days into a lifestyle choice. Bed-rotters boosted their serotonin levels by staying tucked under the covers. And yes, John Lennon and Yoko Ono had tried to make bed-rotting a thing years earlier, but theirs had been a peace protest. The world hadn't yet invented a website crammed full of inane videos of people who thought they were funny. Hardcore bed-rotters doom-scrolled while binge-watching *Emily in Paris* or something equally trite. They consumed tear-and-share bags of over-salted crisps or road-tested skincare samples from glossy magazines. The point was to never leave your fetid pit, save for the occasional toilet break.

For Jake, an afternoon spent bed-rotting and staring sent out a clear signal that he should delete TikTok from his phone and stop paying any attention to people under the age of 24. They were not his tribe.

Familiar smells and sounds filled the house: laundry drying on a rack on the landing, his father's aftershave in the bathroom, a radio in the kitchen that only ever got turned off when the living room TV took over.

His parents hated silence. Jake craved it. He missed the Serenity Retreat.

Moving his grown-up life into his childhood bedroom had been like travelling back in a time machine that had just about scraped through its MOT. The walls, once a vibrant blue, had faded to a duller shade. A canary yellow duvet cover contrasted with silver-grey curtains. Tatty school textbooks lined a wooden bookshelf.

There had been a gentle knock at his bedroom door, followed by an exaggerated clearing of the throat. His mother had started doing this after barging in with laundry and catching teenage Jake enjoying quality time with an *Attitude* Robbie Williams photo spread.

'I'm decent,' he called, not lifting his head from the scratchy pillowcase.

'There's macaroni cheese in the fridge,' she said, placing a pile of white towels on a chair—enough to last him through to the first snows of winter. 'Your dad and me are off to see Rod Stewart at the NEC, so you'll have the house to yourself. You know... if you wanted to invite any of your friends over.'

Jake's parents went to concerts at least once a month. And not the usual mum-and-dad 60s tribute acts. They shunned a recent Stourbridge Town Hall set by The Strolling Bones. When they weren't being fleeced for hospitality suite tickets at the NEC, they found other reasons to be out—dinners with friends, last-minute weekend breaks, yoga, and am-dram. Sometimes he forgot his dad was sick, and he liked that a lot.

He hadn't told them about the stand-up comedy class. For one thing, they wouldn't understand why anyone needed to learn how to get up on a stage and tell jokes. And comedy wasn't their thing; his mum had once walked out halfway through a *Black Country Night Out* chicken-in-a-basket show, loudly declaring the elderly male comic too blue.

INT. LGBTQ+ OUTREACH CENTRE – NIGHT

The Outreach Centre was one of those places he always meant to visit, knew he should support, but had never quite made time for. When he reached double doors, his eyes took in a laminated sign:

COMEDY COURSE
START TIME: 7 PM SHARP
NO EARLY ADMISSIONS. NO ALCOHOL
DOORS OPEN AT 7 PM
LATECOMERS NOT ADMITTED
NO EXCEPTIONS

Miranda Ratchett's comprehensive joining instruction email had done away with pleasantries, focusing instead on house rules: *I expect full attendance. Comedy is serious business, and I only want dedicated individuals who trust the process. My course is a safe space for aspiring comedians, not time wasters.*

Nerves took over as a young guy staple-gunned a pride flag to the far wall. Jake was early. Over half an hour early.

He ducked back through the doorway, descended three bare wooden steps, and stepped out into the street.

    INT. THE LOFT LOUNGE - NIGHT
    A modern Birmingham LGBTQ+ bar, decked
    in rainbow flags in the heart of a
    central Birmingham area known as The
    Gay Village.

There were three bars Jake knew and still loved in Birmingham. He'd sort of become what he used to ridicule—a non-scene gay. But when the mood took him, whenever Tom had suggested they dress up and go drinking and maybe even dancing, his absolute first choice was The Loft Lounge. On a busy Saturday night, they could combine the drinking and dancing and then not feel like they missed out when, by mutual consent, Tom and Jake hailed a cab and found themselves in bed before midnight.

Jake pushed open the glass doors, stepping into a space that straddled the line between trendy and homely: Industrial New York loft meets the contents of a charity shop donation bag. Plasma screens showed football, and fluorescent pink posters promised 2-4-1 cocktails.

Monday night was nothing like Saturday. In one corner, a table of younger guys nursed bottles of beer, glued to their phones. An older couple looked to be filling time before going somewhere else. Together. Like a film or a play or someone's house party. Because some people do throw parties on a

Monday. Dinner parties mostly. Not loud, banging parties; not crawling home at three in the morning, head broken, mouth dry with some stranger you think might be called Greg parties.

Miranda Ratchett's rules had been clear, though; he couldn't risk smelling of drink and being refused admission, so he ordered Diet Coke.

A guy on his own stared over, smiling, and Jake realised they'd sort of dated for two drunken weeks. Eight years ago. By dated, he meant they had a handful of drunken shags, and two or three forgettable ones. What was his name? Cameron, Caleb, Ciaran, Chris? When he smiled back, it was clear the guy had been looking at someone else.

He ordered a Coke and managed not to bite back when the barman asked if he meant Diet Coke, instead insisting on ice and a slice. It was his first night out alone in a gay bar since... since he couldn't remember. Tonight could well be the first of many.

INT. LGBTQ+ OUTREACH CENTRE – NIGHT

Back in the Centre, Jake followed a girl with red hair into a utilitarian room. Leaking water had stained the once-white ceiling tiles brown, and paint peeled from the frame of a cracked window. Mismatched chairs lined up to face a small, raised platform. A rickety table held a pitcher of water and paper cups.

A woman with close-cropped grey hair was holding court. 'Yeah, well, I've like written a one-person show, and I'm looking for Miranda to help me polish the script before I take it to Edinburgh.'

A guy in NHS glasses enthused about being famous. 'But on my own terms. Like Jesus.'

Everybody else looked to be sick with nerves. Jake had found his people.

A door on the far side of the room opened, and in walked someone he vaguely recognised from an airbrushed photograph on the comedy class website. In the flesh, Miranda Ratchett was older—a walking, talking embodiment of beige. From a shapeless top that screamed apathy to culottes that hung with the enthusiasm of a deflated balloon.

'Funny for life?' She framed her first words as a question.

Every single person fell silent.

'Right then. Let's all find a chair. And sit in rows. Imagine you're part of the audience in my comedy club.'

Miranda dumped a shapeless canvas bag next to a wooden stool and pulled out papers.

'Contracts,' she said. 'The knowledge I impart has huge value. You have paid for access, but you haven't paid to share it with any Tom, Dick, or Harry.'

Jake flinched. He'd have shared anything with Tom.

'Before I start, the rule is each of you signs a non-disclosure agreement to say you will keep safe all handouts and not discuss the course content with any third party. Up to and including your partners.'

A hand shot up—a studenty girl with pigtails and piercings. 'What if my girlfriend asks how the class went?'

'The rule is you ensure no unauthorised person gains access to my printed materials.'

Jake shared a smile with a red-haired guy, who looked about the same age—a smile that he hoped conveyed how weird all of this seemed.

'If this is a problem for anyone, including you...' Miranda jabbed a podgy finger in Jake's direction, 'you are free to leave. But the rule is strictly no refunds.'

Because his job involved dealing with Horizon Seeking Holidays' customer complaints, Jake had a solid grasp of consumer law, and if he wanted a refund, he'd jolly well get one... but Lucy's wedding guests needed to be wowed, so he mumbled an apology.

Miranda circulated paperwork. 'Sign at the bottom of the third page.'

Jake folded his copy in four and slipped it into his jacket pocket.

Miranda saw.

'We won't be able to continue tonight until everyone has signed and returned their binding contract. There is an option to submit paperwork at our next session. That will mean leaving now. You will be welcome tomorrow evening. 7 PM sharp. No early admission.'

Jake cracked and signed her ridiculous contract. And the course began.

Miranda spent an hour droning on about how stand-up comedy was a serious business, grunting at anyone who asked questions, before getting to her feet to announce a thirty-minute comfort break.

Jake raised his hand. 'Are we still finishing at nine?'

'On the dot.'

He glanced at a clock. 'So maybe we don't need the full 30 minutes? We are here to write jokes, right?'

Miranda's eyes narrowed. 'Comedy isn't something that simply happens. Like a good wine, it takes time.'

'I thought—'

'I've taught this course a hundred and three times to date. Trust the process.'

With that, she grabbed a chair, dragged it over to the far corner of the room, and reached into one of her beige bags for a yellowed Tupperware box, then began picking at limp salad leaves, avoiding eye contact.

Nobody else had brought food, and nipping out for a quick pint was almost certainly not the rule. His only option was to mill around, nodding and smiling hello. An older woman with a blonde bob studied a timetable pinned to the wall, her lips pursed in concentration. She turned around and went to talk to Miranda.

'Would you mind if I interrupt your supper?'

The request met with a face that said yes. She continued regardless.

'Next Tuesday is an audition?'

'For the showcase.'

She frowned. 'When you say showcase, is that the thing we're doing at the end of the course? The show for our family and friends.'

Miranda's jaw clenched. 'Unless you're aware of some other showcase.'

The woman's shoulders slumped, and her confident stance faltered. 'It's just that my eldest has a ballet recital next Tuesday, so I might have to audition on Wednesday. I'm happy to get here early or stay late. Whatever works for you.'

Miranda snapped shut her Tupperware and reached into her tote bag for a lip balm.

'The rule is that the auditions happen on Week Two, Tuesday evening.' Her voice stayed even. 'I allocate equal minutage to each student. Pushing your slot to Wednesday would throw off the entire schedule.' The woman opened her mouth to protest, but Miranda raised a hand. 'The showcase carries my name. I can't let just anyone take to the stage. Each comic needs to earn their time in my spotlight.'

Jake looked around. The room lacked anything approaching a spotlight.

'If you are unable to make next Tuesday's audition, you may attend the showcase as an audience member free of charge. I'm prepared to waive the ticket price, subject to availability. If the show sells out, you'd need to stand at the back of the room.'

The blonde woman opted to haggle. 'I'll pay for an extra five minutes of your time on Monday, then. How much will that be? Ten quid? Twenty?'

The suggestion met with pursed lips. 'The rule is clear. If you want to take part in the Miranda Ratchett Funny for Life Showcase, it's a requirement that you make yourself available for audition in line with the published schedule.'

'My daughter has been practising for months. The recital means everything to her. I can't let her down.'

Miranda's eyes flashed with irritation. 'You signed a contract.'

'We all did. You didn't give us time to read it.'

'I made it clear that anyone who required more time to absorb the contents was free to leave and return tomorrow.'

The woman's shoulders sagged in defeat, her face reddening as she sniffed down what sounded like tears. 'Fine. It's your show. Your rules.'

Miranda's expression refused to waver. After putting away her salad box, she wiped her hands and tottered back over to her special table. Jake glanced around, wondering if he'd walked into some new version of hell. Miranda had sold the course as *fun fun fun*. A chance to laugh and hang out with like-minded jokers. There hadn't been many online reviews—especially if she had delivered this course anything like as many times as she claimed. He'd assumed stand-up comics were rebels. The sort of free thinkers who refused to rank and rate.

A chair scraped across the floor. Jake looked up to see the woman with the diary clash gathering her things before leaving. Past somebody making their way in. Laden down by heavy boxes, and looking out of place. But someone who was so very welcome.

When Miranda dismissed her class, Jake set off to find Vicky.

She was standing near the coffee machine, chatting to another volunteer, and when their eyes met, she screamed, and they stumbled into a messy hug, dancing in a circle.

'Small world,' he said. 'Of all the gay centres in all the towns, you had to walk into mine.'

'I thought I told you I did this...?' she said, straightening her jacket—Chanel Fall/Winter 2023, black bouclé with pearl-studded pockets.

He shook his head. 'I thought you were all about the corporate world.'

Vicky nodded hello to someone and signalled to a quiet corner.

'So, because my day job robs me of any moral compass, I volunteer,' she said. 'It's my Plan B to get into heaven or be reincarnated as something other than lice. I assume you're here for the fabulous coffee and stunning décor?'

Jake ducked his eyes. 'Would you believe I'm trying to become a comedian?'

'That's... unexpected,' Vicky raised an eyebrow. 'Listen, I was only here to grab files, but do you fancy a quick drink?'

He hesitated, then let a smile take over. 'Try stopping me.'

INT. MISSING BAR – NIGHT
The eclectic décor blends pride flags
and vintage posters. Patrons gather by
small tables. Upbeat music plays.

Jake couldn't recall the last time he'd ordered a pint at Missing Bar. Photos of long-retired drag queens and yellowed flyers from past events papered the walls. He remembered being there on opening night, years ago, with Stu and Fred. Back then, Missing had been *the* Birmingham gay bar, the place to be seen. Time had not been kind.

Getting served took forever. The boyish bartender seemed to favour anyone younger and prettier. Had he become what his mum always complained about? At 42, was he past it? Invisible?

He'd stumbled around this bar, drunk on cheap vodka, chasing something—or someone—while most of the guys here had still been in nappies. Before Tom, a successful night ended with a splitting headache and a night bus ride home, his boxers balled up in his pocket.

'So,' Vicky took a sip of wine. The face she pulled suggested it came with an aftertaste of malt vinegar. 'You're going to be the next Joe Lycett?'

Jake's cheeks were on fire. 'I agreed to be Colin's best man. Lucy caught me at a low ebb.'

'Wait.' She wiped her mouth with the back of her hand. 'The guy doesn't have friends?'

'His brother's had an accident. I said yes without thinking it through.'

Vicky leaned back, laughing hard enough to draw glances from nearby drinkers. 'Does it ever cross your mind to say no once in a while?'

He forced a smile, but the words hurt. He'd dug in his heels when Tom wanted to stay over in Bristol. And look how that played out.

She was frowning. 'Did I say the wrong thing?'

He blinked away what might be tears. 'No. And yeah... you're right. I need to get a backbone.' He needed to sit and nodded over at an empty booth.

A sticky-to-the-touch table bore the scars of countless wild nights. For an awkward minute, silence dominated. They'd become first-date strangers, exchanging polite smiles, struggling for stuff to talk about. Vicky spoke first.

'Correct me if I'm mistaken, but we *do* know each other,

right? You're acting like you caught your geography teacher buying top-shelf porn in the local newsagents.'

She was right. He wasn't being himself. And he knew why.

'If there's a road accident and they do toxicology reports, that means they think the driver was drunk, right?'

'It's routine, Jake. The police have to explore every angle. Reports rule shit out, not in.'

'What if Tom had been drinking?'

Vicky's face softened, and she reached across the table, her hand stopping short of his. 'Stop letting the "what ifs" take over. Accidents happen. There doesn't have to be a reason.'

Jake swallowed hard, doubt catching in his throat. If Tom had been drinking... was it because he was unhappy? Unhappy with him?

A drag act took to the stage—some guy in a slinky silver dress and a towering wig, miming to Cher. The crowd whooped and whistled, and for one fantastic moment, everything blurred, and Jake saw Tom at the bar, waving a tenner, calling out to be served, before turning back and giving him a playful wink.

He forced a smile. 'You're right. Overthinking, as usual.'

Vicky squeezed his hand. 'Love is messy, complicated. But don't let it eat away at the good stuff.'

They switched to bottled beers, weaving through the crowded pub. The music got louder, and Jake watched two guys dancing, leaning in to yell in each other's ears. He remembered when that had been him and Fred—two friends, never ever thinking things might change.

Vicky leaned in. 'You want to go somewhere we can actually hear ourselves think?'

Jake grinned. 'OK, boomer.'

INT. VICKY'S FLAT – NIGHT

Jake stood by the window, looking down at the rain-slicked city streets. Opposite, a billboard flashed, and the fancy hotel two doors down glowed with warm, golden light. 'You're a big deal, right?'

Vicky rolled her eyes, leaning on the counter as she poured two glasses of wine. 'I paid way over the odds for this place, and as Lucy's lovely father never tires of telling me, got myself royally screwed by taking on the lease.'

He turned and smiled. 'You do know she's got no intention of signing the prenup.'

'I'm aware of the current state of negotiations.'

'But you think you can change her mind?'

'Penrose kind of has good reason to worry.' She returned the wine to the fridge. 'The family Lucy's marrying into might not be the greatest.'

Jake's smile faded. 'Does she know any of this?'

Vicky raised a hand. 'People love to shoot the messenger. I'm leaving it to her father.'

'What are we talking about here?' He frowned. 'Tax evasion, sweatshops, shady business deals...?'

'They hate people like me.' She handed him his wine and took a slow sip of hers. 'And they probably don't have much love for the gays, either.'

His eyes widened. 'Wait—hate people like you? What are you saying?'

She sighed. 'There's a possible link... between Patricia Macluskey and some far-right nutjobs. Nothing proven, but enough to raise serious red flags.'

'Does Lucy even know?' he pressed, his voice low.

'Like I said, people take it out on the bearer of bad news.

Penrose wants me to dig around and report back. What he does with anything I find out is his call.'

Jake moved to the sofa, lowering himself down, feeling unmoored, as if he'd woken in a strange place. 'I guess... I could tell her.'

'Why would you do that? Nothing's proven. Not yet.'

'But she's my friend...'

'And what do you reckon is going to happen if you tell her that the man she's marrying is Oswald Mosley in a shift dress, and it turns out to be a pack of lies? She'd never forgive you.'

He took a long drink of wine. 'How do you deal with stuff like this? I mean, I get to pass by on the other side. When people see me, they don't think, Oh, look, there's a gay guy. But you...'

'I let myself get angry.' Vicky came to sit beside him. 'And then I take a step back. I rise above it, listen to what they're really saying. When I do that, it's just noise—words designed to hurt. Racists crave a reaction. It's not my job to give them one. I hear the fear behind all the hate. The insecurity behind their bigotry. And that's where I find my power.'

Jake stared. 'I don't get it. Isn't that the same as letting them get away with it?'

Vicky shook her head. 'It's about exposing them. When they show who they are, everyone sees. I make their prejudice look small and pathetic.'

She flicked on her vape, took a puff, and exhaled a slow cloud. 'I'm a senior partner at the second-biggest law firm in Birmingham, and I just so happen to be black and trans. The higher up I go, the more times I see it—the surprise in their faces, like I shouldn't be there. I can't tell you how often I get given coffee orders.'

Jake leaned in, still unsure he understood. 'And you... put up with that?'

'I never play the race card,' she said, her voice steady. 'I let my work speak for itself. Every case I win, every agreement I sign off, is a victory. It proves them wrong without me having to say a word.'

She paused, looking out at the rain. 'But the hardest part… it wasn't in a boardroom or a courtroom. It was when my mother called me a liar. Told me to stop dressing like a whore. Refused to use my name, only the one she claimed the Lord gave me.'

Jake swallowed. 'Your family's religious?'

She laughed, a dry, brittle sound. '*Songs of Praise* on Sundays, but otherwise no. And as far as I know, the Lord wasn't there when she gave birth. He didn't whisper in her ear. I got named after her grandfather.'

Jake's heart ached. 'That's shitty. Families are why we make friends.'

She took a sip of her wine and managed a small, warm smile. 'Cheers to that.'

INT. LGBTQ+ OUTREACH CENTRE – NIGHT
SUPER: '20 AUGUST 2024'

As Miranda waddled to the middle of her pallet-board stage, Jake shifted on his folding chair, the metal frame creaking. At least six people hadn't returned for the second class. She scanned the survivors and launched into another lecture.

'Comedy is an art form.' She brandished her beloved lip balm. 'The language of stand-up is an art form.'

NHS Specs Guy had his hand up. 'Miranda, is it allowed to say you don't want to swear?'

One over-plucked grey eyebrow flickered. 'That isn't what I meant.'

'Yeah, but is it?'

She folded her arms with a deep, dark, heavy sigh. One dredged from the core of her deep, dark, heavy soul. 'There is a rhythm to jokes.'

And so began another half-hour rant from Miranda Ratchett to a class of wannabe comics who had only come here to mess about and make each other laugh. Jake felt like he was back at school with Mrs Evans, the oldest teacher ever employed by Dudley Metropolitan Borough to teach English to disengaged fifteen-year-olds. Kids who didn't care about Lady Macbeth or *Dulce et Decorum Est*, because their hormones were raging, and there had been talk of a porn mag rammed into the hedge behind the science block.

He glanced around at his classmates: a middle-aged woman in a floral dress, scribbling in a notebook; a cute enough guy with sleeve tattoos who kept checking his phone; two friends who sat apart from the others, whispering and giggling. He sensed himself alone in a room full of strangers, all desperate to learn the dark art of stand-up comedy.

'Mr Taylor.'

Jake sat up straight. Miranda was staring right at him.

'Perhaps you could tell us a joke using the structure I just outlined.'

He'd been a million miles away, wishing he'd never agreed to be Colin's best man, wishing every shitty thing hadn't happened, wondering if his offer to talk to Lucy on Vicky's behalf might not be such a good idea after all. Everyone was staring, relieved not to be the one Miranda picked on first.

'When you're ready, Mr Taylor. You were so keen to start writing jokes. This is your chance. Make us all laugh.'

Miranda was a bully. No different to the weasel-faced shits who followed him home from school, hid behind cars, and waited to jump out and call him names or grab his bag and turf the contents onto the pavement.

Poofter. Bum boy. Faggot.

Sweat pooled at the base of his spine. His face was on fire, and his scalp itched.

Miranda buried her hands in the pockets of her beige poncho. 'If you're not ready, we can come back later...'

The simple thing would be to nod, hang his head in shame, and say that she should let one of the others have a shot at telling a joke. But then, she would have won.

One foot managed to lead the other to the stage. His tongue freed itself from the roof of his mouth. He lifted his head and showbiz-smiled.

'Marriage...' He coughed to clear a claggy throat. 'Marriage is...'

And he was a million miles away, floating above, wondering what the hell he was doing there. He had no clue what it meant to be married. He'd joked with Tom about how they might shock everyone and tie the knot, but that was never going to happen. One time, three sheets to an offshore wind, Tom had slurred some righteous speech about how marriage was for conformists.

'I don't want to be equal to my sister and all her miserable mates,' he'd said, throwing a heavy arm around Jake's shoulders. 'I'm better than them. *We're* better...'

Jake could have argued, but what was the point? He liked the fact they *could* get married, and perhaps that had to be enough. Stu and Fred had pushed the boat out big style when they tied the knot, hiring a castle for the weekend, putting everyone up in fabulous rooms, granting free run of the spa and swimming pool, hosting huge dinners and lavish breakfasts. After the ceremony, friends and family danced and swayed along to actual Bucks Fizz—or rather, three members of the original band, court-ordered to perform under some other name.

'Marriage is what?' Miranda prompted, picking dead skin from her thumb.

'Marriage is what you do when you know you've run out of options.'

NHS Specs Guy guffawed. Nobody else laughed.

Miranda rolled her eyes. 'How is that in any way representative of what I just spent half an hour explaining?' She mimed chopping with one hand. 'Set up... punch.'

Red-faced, he mumbled an apology and sat back down. The idea of having to entertain Lucy's wedding guests—who may or may not include a spittle-flecked fascist—was killing him. He barely registered Miranda calling up the next victim, too lost in a downward spiral.

'You.' She jabbed a finger at NHS Specs Guy. 'Show us how it's done.'

His classmate bounded onto the stage like a puppy let loose in a local park.

'I used to play the piano by ear, but now I use my hands.'

Miranda erupted into laughter. Big, gulping gales of laughter. Laughter that didn't sound real.

'That's spot on,' she said, showering him with applause and making the same chopping gesture as before. 'Set up. Punch.'

She carried on clapping until everyone joined in. Jake included.

INT. THE RED LION - NIGHT
A typical back-street boozer with
muted TV screens showing sports.

Jake hadn't meant to hang around after class, least of all to agree to join the others for a pint, but then he weighed up his options. Go home, tiptoe past the living room where Dad would be snoring in his armchair while Mum read a Mills &

Boon. She'd put down her book and corner him in the kitchen to ask about his night, meaning well, but leaving him feeling more and more like his life sucked.

At the far end of Hurst Street, the Red Lion had always looked—from the outside at least—defiant in the face of surrounding pink-pound-chasing bars. An England flag fluttered from a pole over the door, and a poster in the window promised *Live Sports*.

Inside, a handful of locals gathered at the far end of the bar. The *Live Sports* TV screens were muted, and the background music was mid-90s pomp rock. NHS Specs Guy took charge, pulling together two tables.

'I'm Pete, by the way.' He extended a hand. 'Welcome to the Miranda Ratchett support group.'

A ripple of nervous laughter suggested everyone would rather someone else land the first blow. Jake couldn't be that guy. Tom had often called him negative.

'You spend all day reading complaints; it has to rub off,' he'd once said. Possibly in the middle of a fight over why their team never won the local pub quiz. Emma was a nurse, Chris had an A level in geography, and Lucy's dad was *The Scambuster*. Stu ran his own company, and Fred had never missed an episode of *Married at First Sight*. How come they always came last? It had to mean the other teams were cheating.

'I'm Jake,' he said as he picked a chair. 'What brings you to the world of stand-up?'

Pete's smile faltered. 'My wife lost her step-mum a few months back, and... well, she's been struggling. I thought if I could make her laugh again, even a little...'

A lump formed in Jake's throat. 'That's... that's beautiful, mate.'

'What about you?' The woman in the floral dress introduced herself as Susan.

165

'Oh, um, best man duties.' He took a slug from a bottled beer. 'Though I'm thinking I've bitten off more than I can chew.'

'Join the club,' Tattoo Guy—Jordan—chimed in. 'I thought this would be a laugh. But Miranda is a total cunt.'

A collective cheer sounded around the table.

'I felt terrible when she had a go at you, Jake,' Susan said. 'She seems to get off on humiliating people.'

Pete nodded, only half smiling. 'I keep waiting for her to tell us it's all an act. You know, an exercise in how *not* to treat your audience.'

Jake found his mind wandering. He thought about Tom, about all the jokes they used to share. The silly voices, the private references that would have them in stitches while everyone else looked on bemused.

'Earth to Jake,' Jordan's voice cut through his reverie. 'You still with us, mate?'

He blinked. 'Sorry, just thinking.'

'About your best man speech?' Susan asked, her eyes wide.

Jake nodded, then paused. 'Sort of. I'm doing this to push myself. Because I've spent my whole life ducking away from anything tough.' A rumble of agreement did the rounds. 'I'm doing this for my partner.' He swallowed. Should he go on? 'His name was Tom. And he died.'

A hush fell over the table.

'I'm sorry,' Pete gave his arm a blokey kind of pat.

'Tom would have loved this. The class, I mean. He always knew how to have the whole room hanging off his every word.'

'Sounds like a lovely guy.' Jordan raised his glass. 'To Tom.'

The others followed suit, bringing unexpected tears to Jake's eyes.

'You know...' Susan said, showing all the signs of being a dyed-in-the-wool mum, of knowing how to distract when needed. 'That's what your speech should be about. Not just the bride and groom, but your friend. Remind people about how he could make everyone smile.'

'Has to be better than that out-of-options marriage joke you told, mate,' Jordan said.

This raised a laugh. And Jake joined in, feeling a spark he thought forgotten.

'You might be onto something there,' he said. 'Though I'm not sure Miranda would approve.'

'Sod Miranda.' Jordan's declaration met with a chorus of agreement. 'We're here to find our voices, right? Seems to me like you've just found yours.'

Jake raised his bottle in a toast. What if he had? What if he was about to?

EXT. 16 HAVERCROFT LANE – NIGHT

Lights glowed from every window of his parents' house, upstairs and down. His dad was always super strict about turning them off when leaving a room.

We're not made of money. I'm not running Blackpool illumi- nations here.

He hesitated before pulling out his key. The front door opened, and his mother appeared, her eyes darting around as she forced an unconvincing smile.

'Is everything OK?' he said.

Her answer came too soon, too sharp. 'I literally turned my back for two seconds.'

'What's happened? Why are all the lights—'

'Your father needed a screwdriver.'

He didn't buy her explanation. 'It's gone eleven. Why isn't he slumped in front of the telly pretending to be awake?'

She gestured through the house towards the kitchen and then through another open door into the garden.

'He's in his shed.' Defeat laced her words, and she looked down at the floor, picking at the edge of her sleeve. 'Some lads found him. Hanging around by the school. They brought him home. Reckons he's fixing the lawnmower.'

Jake stepped past her, moving along the hall and through the kitchen.

'He might not know who you are,' she called after him. 'It doesn't mean he's forgotten. Not really.'

When he reached the shed, he slowed, unsure if he could face not being recognised by a man who looked like and sounded like his dad.

He knocked on the wooden door. 'Permission to come aboard?'

An eternity passed before a faint voice mumbled to come in.

By the dim light of a battery-powered lamp, his dad sat hunched over a cluttered workbench, sorting nails and screws into piles, his fingers moving with precision. Tools and jars of various sizes lined rickety shelves. This scene had played out countless times, but tonight, things were different. Bad different.

'You look busy,' Jake said.

His dad's head jerked up, and surprise registered.

'Oh, hello there.' The words came out polite and distant. 'You'll have to forgive me; I'm terrible with names.'

Jake released the breath he'd been holding. 'It's me, Dad. Jake.'

INT. 16 HAVERCROFT LANE – DAY
SUPER: 'MAY 1997'

Jake had read the letter three times before folding it carefully back into its envelope. His mother's handwriting—usually so precise—had wavered across the page. *I need time,* and *I don't understand* and, worst of all, *where did we go wrong?* The words burnt. He buried his face in his hands, shoulders shaking.

A gentle knock. 'Jake?' His dad's voice, soft through the door. 'Got you a brew, son.'

He wiped his eyes with his sleeve. 'Yeah.' His voice cracked. 'Just leave it by the door. I'll get it.'

His dad balanced two mugs of tea as he eased open the door with his elbow—a skill Jake had watched him perfect over years of midnight chats and morning wake-up calls. The familiar scent of Yorkshire Gold filled the room.

'You've got mail,' he said, smiling, impersonating a popular advertising slogan. He put down the mugs and nodded at the bed. 'Mind if I sit?'

Jake nodded. The mattress dipped.

'She'll come round,' he said, without making eye contact. 'Your mother. She's just processing a lot of information right now. And hoping for a full house at the bingo so she can pay someone to fix that bathroom window.'

Jake ought to smile. He wanted to. 'I shouldn't have told you both. Should've kept my mouth shut.'

His dad's hand was on his shoulder. 'Look at me, son.'

He turned, expecting... he wasn't sure what. Disappointment perhaps. Instead, his dad's eyes were soft with something that might have been pride.

'You know what makes you brave?' he said. 'Having the balls to tell us. To be yourself.' He took a sip of tea, drinking from the mug with the chipped handle. The one that had

169

become his. 'Back in my day… well, it was different. I must've known loads of gay lads at the factory, the social club. But nobody said anything. Not then. It wasn't done.'

'Dad, you don't have to—'

'No, listen.' He put down his tea. 'Remember my mate Big Steve? Used to come round Sundays to watch the match?'

Jake nodded. Big Steve had been a fixture of his childhood, always bringing Wagon Wheels. Always laughing.

'Found out years later he was gay. Only after he moved away. Never told a soul here. Not even me. His best mate.' His dad shook his head. 'Makes me sad now, thinking how lonely he must've been. Pretending.'

Jake's breath caught. 'Mum said in her letter… she said you must be disappointed.'

'Disappointed?' His dad barked a laugh. 'In what? Having a son who's honest? Who trusts us enough to tell us who he is?' He set his mug down on Jake's bedside table, next to a photo of them at Blackpool, Jake aged ten and grinning with candyfloss-stained teeth. 'Love doesn't come with conditions, son. Not proper love. And I love you proper.'

Something in Jake's chest broke and mended in the same moment. He leaned into his dad's shoulder, like he used to do after nightmares when he was small.

'Your mum…' He sighed. 'She loves you proper too. Just got some daft ideas in her head need sorting out. Give her time.'

They sat in comfortable silence, drinking tea. Outside, a spring evening darkened.

INT. 16 HAVERCROFT LANE — NIGHT
SUPER: '20 AUGUST 2024'

Jake had already lost Tom and the life they'd built together. Now he was losing his father. A cruel disease was draining away a strong, intelligent man, stealing his memories, his personality, every little thing that made him who he was.

Jake had been five when Dad had helped attach glow-in-the-dark plastic stars to his bedroom ceiling, so he could always find his way home.

But where was home now?

He wasn't ready for a drawn-out legal battle with Rona. He couldn't stand up in front of Lucy's friends and family and talk about a man he'd never actually met. And then there was work. Each day he received a text, reminding him to take however much time he needed. Did they even want him back?

How could he focus on any of this when his world wasn't done falling apart?

The back door opened. His dad walked in, clear-eyed and present.

'Make us a brew, will you, son?' he said. 'I've a mouth like the bottom of a birdcage.'

Jake reached down a mug—the one with the chipped handle that had somehow always been his dad's—and opened a box of Yorkshire Gold. His hands shook slightly as he filled the kettle. How many more times would they do this? How many more moments of his father being properly *his* father did he have left?

'I might just watch the headlines before I turn in,' his dad said. 'See what promises Keir Starmer made today.'

If anything, having him back, pin-sharp, just like he always was—just like that night in 1997 when he'd made everything OK with nothing more than a cup of tea and unconditional love—made losing him even more cruel.

He'd gone from having a partner, a home, and some sort of future, to sleeping in a single bed under Sting's watchful eye.

Tomorrow, he'd start looking for a new flat. It didn't mean he loved Tom any the less. But he needed a new start. Something his dad would understand, even if he might not remember saying it: *proper love doesn't come with conditions.*

```
INT. A BIRMINGHAM FLAT - DAY
SUPER: '21 AUGUST 2024'
A modern flat in a recently built
building on the lower end of Hurst
Street in Birmingham City Centre. The
walls are painted off-white, the light
switches are sprayed silver, and the
double glazed windows are anthracite
grey with white vertical blinds. The
laminate floor gleams.
```

The estate agent was gay. Miquel—*call me Micky*—had shown Jake three near enough identical flats in two different blocks, all within The Village. Estate agent talk for: there's a gay bar on every corner, and you can buy milk from a tiny shop that also sells leather shorts and lube.

'Think of the money you'd save on taxis,' Micky had said, jangling a bunch of keys. 'Everything is right there on your doorstep.'

The flats, though, didn't feel like they'd been designed for anyone to actually *live* in. They looked like budget hotel rooms with a bolt-on kitchenette. The bedroom could just about squeeze in a small double bed, but there was no space for storage. The living-cum-dining-cum-everything-else room had the dubious benefit of allowing you to simultaneously watch TV and stir-fry.

'Most of the neighbours are gay,' Micky added. 'You'll have a ready-made circle of friends.'

Jake smiled and nodded. Ten years ago, he'd have jumped at this. Back then, he lived and breathed being out and proud.

And sure, he still loved the occasional wild night, but things had changed. These days, he was more likely to drop hints about hand-knitted slippers and extra-fluffy dressing gowns than lust after XT-6 trainers and Boy Smells candles.

'It's a bit too... small for me.' He tried to sound upbeat.

Micky nodded. 'Fair enough. There's a warehouse unit on the other side of town.'

'Can I think about it?' Jake said. 'Maybe give you a call in a couple of days?'

He didn't wait for Micky to launch into any sales pitch. With a polite nod, he turned and left, only breathing in when he reached the street outside. A gay bar was already setting up for the day, and a handsome guy was arranging tables.

'Are you open?' Jake hoped he didn't sound desperate.

The guy checked his watch. 'Just about. Go on in. I'll be with you in five.'

Inside, daylight streamed through high windows. The disco ball sat idle, rainbow bunting drooped, and the air held a tang of spilled beer mixed with citrus cleaner. Jake ran a hand along the edge of the bar. Viewing a flat on his own had felt every kind of wrong. Why hadn't he brought Fred along? Or Emma? He couldn't make that kind of decision alone.

Losing Tom had robbed him of someone to talk through all the little decisions that made up a life.

Do we order takeaway or reheat last night's pasta? Think I could get away with a medium in this T-shirt? Is ten o'clock too early for bed? What are we watching tonight? The Amazon guy left a parcel with the neighbour, will you get it? Can I go another week without a haircut?

'Mate...' The guy from before was behind the bar, smiling and waiting for Jake to order.

'Diet Coke,' he said. 'Ice and a slice.'

INT. LGBTQ+ OUTREACH CENTRE - NIGHT

'This piece of paper is important.' Miranda shuffled around on her stage. 'If you don't add your name to the list, you don't get to perform.'

She'd spent fifteen minutes of a two-hour masterclass dedicated to creating the perfect punchline, explaining her all-new, *super-important* sign-up sheet. She'd made it sound like an annex to the Geneva Convention.

Upon arrival, everyone needed to print their name. In pen, not pencil. And using block capitals. At the end of each class, they would get stage time, and Miranda would provide feedback. The list dictated the running order.

Jake's phone beeped, earning a raised eyebrow from the stage—'the rule is all phones must be on silent.' When Rona's name flashed up, his shoulders tensed. Vicky had armed him with all the right words, but conflict wasn't his go-to stance. Keeping the phone out of sight, he clicked to read her message.

RONA STAPLES

Coroner's report received. Funeral next
Thursday.

She shared no location. No time. And more than any of that, what did the report say?

'Mr Taylor.' Miranda dragged her stool centre-stage. 'If your phone is more important than being present for class, you are more than welcome to leave.'

He dropped it back into his pocket, but the damage was already done. He could hear himself breathing, hear his heart beating, drowning out Miranda's lecture on timing and delivery. There wasn't enough air, and the walls pressed in. Jake couldn't focus. The room blurred, voices faded into a low hum.

Had Tom been drinking? One simple, awful question

played on a relentless loop. Had Tom lied to him? Lied at every AA meeting. Broken every promise. Had he been unhappy?

Someone else had taken his stage time, and when the others laughed, he tried to join in, despite feeling like he was floating underwater. He grabbed for his phone, squeezing hard, as if that might force out the truth.

'Mr Taylor.' Miranda was staring. 'Let's give that another go.'

She was waiting. Everyone was waiting. Jake's mouth went dry. His pulse thundered in his ears, and his palms were slick with sweat.

'I'm afraid I...'

His chair clattered to the floor, his fist found the door. He was running.

Outside, the muggy August heat still clung to the stale air. The sky was a wash of pale blue, streaked with the burnt-orange glow of a sun that wasn't done setting. Jake pressed his back against the wall and slid down until he was sitting on the cracked pavement, breathing in the stench of hot grease from a nearby chicken shop.

Emma picked up after one ring. 'Rona got the report.' She didn't answer straight away. 'The coroner's report. She's got it back.'

'OK, and... what did it say?'

The world felt like it was spinning too fast, and he was hanging on by his fingernails. 'The funeral is next Thursday.'

Her voice came back, softer now, grounded. 'Breathe, Jake. You're spiralling.'

His fingers scratched the pavement. 'What if he lied to me, about everything? What if he only ever stayed with me because he knew I couldn't handle him leaving?'

'Hey,' Emma cut in, her voice firm. 'Stop. None of that is real.'

He rubbed his forehead, trying to will away the panic. 'What if I pushed too hard, made him drive back, and he...'

'Listen to me.' She had taken charge. 'Tom loved you. You don't spend years with someone out of pity. What happened... it was a tragic accident. You are not responsible for his choices, and you can't let Rona convince you otherwise.'

He tried to inhale, but his breath stayed shallow. Two girls walked past, laughing, not even seeing him. The sky deepened into twilight, and streetlights flickered into life.

There was only one possible next move.

INT. 16 HAVERCROFT LANE – NIGHT

The kitchen clock above the stove ticked towards midnight, its steady rhythm punctuated by the rumble of the kettle rolling to a boil. Jake leaned against the granite worktop, exhaustion seeping into his bones, feeling every muscle ache. The house was too quiet, amplifying the buzz of irritation in his head.

The back door creaked open, hinges groaning in protest, and Jake's father shuffled in, his footsteps heavy and slow. He smelled of crisp night air and cigarette smoke. But Dad didn't smoke. He used to, years ago, but he'd kicked the habit.

'Dad? What were you doing out there?'

His father, hair dishevelled and still in his pyjamas, squinted in confusion. His glasses sat crooked on his nose.

'Have you seen my little boy?' he said, his voice uncertain. 'It's past his bedtime.'

Jake paused, remembering the doctor's advice. There would be moments when Dad got confused, when he forgot who he was or where he was. The answers were simple. Stay calm, show patience, reassure him with gentle reminders of reality.

'Dad, it's Jake. I'm your... little boy. It's late. Mum will be wondering where you are.'

He nodded and smiled, then went over to the cupboard to reach down two mugs—the one with the chipped handle and another Jake hadn't seen in years, a souvenir from Alton Towers.

'Choccy woccy?' his dad said, opening the fridge. 'It always helps when I can't sleep.'

Jake nodded, watching as his father filled both mugs and placed them in the microwave before rummaging under the sink for a tub of drinking chocolate. Was he back with him, or still lost in some other version of now?

The microwave pinged, but his dad didn't move. Instead, he stared at Jake. 'How are you managing, son? It must be hard for you.'

Jake didn't know what might have prompted the question, so he settled for a non-committal shrug. 'I'm getting there.'

A flicker passed across his father's face. He came closer, leaning his hands on the counter as though anchoring himself. 'I was thinking about your friend. About Tom.'

Jake's throat tightened, and he nodded, the familiar ache swelling in his chest. He wanted to remind him how Tom was so much more than just a friend. But that wasn't how they ever talked.

His dad looked down at the floor. 'I never said much, did I? About you. About him.'

Jake swallowed, not trusting himself to speak.

'Tom,' his dad continued, 'was a good one. Anyone could see that. The way he looked at you... well, he didn't just love you, son. He was proud of you. I could see that, even if I never found the right words.'

Jake stepped forward, wrapping his arms around his dad, feeling the frailty of a man who had always seemed unbreakable.

'He loved you too,' he whispered. 'I just wish he'd had a chance to say it.'

INT. BÄCKEREI BRETZEL – DAY
SUPER: '22 AUGUST 2024'

Fred sat back in his chair, staring at Jake's phone, his fingers drumming on the table. 'I mean, I get it.' His voice was heavy with concern. 'But think about it. What if you go to Rona and she refuses to say anything? Isn't that just... twisting the knife?'

'She knows what was in the report.'

Fred set the phone down and leaned forward. 'You really think she'd keep her mouth shut if it said Tom had been drinking? Rona would have thrown it in your face.'

Jake pictured her cold, triumphant glare, the way she'd relish tearing him apart. Fred had a point. But he still needed to see it for himself.

A text message pinged, and they both glanced at the screen.

MIRANDA RATCHETT

Ticket sales poor for showcase. Sell, sell, sell. Or it gets cancelled.

Jake's jaw tightened, a wave of frustration rising. Miranda had badgered her fledgling comics one by one, demanding to know how many tickets each planned to sell. He'd reluctantly said five, then let her bargain him up to ten.

'Do you know anyone who's doing nothing next Friday?' he said. 'Anyone willing to sit through an hour of really shit comics trying to tell their first jokes?'

Fred nodded. 'Put me and Stu down for ten tickets. He can write it off as an office team-building exercise.'

Jake's eyes widened. 'You hate stand-up comedy.'

Fred shrugged. 'True. But I love you. And besides, Stu

could use a night out that doesn't involve talking about supply chains and profit margins.'

A smile found its way onto Jake's face, the first real one in what felt like ages. 'I don't know what I'd do without you two.'

Fred leaned back once more, his fingers resuming their table-top drumming. 'Just promise me one thing. If things get too much, or if... if you feel like you're drowning, call me. Don't be a hero.'

Jake swallowed his urge to deflect. 'I promise.'

INT. LGBTQ COMMUNITY CENTRE – NIGHT

Jake had arrived early, hoping Thursday might be one of Vicky's karma-cleansing nights. He'd started to text her a dozen times, but the words just wouldn't come out right.

The internet said grief came in five neat stages. He'd sailed through denial. Anger had lost its power. He ought to be deep into bargaining, making deals with God. But losing Tom had scrambled any rulebook. Grief wasn't linear. It could knock him sideways on a sunny day, forcing him to sit down on someone's garden wall before his legs gave out. Triggers lurked everywhere—a song playing in Tesco, someone wearing the same aftershave on a bus.

That morning, Jake had woken angry. Not at Tom. Not even at death. At Rona, for making everything so much harder than it ever needed to be.

Jordan appeared, landing a matey punch on his shoulder before pulling him into a hug that reeked of weed and Lynx Africa. Through the main doors, Vicky appeared, juggling a water bottle and a box of papers.

'I'll catch you in class,' he said.

He caught up with her at the door marked 'Private', earning a smile that looked as tired as he felt.

'Any chance I could pick your legal brain?' he asked.

She dumped the box on a chair. 'I've had a pig of a day, so you're welcome to what little remains.'

'Rona got the toxicology report back.'

Her expression sharpened. 'And?'

'That's all she wrote.' He held up his phone, showing Tom's sister's curt message.

'Classic bait.' Vicky's lip curled. 'At least now the funeral can happen.'

Grief was back, swamping his head, turning his brain to goo. 'I called. Left a voicemail. She hasn't got back to me.'

'Let me write to her solicitor…' She hesitated. 'Thing is… legally, if she doesn't want you there—'

'She can't just erase me from Tom's life.' The words came out harder than he meant.

'Mr Taylor.' Jake turned to see Miranda tapping her watch by a door. It was five past seven.

EXT. BROAD STREET – NIGHT

Jake had every intention of heading home. The class had been a total downer. Miranda had spent the first ten minutes berating latecomers—by which she meant Jake. She'd turned it into a masterclass on professionalism, setting out what she called 'the rules of being a comedian'. They sounded an awful lot like the rules of being someone happy to let the rest of the world treat them like a doormat: turn up early, offer to help set up the room, avoid drinking, thank the organiser in person and again by email. Above all else, don't expect payment. Work for free.

He'd sort of decided midway through the follow-up lecture on what was and wasn't allowed in jokes that he needed to tell Lucy he wouldn't be able to step into the best man role. Jordan had wanted to talk about his nan dying. Miranda had shut him down.

'Never talk about death. Or serious illness. You'll make the audience nervous. They want to like you, not fear you.'

That ruled out any chance of talking about Tom. When the class ended and everyone headed for the nearby pub, he'd lied and claimed a headache. It had all felt so final, and he'd known he would never see any of them again. He would join the growing list of faces that just stopped turning up to class.

And then he'd had a change of heart.

INT. THE RED LION – NIGHT

There had been a cheer, a wolf whistle, and all-round whoops when Jake peered around the pub door.

'Get in here, mate.' Jordan was on his feet, dragging a chair from a nearby table and calling for a beer from the bar.

Jake sat down, overwhelmed and suddenly shy. 'I figured I couldn't leave without saying goodbye.'

Susan put down her glass of red. 'What do you mean, goodbye?'

'I figured that was my last class.'

Most everyone protested. Everyone except Jordan, who held up a hand, signalling for quiet. 'If Jake's made up his mind, we need to respect the decision.'

Susan wasn't having that. 'You can't let Miranda bully yet another one of us into dropping out. The showcase will be over in fifteen minutes at this rate.'

'My reason for doing this changed,' he said. 'And Miranda might have a point. Who wants to listen to stories about dead people?'

Next to him, Pete placed a manly, awkward but reassuring

hand on Jake's leg and patted. 'You're in charge of your five minutes, mate.'

'But she'll just fail me at the audition.'

'Who says you need to audition with the set you plan to deliver?'

Jake shook his head and reached into his bag, pulling out a copy of one of Miranda's handouts. 'It says here that the audition is the final opportunity to modify material. Once signed off by Miranda, this is the set you must perform at the showcase. No changes are permitted.'

Susan shook her head. 'What's she going to do? Drag you off the stage?'

Pete cut in. 'But at the same time, you need to know that you're doing it for the right reasons.'

Jake understood. A dull, dark ache had replaced Tom in his heart. Nothing specific—just a void. Emptiness. How did anyone move through this?

'Do you all think it's too soon?' he said. 'To talk about Tom?'

Susan ducked her eyes. 'Miranda's got no right to take him away from you. She's a bully. And bullies don't deserve to win.'

Jake stared into nothing. And then into something. He stared at the faces around the table, at the bar, at a man perched on a rickety stool watching a muted TV screen, nursing an all-but-empty pint glass. A man trying to decide if he should order another or go home. He was wearing nice clothes. Clean clothes. He might be sitting alone in a dingy pub, but everything about him spoke volumes. He had a wife. A daughter, perhaps. A dog, almost certainly. A mortgage. Someone and something.

Jake had his mum. And his dad. For now. He had Lucy. He had Emma, Fred, and Vicky. He had all these kind people from the comedy class.

'OK,' he said. 'Miranda can do what she wants, but I still want to talk about Tom.'

Susan smiled. 'And we're going to be there clapping, cheering, and carrying you through.'

INT. 16 HAVERCROFT LANE – NIGHT

His digital alarm blinked an accusatory 2:00 AM. He stared up at the always-there stars—relics from a childhood that had come to feel like it belonged to someone else.

His phone buzzed, the screen illuminating the darkness. Who the hell would be calling this late? Vicky's name flashed up, and Jake fumbled, swiping to accept the call.

Her face filled the screen, stripped of any polish. No make-up, her hair hidden under a silk cap, both eyes red-rimmed. Watery. She looked... broken.

'Jake.' Her voice cracked and wavered. 'I hope I didn't wake you.'

He almost laughed. As if sleep were possible on a night like this. 'No, no. I was just... Is there something wrong?'

Her chest rose and fell, her expression twisted, like someone fighting pain. 'I'm facing a complaint to the SRA.'

Jake blinked, his tired brain struggling to process. 'Should I know what that means?'

'The Solicitors Regulation Authority,' she said, a ghost of her usual efficiency creeping in. 'This is nothing I can't handle. Occupational hazard. Disgruntled client.'

Jake propped himself up on an elbow. 'You gave someone advice, they took it, and now they're blaming you for whatever fuck-up they made of their life?'

Vicky's eyes connected through the screen, and for a moment, Jake saw past the mask. Past the strong, black woman. To fear. To something else.

'They're threatening to report me for professional misconduct.' Her voice stayed steady but soft. 'Claiming I've hidden things. About my former sex.'

'Oh,' he said, eloquence deserting him. 'That's... that's awful.'

Her lips curved upward, but her eyes remained dull and lifeless. 'I've faced worse.'

Jake wanted to reach through the screen, to offer comfort. 'Is there anything I can do?'

She shook her head. 'No, but thank you. For picking up. For listening. For not...'

She trailed off, leaving the sentence unfinished.

Two insomniacs sat in silence, sharing the stillness that belongs to the smallest of hours in the darkest part of any day.

'Vicky,' he said. 'Whatever happens, I'm here. OK?'

She nodded, a genuine smile moving across her face.

FADE TO BLACK

vicky

Vicky stumbled into her flat, the door closing with a soft sigh that matched her exhaustion. She flicked off her heels—one clattered down the hallway, the other skidded toward the bedroom door.

The kitchen was in darkness, save for the green glow of the microwave clock, and she fumbled for a light switch. Unforgiving brightness served only to highlight the clutter she'd been avoiding. A half-empty bottle of wine stood sentinel beside a stack of unread post.

Vicky filled a glass with water, downing it in one go, her

eyes closed, willing hydration to dull the lacerating headache throbbing at her temples. A faceless, nameless, gutless somebody had complained to a professional body with the power to take away her job.

Who knew her well enough to know when, where, and how to strike? To cause the most pain. She didn't give a damn about who knew she was trans. What hurt was having that knowledge turned into a weapon.

'You've clearly rubbed someone up the wrong way,' Tarquin Walker had said when she went to him for advice.

She was facing an investigation. At best, an unfounded complaint would follow her around for the rest of her professional life.

'I got a couple of text messages,' she'd told Walker. 'But that was weeks back, and I ignored them. They stopped.' He'd shaken his head, like she was the one in the wrong. 'I assume you have a longlist of culprits?'

She unfolded the letter, smoothing it out on the kitchen counter.

The allegation is that, by failing to disclose your transgender status, you acted in bad faith and provided misleading advice.

On the surface, the complaint was absurd. Gender identity had no bearing on legal expertise or client advice. As a progressive firm, Walker, Haynes & Dobson would have her back. But that didn't matter. If people saw smoke, they assumed there must be a fire. Her name would disappear from any list of potential named partners.

She did what Walker suggested and compiled a longlist, replaying her recent client list. Seven divorces, one messy, the others civil. A fight over who got to keep their late mother's ashes. An asset division that had taken forever but ended with both sides sending her flowers. A protection order. And the Penrose prenup.

Gerald Penrose knew she was trans. But he wouldn't do this. And what was it he always said? *Pay no attention to the man on stage; keep your eye on what's happening in the wings.* The first time he'd shared these words of wisdom, Vicky had misunderstood.

'Not a huge theatre-goer,' she'd told him.

Penrose had fixed her with his kindly uncle smile. 'I'm talking about life. Keep your eye on what's going on behind the people making all the noise.'

```
INT. VICKY'S FLAT - NIGHT
SUPER: '1AM'
```

Sat cross-legged on her living room floor, Vicky studied three neat piles of sticky notes. She'd organised recent clients into three categories: grateful, indifferent, potentially deranged.

The third pile was the one she feared the most. And it was the biggest. Her professional superpower was, it seemed, an ability to piss people off. It was impressive in a 'maybe invest in a good security system' kind of way.

'Congratulations, Harper,' she muttered to herself. 'You've managed to alienate half of the local legal community. Mum would be so proud.'

As she stared at the names, playing a mental game of 'who would most like to ruin my career', nothing clicked. Perhaps this wasn't about a disgruntled client or a bruised ego. The threat felt personal and specific. What if, without knowing, she'd poked around where she wasn't welcome?

Her laptop pinged, and Vicky shuffled around. Most likely a *Net-a-Porter* discount code, but she needed the distraction. And buying clothes was always a great distraction.

Vicky scrolled through the usual spam—penis enlargement and off-label drugs. One message stood out: the sender's name was a string of random letters and numbers, the kind of thing she deleted on autopilot. But the subject line stopped her cold: *The truth about Rona Staples - Urgent.*

Her finger hovered over the mouse. This had to be a scam. She cancelled a requested read receipt and opened the message anyway.

+1 (800) 555-0198

Ms. Harper, Rona isn't just after money. She's hiding something bigger. Dig into Ravenswood Enterprises and their links to True North. CLF is just the surface. Be careful. Some truths come at a cost. - A friend who hates to see someone in trouble

Vicky typed "CLF" into a search engine. Three entries down, she spotted *Covenant Light Fellowship*—an American megachurch with recent police raids and cleared links to the far-right. This was no coincidence. She re-read the email. Was this connected to the SRA complaint? Was Vicky the 'someone in trouble'? And how did any of this link to Rona Staples?

INT. VICKY'S FLAT - NIGHT
SUPER: '2AM'

At school, Vicky had brought home few badges or trophies for her mum to display with pride on the thin wooden mantelpiece above an ancient three-bar electric fire. She hadn't been sporty, preferring to bury her head in books or research online. In year ten, a sympathetic teacher invented the 'Digital Scholar Award', a special commendation given in recognition of her exceptional ability to conduct thorough and accurate online research. She was declared good at Google.

That skill had never left her, and spurred on by an uninvited email, giving up and going to bed was no longer an option.

'OK then, Rona.' She cracked her knuckles—a habit she'd been called out for many times. 'Let's see what you've been up to.'

A quick search brought up Rona's Facebook and LinkedIn profiles. After six years bouncing from one admin role to another, she'd switched to full-time voluntary work for a local branch of the Covenant Light Fellowship. So far, so underwhelming. Vicky scrolled down to *Interests* and clicked on *Groups*. Rona listed the Christian Women's Fellowship along with a hymns and worship music group. Alongside these, she'd joined the Anti-Censorship Alliance and the UK Sovereignty and Independence Group. Unsurprisingly, Rona had posted plenty of "Vote Leave" memes. She was about to try another search when she spotted a fifth thumbnail: the letters TW in a gold serif font, against a laurel leaf logo. The Traditionalist Women's Network was set up to "empower women through timeless traditions and strong moral foundations." She clicked.

At the Traditionalist Women's Network, we celebrate the strength, grace, and wisdom of women rooted in time-honoured traditions. Our community fosters a supportive environment where women can thrive in their roles as leaders in the home, church, and society. We believe in the power of family, the importance of nurturing strong moral foundations, and the value of maintaining cultural heritage.

'Well, that sounds suitably ominous,' Vicky said with a snort. 'Handmaids United.'

The website listed events and showed thumbnails of group

members who'd attended each. Rona's face appeared next to a 2021 leadership seminar: *Preserving Our Heritage.*

She typed that into her search engine, finding a dedicated page. In 2021, the seminar took place in Detroit. A warning bell rang in Vicky's head. How could someone with what she assumed to be a low-paying admin job afford to fly halfway across the world for a random meeting?

She scrolled through stock photos of diverse businessmen and women and clicked on buzzword articles promoting traditional values and cultural preservation. The sponsor's list thanked the True North Institute for taking care of catering.

Bingo.

Vicky had learned a thing or two from Gerald Penrose about accessing public records and soon found herself on the Elections Canada website, studying True North's most recent financial returns. It didn't take long to find a sizeable 2021 donation from Ravenswood Enterprises.

'Curiouser and curiouser,' she whispered, reaching for her now-cold coffee.

She clicked back to Rona's Facebook. Amid posts about fundraising car boot sales and coffee mornings, she spotted a reposted article from *The Spectator*: *Standing Firm: Defending Faith and Family Values in a Changing World.*

'Oh, Rona,' Vicky said with a sigh. 'The thing about social media is everyone gets to see what you do.'

On a neglected page for the Edgbaston House of Hope Ministry, she found archived listings for meetings on "heritage preservation." Harry Staples featured as both organiser and speaker. It was hard not to notice the way each event was branded like a product launch, with titles crafted to hook the unwary, drawing them in with promises of "unity" and "unbreakable community," as if their flavour of faith could be packaged and sold.

True North had its fingers in many pies, including a charity called Future Leaders of Tomorrow. Vicky enlarged a group shot of attendees at its most recent meeting. One that took place in Toronto. There, in glorious high resolution, stood Rona Staples, smiling next to a stern-faced woman. The caption below named her as Patricia Macluskey.

Vicky ought to call Penrose, but he wouldn't welcome a babbled conspiracy theory at this time of night. She'd text first thing and suggest a meeting.

First, though, she needed to clear her head. And possibly bleach her brain. The company gym would be empty at this hour. Perfect.

```
INT. WALKER, HAYNES & DOBSON - NIGHT
SUPER: '3AM'
Fluorescent lights cast a sterile glow
over the empty company gym. Machines
stand silent and waiting. Weights rest
in perfect order. Motivational posters
urge users to 'Push Harder' and 'Never
Quit'.
```

Just like always, Vicky had the place to herself and made a beeline for what she thought of as *her* treadmill, catching her reflection in the mirrors. Dark circles betrayed sleepless nights. With a resigned, heavy breath, she punched the 'start' button, and the treadmill hummed to life.

She began at a brisk pace, easing into the rhythm, but it wasn't enough. She needed to push harder. Vicky came here to outpace swirling thoughts. A jab at the controls cranked the speed, matching her mood with each pounding step. If she ran hard enough, maybe she could outrun the gnawing doubts about what she'd uncovered. Sweat soaked her forehead, her breath came in sharp bursts. *Never quit.*

The podcast playing in her ears featured an interview with Al Whitmore, the founder of True North. The host was giving him an easy ride.

'We're not against diversity,' Whitmore said. 'We simply believe in prioritising those who share our values, our way of life.'

Her chest tightened, but she didn't slow, pushing harder, her legs burning, lungs screaming. Every muscle hurt as she pushed the treadmill into a brutal incline.

Her body gave in before her will to push harder, and Vicky yanked out her earbuds as she hit the 'cool down' button, slowing the rattle of the machine. She wiped her forehead with the sleeve of a faded WHD hoodie, then reached for a towel, wrapping it around her neck.

A door swung open, a quiet hiss in what had been blissful silence. Vicky glanced over, expecting a security guard doing his regular round. A guy dressed for a workout raised a resigned hand in greeting. He looked as worn out as she felt, with a day's worth of stubble shadowing a strong jawline.

'Oh, hey,' he said, setting down his water bottle on the treadmill furthest away. 'Didn't expect company at this hour.'

Vicky blinked, her mind still struggling to slow down. She ought to say something. That was how conversations worked, after all. 'Guess I'm not the only insomniac on the payroll.'

What was she thinking? This wasn't the start of an office romcom, and he definitely wasn't the rural Romeo to her uptown girl. He was just another lawyer in a firm of hundreds, a stranger she'd likely never see again.

He draped a towel over the treadmill handrail. 'Alex Bonner. Corporate Strategy.'

She wiped her forehead, her defences melting. 'Vicky Harper. Family Legal.'

What if she was the country bumpkin, and he was the city slicker? She'd grown up in Brixton, near a park where she fed the ducks and dreamed of one day keeping chickens. Back when she allowed herself dreams. Take away the mussed-up hair and stubble, he was borderline cute. If only she didn't look like a walking, talking puddle.

This was not a romcom.

'What brings you to the land of the sleepless?' he asked, starting his warm-up with practiced ease.

Vicky shrugged, blinking away the Hollywood glitz and willing her heart rate to settle. 'Stress, deadlines, impending doom.'

'The WHD holy trinity, then?' His eyes lingered on hers for a long moment. 'I find a run helps keep the demons at bay. That, and the occasional midnight raid on the vending machines.'

Vicky let out a half-laugh, exhaustion sending her giddy. 'Did you know they have Monster Munch on the 21st floor?'

Alex feigned shock. 'And all this time I've been making do with Hula Hoops?'

'Not beef and onion flavour?'

'I'm not a monster.' He faked disgust. 'I'm strictly ready salted. Cheese and onion when I'm feeling reckless. You?'

'Smoky bacon all the way.' The smallest smile crept across her face.

'Now we're talking.' He hit a button, upping the treadmill pace. 'Well, if you ever need a partner in crime for a late-night snack heist, you know where to find me.'

She nodded, adjusting the towel around her neck, telling herself it was the company that kept her there a little longer. Maybe it was. Or maybe it was the small respite from an investigation she ought to forget. She was a solicitor, not a freelance detective.

As she readied herself to leave, Alex hit stop on his treadmill.

'Good to know there's another night owl on the team.' His voice was warm and friendly. 'Makes the small hours less lonely.'

Vicky paused, halfway to the door, before flashing a final smile. 'It really does.'

INT. WALKER, HAYNES & DOBSON – NIGHT

SUPER: '4AM'

Vicky stood in the doorway of her office, eyeing the couch with the kind of longing usually reserved for a last slice of communal pizza. Pale pink and inherited from the previous occupant of her glass box, she'd transformed the brushed velvet monstrosity into makeshift storage for files and folders. Her keen legal mind had spotted a loophole in the company-wide clear desk policy— a loophole big enough to drive a forklift through.

A couch wasn't a desk.

Neither was her desk a couch, and more than anything, she craved a power nap. As she relocated the chaotic stack to the floor, her caffeine-fuelled brain refused to power down, whirring and clicking like an ancient hard drive.

She abandoned *Operation Nap* in favour of *Operation Caffeine I.V. Drip.*

The communal kitchen was a fluorescent-lit oasis in the desert of an empty office. As the off-duty coffee machine gurgled and hissed, Vicky spotted a ball of twine lurking behind a catering pack of teabags. Next to it stood a box of coloured index cards and pins marked: *Property of Emmaleigh. Return if found.*

She glanced around to confirm she was alone—that romcom guy hadn't followed her from the gym—then reached for them. And then put them back.

'I am not doing the clichéd detective board,' she muttered. 'I'm a professional.'

She turned at the sound of footsteps and saw Corporate Strategy Alex, still in his gym kit. His sweaty gym kit. And somehow, the look was totally working for him.

He reached past her for a tumbler and filled it to the brim with iced water. 'We meet again.'

'Small world.'

Vicky rarely found herself tongue-tied. The words bouncing inside her head refused to form full sentences. 'Coffee, I'm making... for you, one too, perhaps?'

She'd turned into Yoda.

His gaze lingered, noticing the subtle, almost languid shift in his stance, the way he leaned against the counter. One arm crossed over his chest, the other mussing still-messy hair.

'Is that your way of asking,' he said, 'or are you a secret Jedi in your spare time?'

Vicky swallowed, trying to focus on anything but him. The flickering kitchen lights. The laminated passive-aggressive signs denying the existence of "dishwasher fairies" and requesting everyone "leave the kitchen how you found it."

'I'm no Jedi.' A half-smile crept onto her lips. 'But I do know my way around Guatemalan beans.'

Alex laughed, a low, unhurried sound that felt intimate. He turned to face the counter, his fingers tracing the edge. 'Well, if your coffee's anything like your Yoda impression, I'm in for something memorable.'

Her breath caught, though she couldn't pinpoint why. It was a harmless remark, a simple joke, yet the kitchen felt different, the air heavier. Conspiratorial.

'I'll take that as a challenge.' Vicky reached for matching *Sports Direct* mugs. 'I figure as it's out-of-hours, we can go big.'

He hadn't moved closer, yet she was sure the space between them had grown smaller. Her pulse raced, unbidden, a secret she hoped wasn't plastered across her face. She bit her lip, focusing on pouring the coffee, hyper-aware of every little movement. The way his fingers drummed on the counter. The way his gaze followed her—not in a creepy way, just enough to make her feel... seen.

She slid one mug across the counter, and their fingers brushed. Brief. Innocent. Yet it sent a jolt through her, an electric current that left her holding her breath.

'Thanks.' He raised his coffee in a small toast. 'Next time we'll do Hula Hoops.'

Vicky forced herself to smile and reached for the three balls of twine before walking back to her office, fighting the urge to look back.

With the door safely shut, she let out a groan and slumped onto the edge of the couch. She was a kick-ass lawyer, not some love-struck sap. What was that all about? An office romance would be tacky. HR would step in, citing policy. And if they broke up, things could get awkward. Especially if she needed something from Corporate Strategy. Not that she'd *ever* needed anything from Corporate Strategy in almost five years of working there. Had it really been that long? And what if the break-up happened down the line after they'd moved in together and got a dog?

Slow down, Harper. And maybe give the coffee a rest.

She fired up her email, hitting delete on reminders to complete her diversity and inclusion profile. Even as she tried to focus on routine client comms, Vicky found herself clicking back to the Rona Staples message.

What exactly was the "something bigger"? She'd uncovered

a possible True North connection in just three clicks—surely there had to be more. Or was she overthinking it, and letting her friendship with Jake skew things? Coincidences happen: Rona attending the same event as her client's future mother-in-law could be nothing more than chance. Fact often defied fiction, but what if there *was* some deeper link?

As soon as the sun came up, she'd call Penrose.

Except... what would she tell him? He'd already written off the Macluskey clan as money-grabbing. He'd demanded a watertight prenup, fearing the worst. Lucy knew nothing of this. All she saw was her father sticking his nose in where it wasn't welcome.

People love to shoot the messenger, she'd told Jake. Nothing proven, but enough to raise serious red flags, she'd insisted.

And now there was proof. Of sorts. Was Colin Macluskey a willing participant in his mother's xenophobia, gussied up as cultural preservation?

Fuck it. Fuck it. Fuckity fuck.

Vicky took a long swig of coffee, grimacing at the bitter taste.

She'd untangled messier cases. Like the Johnston estate— two warring wives, one horrible husband, and a parrot with claims to power of attorney thanks to a dodgy do-it-yourself will. But this was more than marital discord and avian supremacy. This was bigger and darker, with tendrils reaching into places she'd rather not think about. At 3:15 in the morning.

Or at any time, really.

She put down her laptop and stared at the far wall of her glass box. She had index cards. She had pins. She had twine.

And a desperate need to make sense of it all.

INT. VICKY'S OFFICE - NIGHT
SUPER: '5AM'

Vicky stood back, admiring her handiwork with the pride of a five-year-old after creating a macaroni masterpiece. Her off-white office wall resembled the fever dream of a conspiracy theorist with a penchant for colour-coding.

'And they say lawyers have no artistic talents,' she huffed, taking a sip of her third oversized mug of coffee, and watched office lights in nearby buildings wink out one by one as cleaners finished their rounds.

Twine criss-crossed between index cards, news clippings, and scribbled names. At the centre of the web sat two words, circled multiple times: *TRUE NORTH.*

She squinted at the mess, willing it to make sense. Lines connected Rona Staples to the Edgbaston House of Hope Ministry, to Harry Staples, to the Traditionalist Women's Network. Another strand linked True North to the Preserving Our Heritage conference and various far-right political groups. She'd colour-coded each link—red for confirmed, blue for maybe, yellow for where questions remained.

One connection remained elusive.

'Come on, Rona.' Vicky paced the length of her evidence wall. 'How does any of this link to Patricia Macluskey?'

The trail couldn't go cold. It couldn't just be that Rona had stood next to the woman in one random photograph posted online. She'd scanned the conference attendee list at least a dozen times, but found nothing. It became maddening, like an itch she couldn't quite reach.

And then, like a bolt from the blue, she spotted another familiar name.

```
INT. HARRINGTON, THORNE & PARTNERS -
DAY
SUPER: '2021'
VICKY, looking younger and more
nervous, sits across from NIGEL
HARRINGTON, a man in his late 40s with
thinning hair and an ill-fitting suit.
```

Nigel Harrington leaned back in a high-backed leather chair, his pale, watery eyes bulging as they made no secret of where they'd come to rest—squarely on her chest.

'Well, *Victoria,*' he pronounced each syllable of her name with a mocking drawl, 'you certainly look the part.'

Vicky shifted in her seat, wanting to fold herself in two and hide, wishing she'd dressed down, not up. She could have worn a Brixton Law Centre sweater, not a tight shirt and a jacket cinched at the waist.

'Thank you, Mr Harrington. I believe I'd be a valuable asset to your firm.'

He leaned forward, as if trying for a better view. 'Oh, I'm sure you would be, Vic-tor-i-a. Very valuable indeed.'

Then he got up.

First, he went to stare through his office window, then came to perch on the edge of his desk. Closer to Vicky. *Too* close.

'I often conduct the final stage of interviews in a more relaxed setting.' He flashed a yellow-toothed smile. 'There's a little bar. Very discreet. What do you say we continue this discussion over drinks?'

'I probably ought to get back. I'm on an extended lunch.'

He inhaled, throwing back his head. 'You're a good liar too. That's an asset in our line of work.'

Harrington didn't move. His bony knee brushed her elbow.

Vicky picked up her bag and rose, shuffling from the chair,

squeezing past, tottering on borrowed heels. 'Thank you for taking the time to see me.'

'I mean... let's talk about that other big lie you told. The one in your letter of application.'

She froze.

'I'm struggling to understand how *Victor* Harper enrolled at Queen Mary's in 2012, and yet *Victoria* Harper picked up her LLB three short years later.'

She gripped the door handle. *Stiff*. Locked?

'My firm carries out background checks. And nothing about your past proclivities suggests you wouldn't make a shit-hot associate. Primed for the fast track.'

Why was she still smiling? Why did she care what he thought? Why hadn't she kicked the tosser in the balls?

'Come now, Vic.' He winked, like her uncle Brian used to wink at Christmas after too many drinks, when his hands wandered. 'Don't you want the job?'

She tried the handle again. This time, the door opened.

'I don't think I'm the right fit for your firm.'

Harrington's snark followed her out. 'Your loss. Good luck finding a position elsewhere with your back story.'

INT. VICKY'S OFFICE – DAY
SUPER: '6AM'

Nigel Harrington. There it was, in black and white. Harrington hadn't just attended the Preserving Our Heritage conference; he'd been a speaker. And now he was Rona's solicitor, working to oust her friend from the flat he'd shared with the man he still loved.

Her heart pounding, Vicky lunged for her laptop. The warning email took on a new, sinister meaning:

+1 (800) 555-0198

Rona isn't just after money. She's hiding
something bigger. Dig into Ravenswood
Enterprises and their links to True North.

A few frantic keystrokes later, and she was deep in the bowels of Companies House records. At first glance, Ravenswood Enterprises seemed innocent enough: property management and community development. Standard corporate speak that could mean anything or nothing. But as she traced each subsidiary and scanned through board member names, a familiar pattern began to emerge.

Vicky clicked on *people of interest,* her pulse quickening. The records listed two directors: Nigel Harrington and Harold Martin Staples.

She sat back, absorbing the implications. This wasn't just about Jake's flat anymore. This was about money laundering, about hiding far-right funding behind legitimate business fronts.

Three mugs of coffee and no sleep set her mind spiralling. One minute everything linked up; the next, it all fell apart.

She needed Penrose. If anyone could make sense of this financial labyrinth, it was him. The man could smell creative accounting from three counties away.

By habit, he was an early riser.

Vicky reached for her phone, her hand trembling. From caffeine, exhaustion, or good old-fashioned fear, she wasn't sure which.

'Good morning,' she said when he picked up, trying to sound more composed than she felt. 'I might have found what you're looking for.'

INT. VICKY'S OFFICE - DAY

SUPER: '7AM'

As sunrises went, the one she'd watched had been spectacular. A bolt of bright yellow set fire to the far horizon, silhouetting grey buildings before bathing the city in a warm orange glow. Empty roads filled up fast, lights flickered on behind countless windows. The forecast promised temperatures in the lower 30s —a stark contrast to what had been a washout summer. Rain, then cloud, then more rain. And when the sun had deigned to shine, it hadn't been the good kind of sun, instead blanketing the city with hot, heavy humidity. Leaving her air-conditioned office meant sweat-drenched clothes and frizz for hair.

Vicky rolled her shoulders, wincing at the stiffness. Her eyes were gritty, and a too-much-caffeine headache pulsed at her temples. She'd pushed through all-nighters before, but this one felt different—heavier, more consequential. Still, she straightened her back, determined not to let anything cloud her judgement.

After talking to Penrose, she'd dared herself to pull up the SRA code of conduct. Long, dry paragraphs focused on honesty, integrity, and professionalism. There had been nothing specific about gender identity, but anyone with a score to settle could twist words. Lawyers were paid to find loopholes, to block or exploit, according to need. And that meant someone— like, say, Nigel Harrington—could bring a claim against her for not acting with integrity. That same someone could use it to force her hand and shut down any claims that might stop his client getting her hands on property she could go on to sell and line True North's pockets.

She glanced at her phone. Penrose had promised to make calls. Vicky clicked to her inbox, dismissing Emmaleigh's latest early-morning reminder email and accepting meeting invites.

Tarquin Walker had dumped a first directions appointment on her, as if she had nothing better to do than deal with yet another contested divorce. He would be playing golf, and she needed to be on the other side of town.

'Hey there.'

She looked up, startled from her thoughts. Alex stood in the doorway, fresh and shaven, his shirt crisp and his hair gelled. When he spotted her evidence wall and raised an eyebrow, she understood how it might send the wrong message. *The gym lady. She's a crazy person.*

'School project,' she lied. 'For a nephew.'

'True North?' His tone was serious. 'Don't tell me we're representing them now?'

Vicky swallowed. 'You've heard of them?'

'Walker somehow managed to sweet-talk one of our corporate clients into a questionable partnership. It was supposed to be back-channel, all very hush-hush. I got dragged in to do the due diligence.'

She sat to attention. 'What did you find?'

Alex narrowed his eyes as he studied her wall. 'Some of these names sound familiar. I flagged funding funnelled through shell companies. Nothing illegal, but not exactly behaviour that earns anyone a knighthood...'

'Was one of these shell companies Ravenswood Enterprises?'

His expression shifted. 'Rings a bell. I mean... I could check my files if it helps solve...' He gestured at her multi-coloured map and half-smiled. 'If it helps make sense of whatever this is.'

Vicky's desk phone rang, loud and insistent. She didn't pick up.

Alex stepped closer, his voice gentle but persuasive. 'You've been at this all night. Even Superwoman takes a break. Let me buy you breakfast.'

She opened her mouth to argue, but the phone rang again. Her office was getting more claustrophobic by the second. Stepping away was the smart thing to do.

'Why not?' she said. 'But I'm a senior partner. I should be the one paying.'

He laughed. 'You do know I'm head of Corporate Strategy, right?'

Vicky raised an eyebrow. 'Does that come with a cape or just the vending machine code?'

Alex grinned. 'There's a code?'

INT. CRUMB AND BERRY – DAY
SUPER '8AM'

The smell of freshly ground coffee beans mixed with sweet pastries, a welcome contrast to hours spent in her air-conditioned box with three balls of twine.

Alex slid into the seat opposite her. They'd ordered herbal tea and almond croissants.

'I'm not sure I'll ever need coffee again,' Vicky said, rubbing her temples. 'Is caffeine intolerance a thing?'

He grinned. 'You say that, but by mid-morning, you'll be ready to kill for a double espresso.'

She smiled back. 'Thanks for this. I needed to remind myself there's an outside world.'

Her phone buzzed on the table, lighting up with a message.

GERALD PENROSE

My office. ASAP. Have updates.

'I'm going to guess that's one of your clients,' Alex said, glancing at the message. 'The best bit about Corporate Strategy is we have people trained to divert phone calls. No direct contact with the outside world.'

A heaviness settled over her again. 'I might have to put in for a transfer. Some days I love Gerald Penrose. Other days, he's my nemesis.'

'*The* Gerald Penrose?' Alex asked. 'The Scambuster?'

Another message pinged, and her stomach dropped.

+1 (800) 555-0198

Meet me at St. Mary's Row, the abandoned church. 8PM. Don't be late - A friend

She snatched her phone, flipping it face down on the table. His expression didn't change.

'Just Tarquin Walker dumping his cases on me again,' she said.

'The man is a menace to society.'

The knot of tension in her chest loosened. He clearly hadn't seen the message.

Alex leaned back, stretching his arms behind his head with a mock groan. 'We should be getting medals for surviving an all-nighter, you know. Or at least access to a corporate nap room.'

Vicky tried to laugh, but it sounded forced. She held his gaze a moment longer. 'All that stuff... on my office wall. I've been getting messages.'

His easy smile faltered. 'When you say messages...'

She had no idea why she'd even started this conversation. He hadn't seen the messages on her phone. She could thank him for breakfast and go about her day. Trusting people—especially someone she'd only known a few hours—wasn't her strong suit. But maybe saying it out loud would rob the threats of their power.

'Texts,' she said, trying to make it sound like a prank. 'Emails. The usual sort of thing.'

'Saying what?' His jaw clenched.

'Look, Alex. I get this kind of thing all the time. It comes with the territory. I appreciate how you guys in Corporate Strategy are more used to the named partners buying you bottles of vintage Krug, but...'

He held up a hand. 'Tell me what the messages say.'

She tried for a casual shrug, but it felt forced. 'People get upset, say things they don't mean.'

'Is this to do with the nutjobs from True North?'

Vicky shifted, her instinct to deflect kicking in. 'I've handled worse, believe me.'

Another message arrived, and before she could react, Alex reached for her phone.

'Hey!' She stood up, grabbing for it. 'That's personal. You can't just—'

He held up her phone, his face serious as he read the words aloud.

+1 (800) 555-0135

Pretty nose. Getting broken

The blood in her veins turned to ice.

```
EXT/INT MAGISTRATE'S COURT - DAY
SUPER: '9AM'
A stark, imposing modern building, its
glass and concrete facade a deliberate
statement of authority. Wide steps
lead to the main entrance, where secu-
rity guards monitor a steady stream of
people.
```

Vicky sucked on her vape beneath the court's imposing facade, her nerves in shreds. Neoclassical columns rose against a bright blue sky. People arrived for their day in court: men in borrowed suits, women hiding behind masks of make-up. Fake tan was a red flag for older male judges. She always advised her clients to play it safe.

Talking of clients, where was hers?

Tarquin Walker had described Toby Mole as a "lanky streak of piss who thinks the world owes him a living."

What Vicky really wanted was to show Penrose the latest messages, to outline what she'd found. To ask him to make all the bad stuff stop.

She called the office, half-hoping for a message saying Mole's hearing had been rescheduled. No such luck. She took a long drag from her vape, dreading the prospect of telling Walker his client's no-show had landed them with a contempt ruling and the threat of jail time for wasting the court's precious hours—further shrinking her chances of making named partner. Her phone buzzed again.

JAKE TAYLOR

Rona called. She wants to talk. Can we meet?

Vicky stared at the message, her mind racing. *Rona wants to talk.* That was new. Up until now, she'd stayed silent, ignoring emails, phone calls, and two registered letters. If Jake and Rona could settle things, it might tick one item off her ever-growing list.

Mole's name was listed for Courtroom Two. His Honour Judge Alistair Renwick was known for his impatience with time-wasting. Any minute now, an usher would appear, and she'd have to turn on the charm.

The minutes ticked by until, sure enough, a middle-aged man with a stoop called for Toby Mole. She stood, smoothing her skirt and waved him over.

'Is your client here?' he asked, his voice calm but with an edge that suggested he'd seen this situation too many times before.

She offered a tight-lipped smile. 'I'm afraid Mr Mole has been delayed. I've tried calling, but he's not picking up.'

The usher nodded and made a note on his clipboard. 'Would you like me to inform the judge?'

Vicky swallowed her frustration. 'I can keep trying.'

He nodded and walked away. Leaving wasn't an option. Judge Renwick might demand an in-person apology. She texted Penrose, determined to offload her findings. His reply was instant:

GERALD PENROSE

Change of plan. Playing golf with your boss.
Will call later.

She leaned back against the cold wooden bench. Somewhere in this building, His Honour Judge Alistair Renwick would glance down from his bench, note Mole's absence, and hold her responsible. Walker would explode. More so if Penrose had beaten him at golf.

Her phone rang. Jake.

'Tell me what to do,' he said. 'Rona keeps texting.'

Vicky stared at the ornate wooden doors opposite, biting her lip. Why did Rona want to meet up, after everything she'd done to push him away?

'Has she mentioned anything about the funeral?' Vicky asked.

'You think that's why she wants me to go around?'

If she told him to go, would it untangle one knot or tighten another? Jake meant access to Rona Staples. Rona Staples who she'd seen standing next to Patricia Macluskey. And after what she'd found about Ravenswood... But Jake was also her friend. And she didn't have many of those.

'Tell her you're interested, but say you can't get away from work. Suggest tomorrow evening. I'll come with you.'

The usher was making his way along the hall. She stood again, fixing in place her least convincing smile. A decision hit her like a jolt of adrenaline.

'Still nothing.' She held up her phone. 'And I'm afraid more urgent matters require my attention.'

Some battles weren't worth fighting.

The air outside was hot, heavy, and humid. Exhaust fumes mingled with the stench of bacon from a sandwich van. Vicky pulled out her phone and opened her Uber app. She needed to do this before her nerve crumbled.

Professional politeness dictated calling ahead, but when had Nigel Harrington ever been anything but awful? She'd show up unannounced and demand answers. If anyone knew who was trying to destroy her career, it would be him.

A car pulled over. The driver was vaguely familiar—maybe a distant relative of a former client. Her sleep-deprived brain, trained to file and recall the smallest details, refused to cooperate.

'Nice day,' the driver said. 'You work down on Queensway, don't you?'

She nodded, mustering a smile. 'I need to get somewhere fast. Before my nerve goes.'

```
INT. HARRINGTON, THORNE & PARTNERS -
DAY
SUPER: '10AM'
A modern, sleek and soulless commer-
cial space with a long pale wood
reception desk, manned by three iden-
tikit blonde women all wearing head-
sets. A brass plaque orders visitors
```

to sign in and 'wear identity cards at all times'.

The smoked glass doors slid open with a soft hiss as Vicky stepped into the pristine, air-conditioned lobby of Harrington, Thorne & Partners. Her heels clicked sharply against the polished floor as she approached the reception desk, her resolve hardening with each step.

One of the three blonde women behind the desk nodded in greeting, tapped her keyboard, and gave Vicky a practiced once-over. 'Do you have an appointment?'

'Not exactly.' They locked eyes. 'But I'm here to see Nigel Harrington.'

The receptionist's smile wavered. 'Mr Harrington is busy with clients this morning. I'm afraid—'

Vicky leaned in, cutting her off. 'He'll want to make time for me. Tell him Victoria Harper is here.'

The receptionist blinked, taken aback by the directness. She hesitated before tapping a button on her headset. Vicky stepped away, giving her room, watching as the woman's expression shifted.

'Mr Harrington is on a call. If you could take a seat—'

'That's not how this is going to happen.' Without another word, Vicky brushed past her, heading straight for Harrington's office. The receptionist called for security. A man in an ill-fitting uniform appeared, but Vicky was already through the door.

INT. HARRINGTON'S OFFICE - DAY
A plush office, overstuffed with a patterned carpet, bookshelves rammed with plaques and awards and three

giant potted palms dying near a shaded window.

As Vicky walked in, she caught the tail end of a phone conversation.

'I don't care what the press thinks. Things are already in motion. We'll deal with it. Now stop calling me until there's something useful to report.'

He looked up just as the security guard rushed in.

'I'm sorry, Mr Harrington. This young lady—'

'Not to worry,' Harrington said, a slow, smug grin spreading across his face as he leaned back in his leather chair, fingers steepled. 'This young lady is most welcome.'

The way he all but spat the word "lady" made Vicky's insides twist. He signalled for her to sit, but she stayed standing.

Harrington's grin widened. 'I presume *lady* is still how you prefer to be known these days?'

She stiffened, her pulse quickening, but she refused to rise to the bait. Instead, she straightened her back, locking eyes with him. 'Cut the crap, Nigel. I know what you're involved in.'

His smile grew wider, exposing crooked yellow teeth. 'Always so direct, Victoria. You have such a *masculine* energy. Your clients must sometimes feel you've been... less than honest about your—what's the expression we're supposed to use these days?—*gender identity*?'

Her every instinct had been right. 'So you are behind the SRA complaint, then? Trying to discredit me before I expose any dodgy connections?'

His smile didn't fade. '*Come into my lair,* said the spider to the fly.'

Her nerves jangled. 'Why don't you stop pissing around and tell me what you want?'

Harrington's eyes gleamed with something dark, something

unsettling. 'Gerald Penrose has been sticking his bloated red nose into matters that shouldn't concern him. And as his legal counsel, you need to convince him to cease and desist.'

Her breath caught, and she fought the urge to toss every scrap of evidence she'd gathered in his face, to call him out right then and there. But that would leave her exposed.

'You're worried.' She kept her voice level, her smile sweet. 'Worried he's onto something?'

Harrington's mask of smugness slipped—but only for a second. 'Penrose is a persistent fucker, but he's got no idea what a dangerous game he's playing. The stupid old cunt is out of his depth. And so are you.'

Vicky dared herself to step closer, keeping her voice low. 'Your friends need to learn how to cover their tracks. It took me five minutes to link True North with Ravenswood Enterprises.'

A flicker crossed his face, gone as quickly as it had appeared. 'You might think you've got the upper hand, but you don't know who you're dealing with, Victoria.'

She stared him down, refusing to blink. 'Drop the complaint. Tell Rona Staples to sign the flat over to Jake Taylor.'

Harrington shook his head, smiling to himself. 'And why would I do any of that?'

'Because I'm good at my job. I'll win in court, and the SRA will have you down as a time waster.'

'Doubtless,' he said, turning toward the window. 'But it'll throw enough mud your way, and do you know what's so annoying about mud, Victoria?' His voice dropped to a conspiratorial whisper. 'It sticks.'

Vicky's pulse thrummed in her ears. 'When Gerald Penrose exposes the people you mix with, the SRA will be the least of your worries.'

For the first time, his smirk faltered. She turned on her heel and left.

INT. WALKER, HAYNES & DOBSON – DAY
SUPER: '11AM'

The office kitchen buzzed with conversation and the hum of the coffee machine. Vicky weaved her way through clusters of colleagues, exchanging practiced nods and professional smiles. By the counter, two associates were debating Liverpool's chances in Europe, their voices lowering as she slipped between them, senior-partner-style, to grab a bottle of sparkling water from the fridge. The cold glass pressed against her palm, steadying still-trembling fingers.

She'd faced down Nigel Harrington. Called his bluff. But the uncontained rage behind his eyes haunted her. She'd rattled him, yes, but was it enough? *Mud sticks.* She took a long sip of water.

'Hiding from Walker?'

Alex's voice made her start. He'd appeared beside her, his gaze wary, almost guarded.

She managed a tight smile. 'My client was a no-show. The usher wasn't impressed.'

'About earlier...' He lowered his voice. 'The True North thing.'

A chill ran through her despite the stuffy air. She needed to brush it off. 'What about it?'

'You're not getting in too deep?' He leaned in, crossing his arms. 'They're not good people.'

The hairs on her neck prickled. She'd barely known this man existed before today, and now he was everywhere, acting like a concerned friend?

'What I said earlier,' she said, forcing a light tone. 'Ignore it. Blame it on sleep deprivation.'

His gaze held hers a second too long. 'I took another look at your wall.'

Ice crept through her veins. 'You went into my office?'

'They're dangerous, Vicky.' He leaned against the counter, voice low and urgent. 'I don't want you caught up in something that could blow back on you—or the firm.'

Her chest tightened. 'And that's the only reason? You're just doing your Corporate Strategy due diligence?'

A flicker of confusion crossed his face. 'Due diligence? Why would you even...'

She forced herself to look away, studying the rim of her water bottle. 'I'm a nightmare without eight hours of sleep. Ignore me.'

The moment stretched, brittle as thin ice. Carol from the birthday shindig appeared, beaming.

'There you are.' She pulled Vicky into a cloud of perfume, wrapping her in a hug. 'Thanks again for the party. And that speech—comparing me to a ficus plant. I told my husband, and he was tickled pink.'

Vicky turned her back on Alex. 'I was about to make tea...'

INT. VICKY'S OFFICE - CONTINUOUS

The quiet of her office felt like sanctuary after the kitchen's forced cheer. Her evidence wall was just as she'd left it, but now it felt exposed. Violated. Alex had been in here. *Looking.* But for what?

The shrill ring of her desk phone made her jump.

'Victoria Harper.'

After three empty seconds, a woman's voice spoke, low and careful. 'You don't know me. I'm a friend.'

Vicky's pulse quickened as she closed her door. 'Who is this?'

'My name is Karin de Bruin. I worked for Nigel Harrington.'

'Are you the person who's been sending me messages?'

'Listen carefully.' Paper rustled on the other end. 'Tonight. Eight o'clock. St. Mary's Row—the abandoned church. We can help.'

Her stomach clenched. 'We?'

'Others who know what you're up against.' The voice dropped to a whisper. 'This has to be in-person. The phones aren't safe.'

Every instinct screamed at her to steer clear of dark churches and strangers with ominous messages. 'Why me? Why now?'

'You weren't chosen randomly, Victoria. We picked you for a reason.'

The line went dead, leaving only static and a flood of questions.

A soft knock. Alex was in her doorway again, hovering. 'Have I pissed you off?'

Vicky studied him, trust warring with instinct. The morning's easy rapport felt a lifetime ago. 'Ignore me. I'm just knackered, and now I need to tell Walker his client didn't show.'

He nodded, his fingers drumming against the doorframe. 'About me coming in here when you were out...'

'My fault for going full-on conspiracy theorist.' She gestured at the wall with forced lightness. 'Time to pack away the twine.'

'So we're good?'

She managed a smile. 'Of course.'

Only when the door clicked shut did she let the smile drop. Eight o'clock. An abandoned church. And absolutely no way to know if Karin de Bruin was friend, foe, or pure fiction.

INT. VICKY'S OFFICE – DAY
SUPER: 'NOON'

There was something comforting in the predictable cycle of domestic fallout. Trawling through paperwork to negotiate who got what in a bog-standard divorce felt like taking a two-week break somewhere hot and sunny. Her client no longer loved the man she'd married. In her words, he was 'a lousy shag with bad breath who picked his nose and wiped it on the sofa'. There was no conspiracy to unravel, no hidden threats to offset —just the mundanity of dividing furniture, assets, and deciding who got the house. She'd already decided. Not the nose picker.

Her mobile vibrated, and she glanced down, expecting another apology from Penrose or a plea from Jake for advice.

Withheld Number.

Vicky hesitated. The rule of life was to let those go to voice-mail. But being a lawyer moved the goalposts. And what if this was Karin de Bruin with more directions?

'Victoria Harper.'

A robotic voice spoke. 'Hello.'

She was about to hang up. 'I'm fine with my current broadband provider, thank you.'

'You should've walked away, Vicky. Kept your pretty nose out of things.'

She sat up straighter, gripping the phone a little tighter. 'Who is this?'

'You already know,' the mechanical voice continued, every syllable slow and deliberate. 'We warned you to back off. You didn't listen.'

Her throat tightened, the room suddenly smaller. Despite

the distortion, something about the caller's voice nagged at her memory. A cadence she half-recognised. 'Harrington. Is that you?'

A low, digital laugh crackled down the line. 'You think you're smart, don't you? Poking around where you don't belong. But you're in over your head.'

Vicky's mind raced. Whoever this was didn't just want to scare her—they wanted her to know she was being watched. She needed to take control, to make them think she wasn't intimidated.

'You're using a kid's toy to mask your voice. Is that supposed to scare me?'

'This isn't a game. If you don't back off, there will be consequences. You've been warned. You don't know what we're capable of.'

She glanced around her office. The glass walls left her feeling too exposed.

'I'm not going anywhere,' she said, determined to keep the fear out of her voice. 'And if you think this is going to stop me, you're wrong.'

Her heart pounded. She'd faced down tough opponents before, but this was different. Personal. Dangerous. A small voice in the back of her mind urged her to back off, to let it go.

```
INT. VICKY'S OFFICE - DAY
SUPER: '1PM'
```

Vicky hadn't moved a muscle in over twenty minutes. The document open on her screen blurred, words dancing across the page. Someone else's problems belonged in someone else's life. Her hand still shook when she reached for her water bottle.

Twenty minutes since that call. Twenty minutes of wondering who else might be watching.

She glanced up and saw Alex heading her way. Again. Like nothing was wrong. Like he hadn't invaded her space. The same Alex who'd appeared from nowhere in the small hours, all smiles and easy charm. The same Alex who knew far too much about True North.

He didn't knock—just walked in, radiating casual confidence.

'OK,' he said. 'So I get that I crossed a line, and I'm sorry.'

She nodded but stayed quiet, studying his face for tells, listening for any hint he might be connected to the robot voice.

'Fancy splitting a Tesco meal deal?' His smile was warm, genuine. Or a perfect act. 'You can have the Hula Hoops.'

If he was anything to do with the messages, she needed to play along, act like she'd called off the dogs. Vicky forced the corners of her mouth to twitch.

'It is tempting, but—' She caught herself.

'You need a break,' he said. 'All work and no play...'

She hesitated, her mind racing. Keep your enemies closer? Or was she being paranoid? Alex could be what he seemed— just another slave to the machine fighting insomnia. Lunch might be her best chance to figure out whose side he was on.

'Fine.' She shrugged on her jacket before she could think things through and change her mind. 'You had me at Hula Hoops.'

EXT. BIRMINGHAM CANAL – CONTINUOUS

Bright sunshine shimmered off the water, casting wavy reflections of the old brick buildings lining the canal. The air was warm, heavy with the scent of a nearby street food market, and a gentle breeze rustled the leaves of the few trees that dotted the towpath. A faint hum of city traffic drifted from the streets above.

They sat on a low stone wall near the water, Alex balancing a sandwich in one hand and a bottle of orange juice in the other. They'd debated their nearest supermarket chiller options and struck a deal on cheese and pickle.

'I don't think you eat enough,' he said, glancing at her half of the sandwich as he bit into his own. 'No one can survive on coffee and adrenaline alone.'

Her mind was elsewhere. She hadn't agreed to lunch out of hunger. He hadn't done anything outright suspicious, but the timing of his appearances left her unnerved.

'You don't know me as well as you think.' She took a second bite of her sandwich. 'I'm tougher than I look.'

For a moment, Alex just smiled, and there was something almost disarming about him—too easy, too comfortable—but she forced herself to stay cautious. This wasn't the time to let down her guard. Maybe he was just another lonely guy in the city, but what if he wasn't?

'I got a weird call,' she said, wiping her hands on a napkin. 'Some creep using a voice changer. Sounded like Darth Vader with asthma.'

Alex frowned, his sandwich halfway to his mouth. 'What did they say?'

'Told me to back off whatever it was I was working on. Made it sound serious.' She studied his reaction.

Alex just shook his head, pulling a puzzled face. 'I know you're going to jump down my throat, but... you think it's to do with the True North thing?'

Vicky needed to keep her tone light. 'Could be. Or maybe someone's idea of a joke.'

'I don't see you laughing. You think it might be time to involve the police?'

Her mind raced, weighing his words. If he was working for

Harrington, he wouldn't suggest going to the authorities. He'd be playing things down.

'They want to meet me.' The faintest of frowns creased his brow. 'Tonight at St Mary's Church.'

Still nothing but concern. 'You're not going?'

She tilted her head, her hand sweeping through the air, dismissing the question. 'Would you?'

Good question, she thought, because she needed to know. *Would* he?

His stare hardened as if lost in a thought he couldn't—or wouldn't—share. 'You want to know if I'd let someone disguising their voice talk me into going alone to an abandoned church just as night falls?'

She shifted her weight, the space between them suddenly tighter. 'Obviously I'm not going.'

He gave a small nod, and his expression softened. 'You know it could just be a joke. We work with some pretty weird people.'

She grinned. 'Present company included.'

Alex went quiet. He stared at the water. 'When I first moved here, I thought it would be easy to fit in, but it's been tough.'

'You don't strike me as the kind of guy who has trouble making friends.'

This earned her a small, self-deprecating laugh. 'You'd think. But I moved here from Leicester because I figured I wanted to live in a big city. And London was just too expensive. Everyone said the people in Birmingham are super friendly. But... things are harder than I expected.'

Vicky turned to face him, allowing herself the smallest pang of empathy. She hadn't expected this, hadn't expected Alex to peel back the layers of his life in the middle of a supermarket meal deal.

'Is that why you go to the gym in the middle of the night?' she said. 'Working off the loneliness?'

He smiled, but she sensed a hint of sadness. 'Sometimes I meet nice people.'

She so wanted to relax. To trust him. To let someone in. She'd done it with Jake and found her first friend in years, so why not Alex? But she couldn't. It was too easy to believe he was just some guy trying to find his place in the world.

'Nice people, huh?' she teased, trying to shake off the tension. 'So that's me, then. Officially nice.'

The canal rippled as they sat in silence, the sun climbing higher. Despite the warmth of the day, Vicky's instincts held fast. Whatever Alex's role was, she'd have to keep him at arm's length. Trust was a luxury she couldn't yet afford—not with what she knew. She took a deep breath, letting the warmth of the afternoon soothe her tired bones. Maybe she was over-thinking things.

INT. VICKY'S OFFICE – DAY
SUPER: '2PM'

Lunch with Alex had been... fine. His charm was casual, the banter easy. But had she decided she could trust him? Not completely. Was that a problem? No, because she didn't even trust herself.

She opened her laptop, typed in her password, and then stopped.

Something had caught her eye—a piece of paper placed dead centre on her otherwise tidy desk. She reached for it, her fingers brushing the edge of the paper. A single line of hand-writing stood out, stark and deliberate:

Back off or mud gets thrown

Vicky froze, the words searing into her mind. Someone had

been in her office. *Mud gets thrown.* That someone had to be Harrington.

She called through to the front desk. 'I wanted to check if there have been any visitors to my floor in the past hour.'

'One moment, Miss Harper.' The tone was brisk, laced with a hint of irritation. Hold music played.

Nothing else had been moved. Whoever was here would have seen the twine and index cards. They'd know what she'd found.

The line clicked. 'The only guests signed in went to the top floor.'

She hung up. The top floor was home to Walker, Haynes and Dobson—the three named partners, their PAs, and the boardroom. Vicky tried an internal line.

'Debs, this is Victoria in Family and Property. I wanted to check if Nigel Harrington left papers for me to sign?'

She listened to the sound of a keyboard clicking. 'Nothing on my screen, Vicky. I'll check with Suze.' More hold music.

Of course, the note might not have been delivered by Harrington. He had a whole office full of willing goons.

'Vicky. Thanks for holding. Suze says there's nothing on her desk. Shelley's on lunch. I can call you back.'

After hanging up, she stood and went over to her evidence wall, checking for any sign of tampering. And there it was. Someone had taken the card on which she'd written *Rona Staples.*

INT. VICKY'S OFFICE – DAY
SUPER: '3PM'

Vicky stared at her wall. No matter how she tried, she couldn't link Rona Staples to True North. Not directly. Rona had crossed paths with Patricia Macluskey at some far-right conference, the same one Harrington attended. She was a Facebook fan of the Traditionalist Women's Network. Lengths of twine circled, but never once connected with True North. Ravenswood had to be the common denominator.

Her eyes stung from lack of sleep. In five hours, she was due in an abandoned church to face someone or something. Karin de Bruin's sparse LinkedIn profile featured a blurry headshot, taken years earlier in a bar, sunglasses perched on bleached hair. Karin had kept her employment history private to anyone but first-level contacts, but described herself as a life coach. And that could mean anything. But LinkedIn let Vicky scan a handful of Karin's close contacts, and the names were familiar: Don Hayne's PA Shelley, the senior partner whose office she'd taken.

Her phone lit up, and she smiled to see it was Jake. 'Hey you. Sorry about earlier, I was just—'

'Rona won't stop calling.' He sounded frantic. 'Says we need to meet up.'

Technically, he was her client as well as her one and only friend. She never said no to clients, and she wouldn't say no to him. 'You want me to intervene?'

'What if this is her reaching out? Tom always said she had a heart. She just keeps it hidden.'

'For now, hold firm,' Vicky said. 'Don't shut anything down; say you're swamped at work. Apologise. If she keeps up the pressure, I'll suggest a meeting, somewhere neutral.'

After ending the call, she went to sit. God, but she ached. Every bone in her body was screaming out for sleep. Could she risk a power nap? A knock at her door made her jump. It was Carol, armed with a stack of papers.

'Sorry to bother you,' Carol said, her voice cheery. 'Just need a signature on these expense reports.'

Vicky nodded, forcing a smile as she scribbled her name. 'Can I pick your brain, Carol?'

'There's not much there to pick,' Carol said, rolling weary eyes, 'but if this is about last month's overtime, I'm still waiting for Mr Walker to sign everything off.'

'I wanted to ask you about someone who maybe worked here.' Vicky signalled for her to sit. 'A while back, but I figured if anyone might know...'

The implied flattery worked. Carol dumped her papers on Vicky's desk and pulled out a chair.

'Do you remember someone called Karin de Bruin? It would have been before my time, so maybe six or seven years ago.'

Carol chewed her lower lip. 'De Bruin... oh! The Dutch girl. Yeah, she interned for a month or two if memory serves me right. Quiet little thing, always looked like she was about to burst into tears.'

'Any idea where she went after here?'

'Harrington-Thorne was pretty aggressive back then, poaching staff left, right, and centre. Your predecessor was one of them. Wouldn't surprise me if that's where she landed. Why the interest?'

'She's a friend of a friend,' Vicky lied. 'Her name came up. Nothing important.'

Carol nodded. 'I can check our systems, see if we have an address.'

'No, don't stress. Like I say, it was just something a friend said. I sort of half-remembered seeing her name on a document.'

Carol stood and reached for her papers. 'I promise to get Mr Walker's signature on your bonus payment today. I baked cupcakes. That always does the trick.'

As her office door closed, Vicky's mind raced. She turned

back to her laptop, determined to find something—anything—that might fill in the gaps and explain the need for a secret meeting in a derelict church. Each search led to another dead end, each document another puzzle piece that didn't quite fit. She was about to slam the laptop lid shut when her phone lit up with a message.

GERALD PENROSE

Found something big. Need to see you NOW. My office. Don't tell anyone where you're going.

INT. GERALD'S OFFICE - DAY
SUPER: '4PM'

Vicky was out of breath when she burst into Penrose's office to find him hunched over his computer. She'd considered an Uber, checked for her nearest driver, seen a notice warning of surge charging, swapped her office heels for gym pumps, and ran across town.

'Does that bell on your reception desk actually do anything?' she said. 'I've been ringing it for the past five minutes.'

Lucy jumped to her feet. 'Oh, right, so I suppose our private chat is finished?'

Vicky glanced at Penrose, then at her. 'I'm sorry. I didn't know. I can come back later. I—'

'You're going nowhere,' Penrose said. 'But my darling daughter probably wouldn't say no to borrowing my credit card and taking it for a walk around the shops.'

'It's four o'clock,' she sulked. 'They'll be closing.'

'They shut at five, my sweetness. That's more than enough time for you to exact your revenge on my bank balance.'

They kissed, and Lucy left.

'Lock the door,' Penrose said from behind his desk. 'Just in case she works out I've given her the low credit limit one.'

Vicky complied, her heart racing. She had so much madness to share, so many wild theories.

He swivelled his chair to face her, his expression grave. 'I've done a deep dive into True North. Called in favours, spoke to old contacts. What I've found...' He shook his head. 'This is bigger than we thought, Harper.'

He gestured for her to sit, then turned his monitor so she could see. 'True North isn't a bunch of moose-shagging hicks; they've got tendrils in politics, education, even law enforcement.'

Vicky leaned in as he flicked through financial records, email chains, meeting minutes.

'Patricia Macluskey,' he said, 'is more than a talking head. She's funnelling college funds into True North coffers.'

Vicky's eyes widened. 'As in embezzlement?'

Penrose nodded. 'She'll be using a shell company. I just need to find the one missing piece of the puzzle.'

Her heart skipped, and her mouth went dry. 'Try Ravenswood Enterprises.'

He stared at her for a full minute before turning back to his screen, calling up the Companies House website and tapping in the name. 'Bugger me sideways, Harper. You're more than a pretty face.' He clicked some more. 'Nigel bloody Harrington. The slimy little shitehawk. Might have known he'd have his grubby snout in the trough. In league with Harry Staples.' He glanced at Vicky. 'I know that name too.'

She stared past him, out at a hotel opposite, at a woman standing in a window, looking down at the canal basin. She didn't have a care in the world. She was here for a weekend. Time off. Time to relax. If only...

'He's married to Rona Staples, who just so happens to be trying to sell my client's flat from under him,' she said. 'His partner died. Her brother.'

He shuddered. 'Died intestate?'

Vicky nodded.

'This is why I couldn't do your job, Harper. Too many grabbing ghouls all trying to feather their nests. You can hide a lot of cruelty behind fancy legal words.'

She pulled out her phone, scrolled through her emails, and handed it to Penrose.

'Rona isn't just after the money,' he read out loud. 'She's hiding something bigger. Dig into Ravenswood...' Penrose stopped and fixed her with a huge smile. 'You've just found a little piece of the rainbow. The one I was looking for.'

Vicky pulled a face. 'The little piece...?'

'Think of this as a jigsaw puzzle. Rainbows and Lollipops. I needed something to show me how it all fits together. I needed the missing piece.' He held out her phone. 'And that's what you just provided.'

The weight of their discovery settled on her shoulders. 'What's our next move?'

Before he could answer, her phone buzzed. Jake again.

'Something's wrong.' His voice was tense. 'Rona's stopped taking my calls. She sent a text saying she's "done playing games" and that I'll be hearing from her solicitor. What changed?'

Vicky glanced at Penrose. 'Listen to me carefully. Don't respond. Don't contact her. Don't answer your phone unless it's me or someone you trust. I promise you this is under control.'

She ended the call, her mind whirling. 'I think Rona might know she's being watched.'

Penrose nodded. 'Then we need to make our move. And bring this whole house of cards tumbling down.'

INT. WALKER, HAYNES & DOBSON – DAY
SUPER: '5PM'

Vicky emerged from the lift, her bag clutched tight. The office was quieter, most people having left for Friday night drinks. She headed for her office, hyper-aware of every sound, every movement.

Alex appeared from the kitchen. How come he was everywhere today? Until this morning, she'd never laid eyes on the guy.

He shared an easy smile. 'I came to see if you fancied a cocktail.'

'Would love to.' She tried for a sad face. 'But I have a late client call.'

'On a Friday?' His eyes searched hers. 'Is everything OK? You seem... tense.'

She waved a dismissive hand. 'High-stakes divorce. Client's convinced his wife is hiding assets in the Cayman Islands. Hence the Friday night at eight thing.'

'How the other half live, eh? But that gives you three hours; we could still grab that drink.'

Why did she say eight o'clock? Think, Vicky, think. 'I've got to email a consent order.'

'That's only going to take a minute. I don't mind waiting.'

'No, really,' Vicky said, her voice a touch too bright. 'I might be a while. You head on out. I'll catch you guys up. The Old Joint Stock, right?'

Walker, Haynes and Dobson people always went to the same pub. It had become their territory. Other city firms stayed away.

He hesitated, then nodded. 'OK, so I'll order you a mojito. Don't work too hard.'

Vicky let out a breath she didn't realise she'd been holding. She waited three minutes, pretending to gather papers, before heading for the stairs instead of the lift.

EXT. CITY CENTRE – DAY
SUPER: '6PM'

Every instinct screamed at her to turn back, to forget this mess. The safe, familiar beat of divorce cases and custody battles offered an easy escape. Yet she couldn't walk away. Not now. Not when she'd come so close to whatever the truth turned out to be.

Her father chose that moment to pop into her head. 'Why you put yourself in other people's business?'

Now of all times. He was never there when it mattered. How come he all of a sudden had an opinion?

'I'm doing what any decent person might. Not that I'd expect you to understand that.'

Was she actually talking to someone who wasn't there?

'I understand more than you think.' He'd been drinking; she could hear it. 'This ain't your problem.'

She'd once read a magazine piece about sleep deprivation psychosis—ironically, during a sleepless night. Lack of rest, it claimed, disrupted brain function, leading to sensory distortions and hallucinations.

'This is my problem,' she said. 'Groups like this hate what I am. They tell people it's cool to ignore my humanity. They put my life at risk.'

There was no answer. He was gone.

Vicky walked fast, her eyes darting around, checking for any sign of being followed. At the first corner, she changed direction, heading down a side street, before zigzagging through alleys and backstreets, doubling back twice, on high alert.

She ducked into an open-late department store, weaving between counters and exiting through a different door. Back on the street, she hailed a taxi.

'Where to, love?' the driver asked.

'St Paul's Square.'

As the cab pulled away, she glanced out the back window, scanning the street. No sign of anyone following, but she couldn't shake the sense of being watched. Of always being watched.

'If you are keeping guard, now might be a good time to act like a dad,' she whispered.

'Sorry, love?' The driver's eyes met hers in the rearview. 'You say something?'

'Just... talking to myself.'

The taxi wound its way through city streets, and Vicky's mind raced. What would she find at the church? And more importantly, could she trust Karin de Bruin?

When they reached St Paul's Square, she spotted the nearby spire of St Mary's.

```
EXT. ST. MARY'S CHURCH - DAY
SUPER: '7PM'
The abandoned church loomed, its crum-
bling spire a dark silhouette against
the dusky sky. A cool breeze rustled
through overgrown weeds that choked
reinforced panels designed to keep
anyone out.
```

Vicky had circled the block twice, checking she hadn't been

followed. Now, with the appointed time drawing near, she found herself rooted to the spot.

'Come on, Harper,' she whispered. 'You've faced worse.'

But had she?

A cat yowled in a nearby alley, and she chided herself for being on edge, but every instinct screamed caution. Run away. Go back home. Be safe.

This was Alex's fault. She'd planned on hiding out at the office for an hour, catching her breath, talking herself up. *Why had he still been there? Waiting.* Once again, she wondered if he knew. If he was part of this.

Her eyes darted to each passing car, each pedestrian.

Jake texted, and Vicky's fingers hovered over her phone screen. What could she tell him? That she was about to meet a stranger in an abandoned church because she was Black and trans, and this might change everything. Did her father have a point?

It was now or never.

She crossed the street, her footsteps echoing. A side door hung open, and a faint light flickered from within. Was she walking into a trap? As her fingers brushed the worn wood, a voice caused her to freeze.

'You came.'

She whirled around, her heart in her throat. The woman's features were half-hidden in shadow, but when she stepped closer, Vicky recognised her from the LinkedIn profile. A little older. A lot less carefree. But this was Karin de Bruin.

```
INT. ST. MARY'S CHURCH - SUNSET
SUPER: '8PM'
```

The door creaked, its hinges protesting. Karin used her phone's torch to reveal dust-covered pews. The nave stretched into darkness ahead.

'What do you want from me?' Vicky said. 'If you wanted to talk, couldn't we have met in Starbucks?'

Figures emerged from the shadows near the altar. Vicky squinted, her nerves long past the point of being frayed.

'I couldn't risk us being seen together.' Karin's accent was more pronounced in person. 'Some of us are forced to hide in the shadows.'

Faces came into focus. A young Black couple held hands, their smiles uneasy. An older man in a wheelchair was pushed by his partner, both wearing rainbow pins. A woman in a hijab raised a hand in greeting. Next to her, someone taller with close-cropped hair stared at the rubble-covered floor.

'We're the ones they'd rather keep in the dark,' Karin said, 'but we refuse to be silenced.'

Vicky's guard remained up. 'And who are "they"?'

The man in the wheelchair laughed. 'You don't know who's out there chucking shit our way?'

'The UK Sovereignty League,' Karin said. 'Or True North... whatever respectable-sounding name they're hiding behind this week.'

'I'm Amira,' the woman in the hijab said. 'Last month, my mosque was vandalised. Swastikas spray-painted, bacon left to rot on the doorstep, windows smashed. The police said there wasn't enough evidence to bring charges.'

'My name is Devon,' the young Black man said, his voice tight. 'My partner and I were attacked outside a pub. Not anywhere rough. Harborne. We were told to "go back where we came from." I was born in bloody Nottingham.'

A chill ran down Vicky's spine. 'I'm not sure how I can change any of that.'

Karin's voice was firm. 'You know about True North.'

'I do, but—'

'Are you going to tell me they're nothing to do with this? That they're based in Canada?'

Vicky didn't answer.

'They might be miles away,' Karin continued, 'but hate doesn't respect borders. Money raised at a bake sale in Toronto ends up paying for the spray paint Amira got to scrub off walls.'

The tall person introduced themselves as Jonah. 'They use the same playbook. Stirring up fear about trans people in bathrooms, spreading lies about children being indoctrinated. Every bit of hate divides communities, makes us afraid of our neighbours.'

Vicky nodded. 'But how can I make any real difference? The people I've found... they're small players.'

George, the older man, smiled wryly. 'Every brick we remove weakens their wall. Nigel Harrington isn't what you'd call a small player. He's been providing legal cover for these groups for years.'

Karin nodded. 'The police won't act without hard evidence. They see us as cranks. But you're a senior partner at a major law firm. People will listen to you.'

'And Black and trans and a woman.'

'But you have respectability. And respectability equals power.'

Amira's eyes met hers. 'And Gerald Penrose... he's rich and white. In this world, that's the voice that carries furthest.'

Vicky understood. She'd often been mistaken for a shop assistant while browsing designer clothes. Hotel security frequently insisted she couldn't be a conference keynote speaker. Last week, a new temp had asked her to empty his bin. Each represented nothing more than a paper cut. In isolation, nothing more than an irritation. Add them together and they hurt.

Karin stepped closer. 'You understand how it feels to be othered, to be treated as less than human.'

'OK,' Vicky whispered. 'I'm in. I'll do whatever you need. I just don't know if me *being in* is enough.'

INT. ST. MARY'S CHURCH - NIGHT
SUPER: '9PM'

Moonlight filtered through cracked stained glass. Even on a warm summer evening, the air blew cold, and Vicky shivered as Karin pulled a battered laptop from her bag.

'What I'm about to show you is the result of months of digging. Some of it obtained... unconventionally.'

Vicky's fingers twitched, her legal instincts flaring. 'Probably better for me not to know the details.'

'Plausible deniability,' George said, his wheelchair squeaking as he leaned forward. 'I used to be in the business.'

Karin opened a document, numbers and names scrolling past. 'This is a trail of financial transactions linking True North to local hate groups.'

Vicky's eyes widened, taking in the numbers. Hundreds of thousands of pounds routed through a dizzying maze of shell companies and offshore accounts. Her heart raced as she spotted a familiar name.

'Ravenswood Enterprises,' she said.

Karin nodded, her face grim. 'The linchpin. Set up by Harrington as a front.'

More documents flashed across the screen: conference attendance lists, bank statements—some familiar from Vicky's own investigations, others new. The pieces of what Penrose had called a puzzle clicked into place. A sinister jigsaw of hate.

'This proves Harrington is in bed with the UK Sovereignty

League,' Karin said, her voice tight. 'And through them, to True North. It's all connected.'

Vicky's head filled with cotton wool. 'The police will refer this to an anti-terrorism unit. It's compelling, but it won't be a quick fix.'

Amira stepped forward, her hijab rustling. 'Show her the emails.'

Karin hesitated, then opened a new folder. The messages made Vicky's blood run cold. Harrington's words, clinical and detached, detailed 'target areas' and 'sending a message.'

Devon's fists clenched at his sides. 'They're careful. Never explicitly calling for violence. But the intent is clear.'

Vicky's stomach churned as Karin clicked on a scanned document. A familiar scrawl detailed payments, and Karin's notes matched each transaction to reported assaults.

'They call it community protection,' Jonah spat, their voice trembling with anger.

Vicky stared up at the patchy church roof, moonlight peeking through like accusing eyes. Whoever had kept books for this group of shadows had also written the note she'd found on her desk. 'Whose handwriting is that?'

Karin stopped. 'You won't know her.'

'Try me.'

'Her name is Rona Staples. She's part of—'

'The House of Hope Ministry,' Vicky finished her sentence. 'And believe me, I do know her. I know her too well.'

Rona had somehow been in her office. She'd seen her evidence wall. Was that why she'd stopped calling Jake? Because the game was all but up?

George wheeled closer, the floorboards creaking under his chair. 'We need someone with the legal know-how to make this stick.'

Amira's hand on Vicky's arm was warm, grounding. 'You don't have to decide now.'

She inhaled the musty air. 'I'm not saying I can't help. I just need time to process.'

Karin nodded, closing the laptop. 'Don't think too long. They're getting bolder.'

INT. VICKY'S FLAT – NIGHT
SUPER: '10PM'

Vicky barely had time to kick off her heels before Penrose arrived. Summoned by a phone call, his usually pristine suit was rumpled, his eyes wild.

'Tell me everything, Harper,' he said, sinking into an armchair. 'Your message was cryptic, even for you.'

Her hand shook as she poured wine. 'I've found the missing pieces.'

She turned her laptop, revealing a handful of documents. Karin's curated selection glowed on the screen—a fraction of the whole picture, but enough to implicate without risking anyone's safety.

Penrose leaned in, his breath catching. 'Good God. This, combined with what I've uncovered…'

'It's damning,' she said, her voice low. 'But Harrington's crafty. He'll fight tooth and nail. We can't do anything until we can prove a paper trail linking True North directly to the attacks.'

Penrose's face hardened. 'What's our angle?'

Vicky took a sip of wine. 'I can build the legal case. But we need a face. Someone with clout.'

'Someone the press will fawn over?'

For the first time in what felt like forever, she smiled. 'A man. Probably white.'

His shoulders sagged. 'There are times, my dear, when white privilege becomes something of a millstone around one's neck.'

She snorted. 'Cry me a fucking river, old man. This is your chance to pay it forward.'

He was on his feet, pacing the room, agitation radiating. 'This could ruin Lucy. The man she loves, his family…'

Gerald's voice cracked, his facade crumbling.

'Colin isn't his mother.' Vicky kept her voice soft. 'The soul that sinneth, it shall die: the son shall not bear the iniquity of the father.'

His eyebrows shot up. 'Never pegged you for a Bible basher, Harper.'

'Sundays were sacred,' she said, her eyes distant. 'The pubs shut at two. Dad couldn't drink away the day.'

Understanding dawned on his face. He sank back into the chair, all at once looking older, more fragile.

'You're right,' he said. 'I just wanted better for Lucy. A life untouched by all this.'

She leaned forward, her gaze steady. 'By doing this, we're fighting for that future. For everyone.'

Resolve hardened in his eyes. 'Whatever it takes. I'm in.'

INT. VICKY'S FLAT – NIGHT
SUPER: '11PM'

The buzz of adrenaline ebbed, leaving Vicky hollow. She stood under the shower's scalding spray, willing the water to wash away the day—twenty-four hours that had felt like a lifetime.

Steam billowed as she stepped out, catching her reflection in the mirror. The face staring back seemed different. Weary for sure. In desperate need of skincare, but did she see the same Victoria Harper who'd jumped in a cab and worked out in the company gym at 3 AM? Had she become someone else entirely?

Wrapped in a towel, she padded to the living room window. Below, the city sprawled—a tapestry of light and shadow. Somewhere out there, Harrington would be plotting his next move. Somewhere out there, another hand would smack another face. Was she tilting at windmills? Fighting one small dragon while others lurked in bigger, darker caves?

Her phone buzzed. Alex.

'Can I come by?' His voice was soft, almost unsure. 'I think I might have something useful for your evidence wall.'

Vicky's body ached for solitude and sleep. She craved quiet, time to think. But hadn't she spent long enough shutting people out?

'Sure,' she said, hesitating for a second before sending him her location. 'I'll drop you a pin.'

Her gaze drifted outside. The twinkling city lights flickered against the inky sky, imperfect but alive. It felt like she was teetering on the edge of something—a confrontation, a connection, she couldn't be sure. Alex's name had never once appeared in anything Karin shared. Perhaps he was just another guy, another person struggling to fit in. Someone just as lonely.

The intercom buzzed. She closed her eyes, steadying herself. One step at a time. She pressed the button, unlocking the door, a tentative smile slipping onto her lips.

FADE TO BLACK

lucy

FADE IN:
INT. LUCY'S FLAT - DAY
SUPER: '20 AUGUST 2024'

Lucy refreshed her inbox, telling herself everything would work out fine. The email invitations to her destination hen weekend pitched it as something you'd be crazy to miss. She'd paid a London agency to put together the text and sent it, as instructed, at the optimal time: 6:30 on a Thursday evening.

YOU'RE ON THE WEDDING LIST!!!
Lucy's Greek Odyssey Hen Party

Guess what? You've made the exclusive guest list for Lucy's Santorini Hen Weekend! This will be the stuff of LEGENDS— think epic sunsets, cocktails that never end, and non-stop, over-the- top, goddess-level fun. You didn't expect me to half-arse this, did you?

*🖇 **WHEN:** 4–7 October 2024*
*📧 **WHERE:** SANTORINI, baby!*
*⭕ **WHY:** Because I'm getting MARRIED*

The agenda? Boat parties, rooftop dinners, beaches for DAYS, and spa treatments that leave you feeling as if you've just bathed in liquid gold.

Plus, plenty of time for laughs, stories, and serious dancing under the stars. Oh, and there might be a surprise guest performance from a Greek god or two...

This is going to be the most unforgettable weekend of the year (decade, maybe?), and it won't be the same without YOU. Hit me up ASAP. I'm not kidding... Santorini is calling, and you need to answer! Let's make this hen getaway the stuff of Instagram dreams.

*⚱ **See you in paradise** ⚱*
Lucy
💚💚💚

So far, nobody had replied. Perhaps the internet had failed at the exact moment she hit send, and her friends remained unaware of what they risked missing out on. She'd pulled strings and promised the hotel unbridled influencer coverage to haggle down the inflated room prices. Her guests would enjoy three whole nights of five-star pampering and partying for just £2,680, plus flights, transfers, resort tax, spa treatments, and any non-local beers and spirits.

Should she re-send the email?

Dylan Starr had sworn he'd document the entire weekend for his 60,000 followers, complete with multiple outfit changes.

Sienna Luxe had promised to Insta her signature sun hat collection. Should she WhatsApp them to check they got their invites?

'This is going to be amazing,' she whispered to herself. 'People are still booking time off work. Dylan and Sienna would be busy drumming up sponsor money.'

She had one non-spam email, marked urgent, from Sandrine. And she most certainly didn't feature on the Santorini guest list. Although she'd stormed out of Jean-Claude's pretentious shop, the impulsive move had left her with a huge wedding dress-sized hole to fill. Emma intervened and poured oil on troubled waters. Now it seemed Jean-Claude had been called away. Sandrine's curt message asked her to call to reschedule the next fitting. Lucy was still six kilos from her target weight. This delay meant she could take her time—and up the Monjouro.

She reached for the latest edition of *Brides Magazine*. The editor had promised her the February cover—their Valentine's special. The month that never failed to sell out. The model featured on the September edition wore the most amazing eye shadow.

Within ten minutes, Pat McGrath's Moonlit Seduction Palette was in Lucy's online shopping basket. Along with a Korean beauty cream that promised 20% fewer lines in just three days.

Ping.

That had to be the first reply to her invitation.

No such luck.

Lucy opened an email from Crumb and Berry, explaining there had been an issue with her wedding cake. The specific shade of blue she'd requested for the fondant decorations was no longer available because of the war in Ukraine.

For fuck's sake. Bloody Putin. Why did everything awful have to happen to her?

The whole point had been for the cake to match her newly chosen flowers and contrast the raw silk table runners still held up on a very slow boat from China.

Frustrated and in need of eye candy, she paged through old photographs, finding the first-ever selfie of her and Colin, laughing together on a Toronto park bench, taken two days after they'd first met. She stared at his smile—the easy, carefree grin that had drawn her in. *He should be here,* she thought, a tightness forming in her chest. Helping with the crappy wedding admin. But instead, she was alone, drowning in decisions he acted unconcerned about, leaving her to handle his awful mother. Didn't he understand how hard this was?

Patricia Macluskey had taken to emailing property listings for horrible houses in her beloved hometown of Creemore. Each one she'd shortlisted looked to have been designed by someone who'd binge-watched *The Antiques Roadshow*—and not in a good way.

Lucy did her breathing exercises. In for two, out for three, in for two...

Why wasn't he by her side? The pressure of the RSVPs, the endless wedding admin, the interference from Colin's family—it was all down to her. She blinked, her eyes burning.

Lucy needed someone to tell her everything would be fine, that it wasn't falling apart. She depended on her friends.

INT. BÄCKEREI BRETZEL – DAY
SUPER: '27 AUGUST 2024'

Lucy wasn't sure why she'd felt so nervous. It was just coffee. With Jake. Jake was her friend. They'd known each other for years, yet she couldn't stop checking her phone, refreshing every few seconds, sort of hoping he might cancel their date. Not because she didn't want to see him. Because she absolutely did. Why wouldn't she? But this coffee was pitched as a group affair—a chance to cajole at least one hen or gay man into a Santorini RSVP. And she was rubbish at finding the right words to pay tribute to Tom. She loved Jake, but what if she said the wrong thing?

Emma had been the first to drop out. She'd answered her phone half-asleep, recovering from a night shift, and begged to be excused. Fred kept things simple. He sent her calls to voicemail.

And that meant walking on eggshells. Should she ask Jake about the funeral? It was tomorrow, and no invite had arrived. She'd asked Emma and Fred. They'd heard nothing, either. Lucy had even turned to ChatGPT seeking third-party therapy.

> My friend's partner died. We're meeting for
> coffee. What should I talk about?

> Acknowledge their loss, listen, let them lead,
> offer help, share memories.

She could do that. Would do that. Obviously. But she needed to find out if Jake was coming to Santorini. If he dropped out, it bumped up the price for the remaining participants. Although, then she'd need to send another group email, and if everyone saw how saying no bumped up the price, bookings could rocket.

Lucy reached the café and peered through the window. The guy sitting alone, phone in hand, looked and acted like Jake—same jeans an inch too short, usual quirky socks. But something was different. A heaviness clung to him, dimming his usual brightness. She could text to reschedule, claiming extra cake-tasting duties, or say Jean-Claude was back in town and needed her final sign-off on sequins.

He glanced up, saw her, and waved.

The familiar door chime announced her arrival. She slipped off a light summer jacket, greeted him with a kiss, pulled out the chair opposite, and announced her coffee order. Skinny latte. No sugar.

'I'm glad you got in touch,' he said, eyeing his untouched sticky almond pastry as though it were a puzzle to solve. 'Never, ever move back in with your parents. It's like enforced past-life regression. Except you don't get to be Cleopatra's personal stylist or a Viking with a secret. Mum keeps making my bed, and Dad's taken to suggesting we drink beer together in his shed and watch Sky Sports.'

Lucy smiled, relief flooding through her. His father had been sick—Alzheimer's, but that made things sound OK. 'How's he doing?'

'We have our difficulties, but he's Dad more than he's not. A man came to fix the dishwasher, and he spent half an hour talking me up, trying to get the poor guy to take my number.'

'Was he at least hot?'

Jake grinned. 'More your type than mine. I prefer them beefy, not pale and interesting.'

She relaxed. This was good. She was listening, letting him lead. They were getting along. She still needed to acknowledge his loss, but it's not as if ChatGPT stipulated any order of service.

'So, about tomorrow,' he said, without warning. 'I've thought it through, and Tom wouldn't insist on it, but I'm wearing black.'

And just like that, things between them shifted.

'OK.' She had to tread with care. He'd sounded so matter of fact. Rona might have cracked and invited him. 'And they're meeting at the House of Hope or whatever they call it...'

'St John's in Perry Barr. I only found out the time and place by calling every funeral director this side of the Hagley Road.'

Lucy forced herself to be positive. 'OK, so I guess we could get an Uber.'

Jake focused on the empty table. 'We're not invited.'

Lucy fumbled for her phone. *Acknowledge their loss, listen, let them lead, offer help, share memories.* 'St John's is a church. Anyone can go in. She can't ban you...'

His eyes dodged hers. 'I got to see the toxicology report...'

A profound silence filled the space where words should be.

'It might rain later,' she said in a voice that sounded like it was coming from somewhere near the door. 'Though you just never know. They get it wrong all the time.'

Jake picked at his pastry. When he spoke, his tone was almost hollow. 'It was negative.'

Lucy froze, processing his statement, the weight of it refusing to settle. 'The report...'

'Tom hadn't been drinking,' Jake said, as if he was still trying to convince himself. 'A coroner had to investigate. The accident... it was one of those things.'

His gaze fell to the table. She watched his chest rise and fall in shallow breaths, holding something down, something tangled and twisted. She should reach out, offer help, share memories. Or maybe just touch his hand. But her fingers stopped short. When Jake raised his eyes, everything about him appeared to have changed. He didn't look happy—that was the wrong word. But a weight had been lifted.

'I told myself...' He spoke with care, weighing each word. 'I told myself that if he'd been drinking, it was on me. That I was the reason he was keeping secrets. That he was only staying with me because...' His shoulders shook, and he sniffed, waving away the tissue she pulled from her bag. 'I thought he was unhappy, Luce. He was going to leave me. Rona said...'

Lucy's head jerked up. 'Rona said what?'

'She told me he needed a break. From me. That I was needy and...'

Jake sobbed like she'd never heard anyone sob before. His shoulders shook, raw and unguarded. Not caring that people could see. Not giving a damn about anything. Her own heart pounded with all the things she should have done. All the words she should have spoken. She couldn't find the right way to say what she thought. She might never. But none of that mattered. Not now.

She reached across the table and placed her hand over his, squeezing just enough. His fingers tightened around hers, anchoring them both.

'Jake.' She forced herself to stay steady. Acknowledge his loss. 'Tom loved you. That was real. No one can take that away. Not Rona. Not anyone.'

He looked at her, his face raw.

The world outside could wait. The wedding dress, the hen weekend, the flowers, and the cake—all of it faded, leaving only Jake, her hand in his, and the silent promise that he wasn't alone.

INT. EMMA AND CHRIS'S HOUSE – DAY
SUPER: '28 AUGUST 2024'

Lucy and Fred sat on opposite ends of a patterned sofa, each holding a glass of wine, neither risking more than a single sip. Stu had a rare afternoon off work and stood near the window, his arms folded, his eyes trained outside, even though there was little to see beyond a well-maintained front lawn and a row of identical houses.

Wiping her hands on a tea towel, Emma emerged from the kitchen and glanced first at the muted TV and then at Chris, who was pretending not to be glued to the cricket.

'Turn that off,' she said. 'This isn't the time.'

Lucy twisted the engagement ring on her finger, the perfect little stone catching a slant of fading sunlight. Out of place, sparkling amid so much sadness. This had all been so last minute. After hugging Jake goodbye, she'd called Emma, who'd called Fred, who'd agreed they would team up to show support for their friend.

A friend who had been in the upstairs bathroom for ten long minutes.

'Should one of us go up and check on him?' she said.

Emma shook her head. 'Give him space, eh? Today isn't going to be easy.'

Funerals were always difficult. The last one Lucy went to was for her mother. She'd been fourteen—old enough for it to hurt, but too young to understand how protracted the pain would be.

The toilet flushed, a tap ran, pipes rattled.

'You said you'd fixed that,' Emma whispered.

Chris half shrugged. 'You think they'll do hymns? I mean, Tom wasn't religious.'

Stu glanced up at a clock and back out into the street. 'Is it really ten past one?' he said. 'We'll be late.'

He pulled out his phone to barrack whoever he'd talked into lending them a six-seater car and driver.

Jake pushed open the living room door, and everyone froze, like they'd been caught up to no good.

'Everything OK?' Emma said.

'I'm no fan of economy loo roll, but yeah, otherwise five stars all round. A firm flush and the soap was acceptable.'

From outside, a car sounded its horn. Lucy inhaled and crossed her fingers as she got up from the sofa. Jake didn't move.

Emma turned off the TV. 'We have to go now,' she whispered, and took his hand, like she might with one of the twins having a *Wacky Warehouse* meltdown. 'The sooner it starts, the sooner it's over.'

```
EXT. ST. JOHN'S CHURCH - DAY
Huge cars all but block a narrow lane.
Mourners gather outside the weathered
stone building. Dark clouds bring the
first signs of rain.
```

The sun refused to put its hat on. Heavy clouds hung low, slate grey and unrelenting, delivering drizzle. The mourners, all strangers, were dressed in regulation black, trudging up the path toward the church, carrying umbrellas just in case the weather forecast proved correct.

In their ridiculous pink stretch limo, silence thickened. Stu had turned red with shame when it arrived, apologising non-stop for not being more specific about the favour he'd called in from a friend with a hire-car business.

Jake had surprised them all by laughing. 'Tom will love this,' he'd said, a brief flash of his old self returning. 'We'll open the roof and play "Mamma Mia" full blast.' But that sense of hope passed, leaving them trapped in damp, stuffy silence as they watched mourners file into the church.

Through rain-streaked windows, they could make out Rona by the entrance, greeting people none of them recognised.

She'd texted when she saw the car, warning Jake to stay

away. He'd called Vicky to check her claim that they'd be trespassing if they set foot in the church, and she'd confirmed Rona had the law on her side. Churches might be public spaces, but the service could be declared private.

The car smelled of wet clothes and Emma's perfume. Lucy tried to think of a kind word to say, something to fill the silence that settled in waves, but words refused to come. She stared once more at the church, at the dark stone, at the heavy skies.

Chris shifted in his seat. 'Rona keeps looking over.'

He was right. Tom's sister was by the entrance, greeting mourners. Her lips were thin, her posture rigid.

Jake reached for the door handle. 'Fuck this. Tom was mine. I'm going in.'

Lucy shuffled in her seat. 'Best we go as a group.'

He turned to her. 'Give me two minutes, then you follow. I need to do this first bit by myself.'

They watched him step out into the spitting rain, pulling up his hood as he made his way across the road toward the churchyard. Lucy swallowed, the back of her throat dry. 'What if she's horrible to him?'

Emma shook her head. 'Jake needs to do this.'

INT. ST. JOHN'S CHURCH – CONTINUOUS

The air within was damp and cold, thick with the smell of old wood and wet wool. Rona had spotted Jake the moment they arrived, ducking inside and leaving Harry alone to greet the other mourners. Lucy was first out of the big pink limo.

At the front of the church, a large photograph of Tom rested on an easel—a bright, carefree smile, his face youthful and open. Lucy blinked. This wasn't the Tom she remembered.

'Who's that?' Emma whispered, her voice low and uncertain.

Rona seemed to materialise beside them, her eyes sharp and cold. 'The first ten rows are for family.' Her tone was brisk. 'Perhaps you'd be more comfortable at the back.'

Jake's shoulders slumped, but he held his tongue, turning without a word and leading the way to the very last row.

They shuffled along the narrow pew, Lucy settling on one side of Jake, Emma on the other. They each took one of his hands. A raindrop landed on the floor and Fred glanced up.

'The roof's leaking.'

Buckets were scattered throughout the church, some orange, some blue, collecting rainwater that dripped from the high, vaulted ceiling. In patches, the surface was slick with puddles.

Stu leaned over, whispering, 'Why are we letting her treat us this way?'

The groaning pipes of an ancient organ filled the space with sound. A choirboy, his voice clear and achingly pure, began to sing *Pie Jesu*, his tiny figure dwarfed by the enormity of the church.

Lucy's mind drifted, her thoughts scattering like the rain. She thought about her wedding, about Colin, about the endless decisions still waiting to be made. The Cube was confirmed, the deposit had drained her account. The menu was set. The flowers were on order. None of this stopped her from waking each night at 2 AM in a cold sweat.

The vicar spoke, his voice nasal and small. 'We are gathered here today to celebrate the life of Thomas Carter...'

Jake's hand tightened on hers. She squeezed back, hoping it would be enough.

They stood to sing the first hymn, *Morning Has Broken*. Lucy recalled Tom calling it 'the biggest pile of maudlin shite he'd ever heard. Worse than *The Wind Beneath My Wings*. Way worse.'

They sat, and Rona's voice echoed through the church, delivering her eulogy, a hollow sadness clinging to every word. The Tom she described was a stranger, and Lucy saw how Fred tensed. How Emma dabbed at her eyes. How Stu shook his head and stared down at the floor.

When the service ended and people began to file away, Emma and Chris, Fred and Stu, Lucy and Jake stayed put. Rona stalked past in heels, shooting them a pointed look, but their gaze remained fixed on the photograph of Tom, on a version of their dearest friend—a version unfamiliar to them.

The church became a church again, and Jake took a shuddering breath, his shoulders sagging as the invisible thread holding him up snapped.

Six friends waited, a family woven together by grief and memory, by Tom's presence and his absence. And when they stood to leave, a single sunbeam broke through the stained glass, scattering colours across the empty pews, washing over them—a last tribute to the friend they'd all loved.

INT. LUCY'S FLAT – DAY
SUPER: '29 AUGUST 2024'

The ping of a text woke Lucy from a rare lie-in. For once, she hadn't woken in the middle of the night, gripped by fear. For once, she'd slept through the sound of her neighbours slamming doors and heading off to work.

IRIS FLORIST

Call me.

People never sent that message when they had good news. Had the shop burned down? Were her flowers held up in some post-Brexit snafu?

Iris didn't sugar-coat things. She ripped the plaster off,

quick and clean. 'I can't get the hydrangeas,' she said. 'Not in the shade you asked for, anyway. My usual supplier's out. The best I can do is a darker blue, but I'd have to fly them in from North Africa.'

Lucy breathed in, then breathed out. 'How dark?'

'Closer to purple.'

Purple. Of course. The one colour she hated. And yes, she knew hating a colour wasn't rational. Purple had done nothing specific to hurt her. Perhaps she'd been made to sleep in a purple pram or wrapped in a purple blanket as a baby. Her father maybe force-fed her aubergine as a toddler.

Something inside Lucy tightened. Yesterday had been tough, but turned out fine. After the funeral, they'd jumped back in the limo and driven to Moseley to a pub where Tom used to work. The landlady had been in bits when she heard why they were there and insisted on them drinking the place dry. Now, her head hurt.

'Let me think this through,' she said, hanging up to go in search of water, orange juice, or a new head.

She was mid-glug when Sandrine called. 'Allo, mademoiselle. Je t'en prie, mais I have what you might call such bad news about Jean-Claude.'

Lucy said nothing. The fake French thing was getting on her tits.

'He has to stay a while longer on ze business trip. So we cannot today make your fitting.'

'OK, so when do you want me?'

'Ze shop is not closing down. This is just a rumour. A nasty one, yes?'

She put down her carton of juice. 'I've not heard any rumour.'

'Ah oui. That make me so happy.' Sandrine sounded

anything but. 'I will make the phone calls in a day or two. Perhaps next week, oui?'

The line clicked, and she was gone.

INT. BLOOMING MARVELLOUS – DAY

Lucy sat staring into her cup of tea. Her voice sounded distant, even to herself. 'Is it me?' she asked, her eyes fixed on the table. 'Did I do something wrong in a past life?'

'The sky is always darkest before the dawn,' Iris said, arranging roses with deliberate care. 'Things sort themselves out.'

Lucy forced a laugh. It came across as hollow.

'Have you ever been to Canada?' she asked.

Iris stopped. 'Can't say as I have. Never appealed to me. Not that I've anything against the place. It's just... I suppose, why fly all that way to Canada when you can go to America?'

She nodded. This was what her friends had said way back when plans had hatched for a four-city North American holiday. She'd lobbied hard for Toronto, insisting she wanted to see Victoria Falls. And that was how she'd met Colin.

And that was how come she was sitting in a florist's shop in Kings Heath, wondering what she'd done to deserve sustained bad luck.

'If you had to live anywhere,' Lucy said. 'Where would you choose?'

Iris snorted. 'Well, not Canada, for starters.' She thought for a minute. 'France, if I could. Some place where they grow sunflowers. I love them. They're always so full of hope, and they make me smile.'

'Colin's mother wants us to move to Canada,' Lucy said. She wasn't sure why she needed her to know this.

'Canada?' Iris poised, scissors mid-snip. 'Is that what you want?'

Lucy blinked. The question had thrown her, and she forced down a lump in her throat.

'I don't think it is.' Hearing the words out loud surprised her. 'I've been so wrapped up in planning this wedding... I haven't thought about what might happen next. I guess... I hope people will see how much I love Colin.'

Iris stopped working, her expression softening. 'That's the first time you've mentioned love, Lucy. Most brides, it's the only thing they talk about.' She paused, her voice gentle but firm. 'No offence, but you seem like someone who cares more about a flawless wedding than a happy marriage.'

Lucy felt the words sting. 'Can't I have both?'

'You can,' Iris said, seeming to pick her words with care. 'But when you say you love Colin, are you saying that to convince me, or yourself?'

The question hung in the air, and for a moment, Lucy couldn't breathe. She hadn't thought about things that way. Here, in a florist's shop, drinking lukewarm tea with a woman she'd only met a week ago, she realised how much she missed her mother. Friends were great, but they were always on her side. She needed someone who could challenge her, who could scrutinise her choices, like her mother would have. What would she have said to Patricia Macluskey?

'I've been trying to do everything by myself.' Lucy's voice turned into a whisper. 'I didn't want to bother anyone.'

Iris drew in a breath and smiled. 'Sweetheart, you don't have to do any of this alone. I'm always here for a chat, and what about that lovely young man who came in with you before?'

Lucy sniffed, wiping her eyes. 'Yesterday...' She hesitated.

'Yesterday, I went to a funeral. That young man—Jake—he lost his partner.'

Iris looked taken aback. 'He's just a kid himself. Was his partner a lot older, or...'

'Same age,' Lucy said, quieter now. 'There was an accident. On the motorway.'

Iris shook her head, at a loss for words. 'Was it a nice service?'

Lucy swallowed. It all seemed so far away, dreamlike. Like she hadn't been part of it.

'The whole day was awful,' Lucy said, her voice cracking. 'I didn't recognise the man his sister and the vicar talked about. And I've been such a terrible friend. Every time anyone calls, all I talk about is my dress, my flowers, the bloody cake. Jake is dealing with all this, and I pushed him into being Colin's best man.'

The tears came before she could stop them. She swiped at her face, hoping Iris wouldn't notice. But she did, and pulled out tissues.

'Take a breath, love. You don't have to figure everything out today. Talk to your bloke. Remind yourself why you're marrying him. And be truthful—are your emotions the same as when you fell in love?'

Lucy nodded. She couldn't be sure. Iris was right. She had to stop being such a control freak and let people in. But more than that, she needed to have an honest conversation with Colin about what came next, after the wedding.

INT. LUCY'S FLAT – NIGHT

If she could just haul herself up the ladder, shimmy forward, and stretch a little further, Lucy could reach what she was after.

Gritting her teeth, she strained, cursing her personal trainer's lectures on core strength.

When she'd first viewed the flat, the estate agent—a lanky lad who reeked of cigarettes and Kouros—had raved about the crawl space, rambling on about planning permission and adding another bedroom as if it were a done deal. That was back when decluttering was all the rage, and everything that didn't "spark joy" got shoved into cardboard crates.

The first box she opened was full of books: *The Hunger Games*, *Fifty Shades of Grey*, *Twilight*—all recommended by friends but never read. The next box held her CD collection: Adele, Arctic Monkeys, Ed Sheeran. She cringed. *Did I really own an Ed Sheeran album?*

She rummaged through more—unworn Ugg boots, denim in every shade—and then... a stack of dusty photo albums.

The intercom buzzed. She belly-shuffled back to the ladder.

Her father never visited without a fair amount of negotiation, and he always brought flowers, like a husband making up for missing an anniversary. In the kitchen, she grabbed two mugs, refilled the kettle—a habit Jake mocked, but she'd read somewhere that twice-boiled water ruined tea. As she waited, Lucy opened an album.

There she was as a teenager, sporting a homemade Jessie J dip-dye job—peroxide and a cheap colour rinse that left her hair patchy and brassy. Then came the blunt pixie cut, more angry teenage boy than edgy rebel.

A loose photo slipped free. Her breath caught.

Her mother, radiant on her wedding day, in a satin gown with a sweetheart neckline and lace sleeves. Her hair in a soft chignon, barely a trace of makeup—just blush and pale pink lipstick.

Her father's voice startled her. 'Taking a walk down memory lane?'

She looked up, trying and failing to tuck the photo back inside the album. 'I went to a funeral yesterday, and the picture they used... I guess I wanted to cringe at old haircuts.'

'You've got your mother's taste there.' He picked up the photo and studied it, nodding.

Lucy hesitated. 'I... miss her. Especially now.'

He avoided her gaze. 'Has the kettle boiled, or is it one of those eco-friendly ones that takes forever?'

'I yearn for someone to talk to about the wedding.'

His face hardened, but he stayed silent.

'I have Emma, but sometimes I need... someone who gets it. Someone who gets me.'

His eyes drifted around the kitchen, settling on anything but her. 'Is that an air fryer? People say they're quite useful.'

A knot of frustration tightened in her chest. 'Why can't we ever talk about her?'

He ducked his head. 'You can always ask me whatever you want, darling.'

'Yet every time I try, you find a way to change the subject.'

'That's not fair.'

She pointed at the air fryer. 'Case in point.'

He picked up the photo again, staring at it as if seeing it for the first time. When he put it down, he swallowed. 'Your mother was beautiful. You don't need me to tell you that.'

'What did you think when you saw her walk down the aisle? Did she take your breath away?'

His face flushed. 'I don't remember the exact moment.'

'What?' She folded her arms, frustration flaring. 'Everyone recalls that time. Did you even love her?'

His eyes bulged. 'How could you say that?'

'Because sometimes you act like she never existed. No photos, no memories—just the one picture in your office. You gave all her things away.'

'To charity, Lucy. She would've wanted that.'

'Would she?' She needed to know. 'Is that really what she would have wanted? You never talk about her. I was fourteen when she got sick. Still a kid...'

He turned, retreating to the living room. Anger propelled her to follow him. They'd had this fight before. And every time she'd backed down.

'I'm getting married in two months, and I need my mother around.'

He stood by the window, staring out. 'That can't happen.'

'No, so I'd settle for my father showing a bit of interest.'

He turned, mouth open but silent.

'By "interest," I don't mean paying a solicitor to draft a contract protecting your house.'

He mumbled something under his breath.

'What?' She stepped closer, her vision blurring with anger.

'Patricia Macluskey... she's not a nice person.'

The words just hung there. She stared, but her father simply shrugged. He'd left soon after, the front door closing with a quiet click louder than any slam.

INT. LUCY'S FLAT - DAY
SUPER: '30 AUGUST 2024'

Lucy woke to find an empty Belvedere bottle sharing her pillow like an unwelcome bedfellow. Her laptop screensaver cycled through photos of her and Colin—smiling, laughing, frozen in happier moments. For the second morning in a row, her head was being squeezed in a vice.

Even thinking about coffee sent her stumbling to the bathroom, where she threw up something green. She didn't remember eating anything green.

Her emails confirmed everything she'd hoped was a dream:

258

Pendragon House was booked. The deposit paid. No refunds. Lucy squinted at the one-too-many zeroes. All this, just to prove a point to her father. Though quite what point, she wasn't sure.

She sipped from a lukewarm Evian bottle, staring at her phone. Three missed calls to Colin. She needed someone to tell her she'd done the right thing.

Jake sounded half-asleep when he picked up.

'Is this a bad time?' she said. 'Only... I might have done something silly.'

His silence prompted a full confession. Fuelled by vodka and spite, she'd called The Cube and cancelled her booking. When the Head of Functions quoted terms and conditions, she told him to stuff it up his bum.

'If my wedding moved to Cornwall, would that be a problem for you?'

'Cornwall... as in where they make fudge and argue over scones?'

'I found the most fabulous hotel. Right on the coast.'

'But I thought—'

'I'm not a bloody nepo baby, Jake. Just because my father knows the owner of The Cube...' She forced herself to breathe. 'I found it online. They'd had a cancellation.'

He stayed silent. Lucy needed to rant.

'He told me Colin's mother is some sort of racist. But I'm not marrying Patricia Macluskey, am I? That solicitor looked at me like I was some silly little girl playing at having a career. I work fucking hard, Jake.'

She moved to the window, watching a woman in a blue coat walk her dog.

'Like he's so squeaky clean. He voted Leave. I bet he supports Reform too, on the quiet. And they're just as bad as the people he reckons Colin's mother is helping out.'

'Helping out?' Jake spoke for the first time.

'If he's so bloody sure of himself, why doesn't he go to the papers? Why isn't he on The One Show chucking muck around?'

She slumped onto the sofa. 'I'm thinking about telling him he's not invited to the wedding.'

'What? Why would you do that?'

'Colin isn't his mother.'

'No, but...'

'I'm marrying the sweetest guy anyone could ever hope to meet. He's not like Will... or Gary or François... or Si.'

Static hissed before Jake spoke again. 'We're talking about your father, Lucy. We only ever get one of those. He was only trying to do that legal thing he always talks about. The thing he told Tom to do before buying the flat.'

She sighed. 'Due diligence.'

'Luce. I'm not the person you should be yelling at.'

'I wasn't... I...'

'You need to talk to Colin.'

Jake was right. Lucy reached for last month's Brides Magazine, desperate to change the subject. 'How's the best man's speech coming along?'

'Coming along.'

'If you need help, I can send you stuff about the Heligan Giant.'

'Should that mean something to me?'

'There's this giant who watches over the hotel gardens, keeping strangers safe.'

Jake huffed. 'And that doesn't sound made up at all.'

'Please, Jake, be happy for me.'

'What does Colin have to say about this?'

'He's... cool.'

Half an hour later, she called Emma.

'Cornwall?' Emma made it sound like moving to Alum Rock. 'Could you not just say your credit card was stolen?'

'Juliana gets it,' Lucy said. 'She understood about controlling fathers and wedding pressure. We hit it off.'

'You bonded with your events planner?' Emma's tone was flat. 'The woman you're paying to agree with you.'

'She told me about her father trying to control everything too.'

'So that's a no on the stolen credit card?'

'We're Insta friends. She even DM'd about the cake.'

Emma sighed. 'I guess Cornwall could be nice in October. Though I've got to grovel to the twins' form teacher about taking them out of school. And pay a fine.'

'I'm sorry.'

'Jake already called me. He's freaking out about his speech. Half his jokes were about the Bull Ring.'

Lucy squeezed her eyes shut. 'Great.'

'Also... what's this about Colin's mother being a total Nazi?'

'Is that what he told you?

'Jake said something about her stealing money from the college where she works.'

Lucy groaned. This was how rumours spread. This was how lawsuits started. 'That might not even be true.'

'Babe,' Emma's voice was calm but firm. 'I'm going to ask you a question, and don't freak out, because I asked Fred the same thing.'

'Go ahead.'

'Do you want to marry Colin?'

Lucy's heart twisted in her chest. 'I think so.'

'That's not a yes.'

INT. CRUMB AND BERRY - DAY

Ethan had been so understanding, apologising over and over about the fondant icing mix-up, and refusing to keep the deposit. A part of Lucy wished she hadn't handed everything over to the Pendragon House planner. She would've preferred something just a little off-brand from Birmingham than perfect and impersonal from a bakery she'd never visited.

She was considering a second coffee when Jake arrived, breathless and flustered.

'That Number Nine's a right mare,' he said, pulling out the chair opposite. 'Third time in two weeks it's broken down, trapping me with people who consider deodorant optional.'

Lucy smiled. It was nice, hearing Jake be Jake again.

'I'm just glad you could make it,' she said. 'How's work? Everyone still acting like nothing ever happened. Treating you with kid gloves?'

He rolled his eyes. 'That lasted all of one morning. I'm back to punters sending photographs of flies squashed against windows and demanding full refunds.'

For a minute, they fell silent. And then she placed her hand on his.

'Say if this is a terrible idea, but I thought I might go to the churchyard at the weekend and take flowers.'

A faraway look passed over his face. 'Tom loved yellow roses.'

Lucy remembered her mother's wedding dress, and the bouquet she'd held. 'Iris will get me a discount.'

Another awkward silence. She asked about his comedy classes, and Jake rolled his eyes.

'The woman in charge makes Mussolini look like a slacker. There are rules about rules, and for a comedy class, she's not big on humour.'

Lucy let out a muted laugh, relieved to be back within the familiar rhythm of their banter. 'Are you at least getting ideas for your speech?'

'Kind of, but the showcase night has me worried.'

'Oh God, yeah. Emma was talking about tickets.'

'Don't book online,' he said. 'Miranda adds a fee. Pay ten quid on the door. Even if she says tickets are selling fast, trust me, they're not.'

'So, let's hear your routine. Treat me as your trial audience.'

He blushed. 'It's still a work in progress, Luce.'

'I'm not expecting Jimmy Carr.'

'Thing is, it's not signed off. Not yet. So I don't know for sure this is what I'm going to be allowed to do on the night.'

Lucy wrinkled her nose. 'Signed off? Allowed? What the hell are you talking about? I thought the stand-up thing was supposed to be fun.'

'Miranda has to approve our five-minute set.' He mimed air quotes. 'Once she signs off, we're not permitted to change a word. If we go off-script, she'll literally shut off the lights.' He leaned back, sighed, and stared past her. 'I figured out what I'd like to say, but she keeps rejecting my jokes. I can't mention death because it'll bring the audience down.' Jake paused, as if searching for the right words. 'The thing is... these are my five minutes, Luce. I keep thinking I should be able to say what I want. If I feel like talking about Tom, she can't stop me.'

Lucy's stomach dropped, her voice caught in her throat. She trod with care. 'When you say you're going to talk about Tom... You mean at the showcase, right? Not... at my wedding?'

His expression hardened. 'Selfish much?'

She held up her hands. 'I'm sorry. I get that I've been difficult—'

He cut her off with a grin. 'We've been calling you Bridezilla Penrose.'

Lucy flushed. 'Have I been that bad?'

'Worse,' he teased, then his tone shifted, more serious. 'The Cornwall thing. Is this to piss off your dad?'

It was her turn to blush. 'It's a beautiful hotel, Jake. And you'd be staying in yurts.'

'Tents? In October?'

She tapped at her phone, scrolling through The Pendragon website for photos. 'They're super cute. There's a log burner and 800 thread-count sheets. It's not like camping.'

Jake's phone pinged, and she saw how his expression changed. He showed her the screen.

VICKY

Ravenswood shit hit the fan. Rona in frame.
Can we talk? 💀

Lucy stared at Jake's phone, the name Ravenswood stirring something in her memory. Her father had mentioned it, hadn't he? Something about shell companies and property deals. The same investigation that had uncovered Patricia's activities.

'Jake...' She hesitated. 'What has Rona got herself into?'

CONTINUOUS

Lucy pulled her chair closer, metal scraping against the floor as Vicky Harper spread documents across their table. Despite her tailored suit and usual composure, Vicky's fingers drummed an anxious rhythm, her eyes darting between them.

'Ravenswood Enterprises,' she said, voice low. 'Harry Staples is listed as one owner.'

Lucy studied the papers. Company records, bank statements, a printed email chain. 'So Rona's husband started a business. That happens.'

'Usually after too many beers,' Vicky agreed. 'Then they

forget about it until Companies House demands paperwork.' She tapped a phone number on one document. 'But this traces to a call centre. One that keeps showing up in my investigations.'

Jake remained silent, hands wrapped around a now-cold mug of coffee.

'Your investigation?' Lucy's stomach tightened.

Vicky hesitated. 'The call centre hosts numbers for certain... political groups.'

'Would one of them be True North?'

The café's background noise—espresso machines, customer chatter—seemed to fade as Lucy waited for an answer.

Vicky's silence spoke volumes.

'I've told you what I can,' she said finally. 'The rest has to go to the police.'

'The police?' Lucy was missing something. 'Just because someone registered a company?'

'There's more.' She glanced around. 'Things I'm not supposed to discuss.'

Jake touched Lucy's arm. 'She could get into trouble, Luce.'

But she had already figured it out. This had her father's fingerprints all over it. Anger flared, hot and sharp.

'Did he put you up to this?' Her voice was tight. 'Because I wouldn't sign that stupid prenup?'

'Your father acted on a tip-off,' Vicky said. 'The last thing he wanted was for you to end up involved.'

The café seemed to close in, cheerful chatter blurring to white noise. Lucy had read that no matter how hard you hit what you thought was your lowest point, there was always farther to fall.

Jake broke the silence. 'Tom always called Rona... difficult. I just figured she didn't like people.'

'Patricia Macluskey was arrested this morning,' Vicky said. 'She's in custody in Toronto.'

Lucy's chest tightened. Everything she believed was crumbling.

She turned to Jake, her voice small. 'How are you doing with all this?'

```
INT. THE UNION TAP - NIGHT
A trendy city-centre pub, packed with
weekend revellers. It's three-deep at
the bar, and the air is thick with the
buzz of people ready for their big
night out.
```

Lucy felt every one of her 29 years. The Union Tap had reached that point in the evening where the lights dimmed and the music swelled, transforming from after-work pub to wannabe nightclub. Jake and Fred had claimed a table in the corner, but this was a far cry from their usual cosy catch-ups at the Bäckerei.

'It's eight o'clock,' Fred grumbled. 'Do they need the volume this high already?'

Lucy sipped her mojito, wincing at the sugary syrup. Her ears were ringing, and her patience was frayed. But tonight was supposed to be a reset. That's what she'd told herself—and the others—when she sent out the text invites. But beneath the surface, the reasons were more complicated.

Her future with Colin, once the one thing she was sure of, had become muddled. Until a few days ago, no matter the chaos, the arguments, or her doubts, she knew she was marrying him. That rock-solid certainty had been an anchor. But now, she found herself in unsettled waters. Because the police had come to arrest his mother.

'You OK?' Jake squeezed her arm. They'd agreed not to tell the others anything.

'I'm coping,' she said. 'Just about.'

Fred sampled his drink and pulled a face. 'There is no way this is Bombay Sapphire. Which clueless eighteen-year-old with a charisma bypass do you think is the manager?'

Emma grabbed his glass, sniffed, and declared, 'Gin is gin. That's why everything's half-price. Live a little, Karen.'

Lucy smiled to herself. Once upon a time, the four of them had lived for Saturday nights like this. They'd grown up, not grown apart, but they were all different now. Emma kept checking her phone, worried the twins might have tied Chris to a chair and broken into the drinks cabinet again. Fred had already made it clear Stu expected him home by eleven.

Her friends had stuck by her through all the craziness. They'd been there for dress fittings, cake tastings, and spa days that had turned into health and safety disasters. But tonight, Emma had admitted she couldn't get time off for Santorini, and Fred still hadn't RSVP'd. Without him, Jake would find an excuse.

Her phone buzzed—another RSVP from a stranger she barely recognised. Her guest list had become a patchwork of obligations: clients, distant cousins, Iris from the florist. What was the point of a perfect wedding without the people who mattered most?

She cleared her throat, drawing their attention. 'I need to tell you all something.'

Billie Eilish crooned over the speakers, and heads turned at nearby tables. Lucy hesitated for a beat.

'The Santorini thing... forget about it. What if we just do... this?' She waved her hand to indicate the pub. 'All I want is to be with you guys.'

Her heart pounded as she watched their faces. The music

seemed to fade, as though the moment itself carried more weight. She waited, searching their expressions for disappointment, for resistance.

But Emma was the first to raise her glass, the same easy smile on her lips. 'As long as you're happy, lovely. That's what matters.'

Lucy exhaled, relief flooding her. She lifted her own glass, meeting Emma's eyes. 'And you don't have to wear pink. Turn up in jeans and a T-shirt if you like. Just be there.'

A wave of affection washed over her, warm and grounding. Yes, things were changing. Yes, they were all growing up. But that didn't mean the core of their friendship had to change. They were still here. Together. And that was what mattered.

Fred, grinning, waved down a server and ordered Champagne. Emma called Chris and told him to let the twins have enough of the sell-by-date eggnog to knock them out for the night. And Jake, ever the sentimentalist, pulled Lucy into a tight hug.

'Tom would've lost his shit and insisted on Santorini,' he whispered. 'But I'd have talked him round.'

Lucy drew him close, experiencing a pang of warmth and sadness. This wasn't the ending she'd feared. Just a different beginning.

INT. LUCY'S FLAT – DAY
SUPER: '31 AUGUST 2024'

Lucy had never been a day drinker—a lunchtime glass of wine always sparked a headache, which morphed into a migraine, ending with her hugging the toilet and vowing never again. And yet, after rinsing her breakfast dishes, she found herself pulling a Marks and Spencer ready-mixed gin and tonic from the fridge, adding ice and a slice—because she wasn't an animal.

Her father's radio show started in half an hour, and she'd stocked up with extra pre-mixed tins. A packet of Migraleve sat on the counter, just in case.

"Coming up after the news, we're checking in with the Scambuster…"

Lucy's hand tightened on her glass. She'd been streaming Radio WM all morning, telling herself she didn't care what her father had to say. Her mood was already set to blue—an important client had cancelled despite three expensive lunches, Ethan from Crumb and Berry had called with forced cheerfulness about the cancelled cake, and Iris had accepted the Cornwall thing with a silence that spoke volumes.

She risked a second gin and tonic as the two o'clock news played out, tension tightening in her chest. And then her father's voice boomed through the speaker.

After the usual pleasantries, he launched into his report.

'To most of her acquaintances,' her father began, 'Patricia Macluskey was a pillar of the community. A college principal. A familiar face at charity events.' He paused for effect. 'But beneath that constructed facade lay something far darker…'

By the time Gerald Penrose wrapped up with his 'be careful out there' sign-off, Lucy had finished her fourth gin and tonic on an empty stomach. The room had spun, but her mind stayed clear.

This was huge. Her father had tried to warn her, but she hadn't wanted to listen. She'd dismissed his claims as controlling nonsense, daring him to do what he'd just done if he was so sure.

And he had.

Lucy stared into her glass. She'd been so sure of herself, of Colin, of what her future would look like. Now, nothing felt solid. Her father had only ever tried to protect her, but she wished, for once, he'd let her fuck things up in her own way.

She typed out a text to her father.

LUCY PENROSE

I'm so very proud of you 🩶

Her thumb hovered over 'send' for a full minute before she deleted it word by word.

The intercom sounded. Probably another delivery—something else ordered drunk, destined to be returned. She buzzed them up without checking.

When she opened the door, Jake stood there, looking as rough as she felt.

'You look like shit.' He brushed past, stopping when his eyes landed on the row of empty gin and tonic cans. 'Though not as shit as your recycling.'

'I haven't had the best day.' She swept the cans into the bin. 'Shouldn't you be at work?'

'Told them I tested positive for Covid.' He paused, something in his expression making her stomach twist. 'I need a huge favour.'

INT. JAKE AND TOM'S FLAT – DAY

Left untouched for weeks, Jake and Tom's once-happy home had become a time capsule. Dust motes swirled in shafts of afternoon sunlight. Lucy watched as Jake moved through the space, his fingers trailing over surfaces, straightening a photo frame, removing specks of dirt. His expression stayed unreadable.

'You don't have to do this today,' she said.

'I need to. Before I lose my nerve.'

Vicky's call had come that morning—Rona had agreed to a deed of variation, allowing Tom's estate to pass to Jake. The change of heart seemed to be tied to Walker, Haynes and

Dobson security footage of someone wandering around the 23rd floor before leaving a note on a senior partner's desk.

Jake reached for something on a cluttered bookshelf and froze.

'What is it?' Lucy set down the bills she'd been sorting.

He held up a battered guidebook. *Discover Cornwall*, the cover a vista of rugged coastline.

'We always promised each other we'd go,' he said, his voice unsteady. 'Every summer, we'd say, this is the year, and then... life got in the way.'

She nodded, not trusting herself to speak.

'God, we made so many plans, Luce. Things we were going to do someday.' He held out the guidebook. 'Here. You should take this. For your wedding. It's not the same, but... perhaps you and Colin can use it.'

She took the book, faking excitement. This was a kind gesture from her best friend. So why did it sit like lead in her gut?

For the next hour, they worked in companionable silence, bringing shine to surfaces dulled by two weeks of dust. When they finally sat down with flat cola rescued from a fridge of sell-by food, Lucy took a breath. She needed someone else to hear the question playing on repeat in her head.

'Am I doing the right thing by marrying a man I met less than a year ago?'

Jake looked at her. 'Is this nerves talking?'

'A little.' She downed another slug from the bottle. Now she'd started, she might as well reveal everything. 'Thing is... I got so caught up in planning the perfect wedding, it never crossed my mind to think about what comes after. I'd be living with someone I don't know. You can tell me Tom's favourite movie, right?'

'*Little Miss Sunshine.*'

271

'The music he loved.'

'Bowie, Bush, and way too much Abba for one person to call normal. He even knew the words to *King Kong Song*.'

She shut her eyes and took a breath. 'I know none of that about Colin. He likes waterfalls and rocks and wears a rain poncho, but... that's sort of it.'

Jake remained quiet for a long moment, his gaze drifting to the window, to the world outside moving forward while his own universe stayed frozen.

'I'm not sure we can ever be certain if we're saying yes to the right person,' he said. 'But, the fact you're even asking... Perhaps that means you already have an answer.'

'I don't...' She picked up the Cornwall book, turning it over, wondering whose coffee cup had marked the back cover. And missing Tom more than ever.

'My turn to share a secret now?' he said. 'I've decided not to keep this place.'

'But, where would you...'

'Can't manage with half a life, right? And I'm not sure I want to live with ghosts.'

Lucy squeezed his hand. 'Fred and Stu have about six spare bedrooms.'

He smiled down at the floor, running his finger along a groove scratched into the floorboard. She wondered if he remembered what might have caused that. His smile suggested he did.

'Dad isn't ever going to get better,' he said, and she heard the choke in his words. 'Mum keeps saying she's got it all under control, but you know... I have this sense that if I just let her deal with everything... I don't need another thing to regret.'

She got it. She got it all too well.

Something loosened in her chest, a knot of anxiety she hadn't known was there started to unravel.

INT. LGBTQ+ OUTREACH CENTRE - NIGHT

Six hours after helping her friend say goodbye to the flat, Lucy took her seat in the front row of the makeshift auditorium. She'd been backstage where Jake paced and popped Haribo like off-brand diazepam.

'How is he?' Emma whispered.

'Like everyone else back there – pacing around like he's up before a hanging judge.'

Fred returned from the loo, his homemade *JAKE TAYLOR COMEDY GOD* T-shirt cropped to show off gym-trained abs, earning appreciative glances from half the audience.

'Three phone numbers already,' he said, settling into his seat. 'I should come here more often.'

Rows of chairs—plastic, folding, some that looked like they'd been borrowed from a nearby school—formed the makeshift auditorium. The small stage was little more than a raised platform with a lone microphone stand bathed in the unforgiving glare of a single overhead light.

Fred leaned in. 'I'm back in Year Five, waiting to wet myself in the Nativity.'

The lights dimmed. A hush fell over the room.

Zany music played as a pinched voice welcomed everyone to the *"Miranda Ratchett Funny For Life Comedy Showcase."* Lucy shifted in her seat, the plastic digging into her spine.

The first comic got laughs with a joke about serenading doggers in lay-bys during lockdown by playing *"Frère Jacques"* on his daughter's recorder. The next act—a girl with pigtails— shouted through a sound glitch about goldfish and their flawless memory.

And then it was Jake.

He looked small on the stage at first, fingers fidgeting with his shirt hem. But when he tapped the mic and cleared his throat, something shifted. This wasn't the Jake who'd spent weeks trying to please everyone – Rona, his parents, even Miranda. This was someone else entirely.

'Using moisturiser is like paying into a pension plan,' he said, his voice steady now. 'You've got better things to do when you're 23. When you hit 65, it's too late.'

Laughter rippled through the room, and Jake seemed to grow a little taller. He stole a glance at his friends, and then towards the back. Lucy assumed the shiny-faced woman in beige must be Miranda. She was waving, signalling for Jake to speed things up.

'I was supposed to introduce myself first,' he said, half-smiling. 'So I'm already on Miranda's shit list. I'm Jake, by the way.'

Applause followed. Fred wolf-whistled.

'I'm here to try out some jokes. They've been approved. Signed off.' He glanced toward Miranda, his voice growing stronger. 'I've been warned about what might happen if I change one word. But fuck it. Some things matter more than rules.'

Miranda had turned hypertension red.

'I want to tell you about someone.'

The audience shifted. Lucy held her breath.

'Tom was... everything. Brilliant and funny, but bitchy in a way that made you howl. He hated creatures with no legs—snails, specifically—and he could destroy anyone at karaoke with *"Holding Out for a Hero."*'

Laughter lapped the room.

Lucy spotted Miranda whispering to the guy in charge of the lights. Jake's mic cut out mid-sentence, but he didn't flinch. He just set it down and shrugged.

The audience leaned in, wanting to hear the whole story.

'This is where I'm supposed to tell you he lived as if he were a saint. That he was kind, generous, and cared about the whole world. But cross Tom, and he'd tear you apart with a smile, saying "no offence."'

Laughter, louder now. Support for Jake rolled like a wave.

'Tom had a love for all humanity. I miss him each day. I never got to say this at his funeral, so I'm saying it now. Raise a glass to him, because he always left the party too early.'

The stage went dark.

One by one, people pulled out their phones, lighting up the room with soft, twinkling stars. Lucy, Emma, and Fred joined this quiet tribute.

Jake wiped his eyes, barely holding it together. 'I had seven years with him. I'd do anything for seven more. I want to sit in the sun and listen to him talk about his day, tell me how he saw a cat with two heads, and no, he hadn't been drinking. I want to smell his aftershave in a room and be certain he was just there. I want to listen to him say, "You make me complete."'

A voice from the back called out, 'You go for it, mate.'

Jake smiled. 'Tom was a decent man. Not that he'd ever admit it. He went on about how nuns were the good ones, that he was full of sin and darkness. He ought to know. His sister married a man of the church.'

More laughter. Jake had them now.

'He was the love of my life. And I needed to say goodbye.'
'Thanks for listening. Thanks for letting me tell the truth.'

Music crackled through the speakers—*2Unlimited*. Miranda's attempt to play him off felt small and petty against what they'd witnessed.

The applause was deafening. People stood, clapping and cheering. Tears ticked Lucy's cheeks as she watched her friend take his bow. No longer the broken man told to sit at the back of a church and stay quiet. This wasn't someone who'd spent weeks trying to make everyone else comfortable with his grief. This was Jake, finding his voice again.

INT. LUCY'S FLAT - NIGHT

Lucy dropped her keys onto a side table and, for a moment, didn't move, as if she was waiting for something to happen. Her cleaner had been, and the flat felt different, staged. It reminded her of walking into a hotel room.

In the bedroom, she lit a vanilla candle, and like every other disappointing scented candle, it smelled of nothing much. She sat on the edge of the bed, taking off her shoes as the night replayed: Jake's eulogy, Emma teasing Chris, Vicky with her new man, laughing—really laughing, Fred and Stu bursting to tell everyone about an upcoming party to mark five years together.

She'd known Colin less than five months.

She padded over to the dresser. Her makeup was smudged, her eyes piss holes in snow. Lucy felt worn out, yes, but also something else. She seemed lost.

Emma had suggested sharing their cab, but they lived in the other direction. She'd told them she'd get the next one, and when their car turned a corner, she found the guy in charge of allocating rides and cancelled. Her friends would freak if they knew she'd walked home through empty car parks and taken back street shortcuts. She felt nothing. No fear. She'd grown numb.

In the bathroom, she began the ritual of cleansing her face. Cool water washed away the remnants of the night, grounding her. She patted her skin dry and reached for her best makeup, as if the call she knew she needed to make required her to be at her best.

A text pinged.

DAD

I hope you're OK, sweetheart. Coffee in my office tomorrow? x

Lucy's heart softened. Everything else moved, changed, shifted, but her father was there. No matter what. She texted to suggest she bring cake. She'd swing by the bakery he liked for chocolate brownies.

Her engagement ring sat on the edge of the sink. Just metal and a shiny stone. She stared at it for a long moment, waiting to feel something—a pang of regret—but nothing came. She'd always dreamed of posing for a photograph in her wedding dress, like the picture her father kept on his desk. And one day, she might.

She styled her hair. The tangles gave way to soft waves, and she spritzed sea salt spray, adding texture and life. A swipe of mascara, a touch of gloss.

She was ready.

Moving through the flat, she turned off lights one by one, and after one stiff gin, with the smallest splash of tonic, Lucy picked up her phone. It was seven in the evening in Toronto. The call connected, and Colin's face filled the screen. He looked different. Worried even. Like he knew what might be coming.

'Hey,' was all he said.

She waited two full seconds, giving her mind time enough to change. It didn't.

'I know about your mother,' she said. 'Not just that she's been arrested. I know why. I know about Ravenswood. Your father. Everything.'

Colin didn't so much as flinch. 'This is a huge misunderstanding. She has a great lawyer, we're going to—'

'Please.' She held up a hand. 'I have to tell you something, and if I don't... I might lose my nerve.'

Colin looked so small now. So gawky. Such a baby bird in need of a saviour to swoop in and make things better. And maybe that fragility was what she'd fallen for on that boat under

277

the waterfall, wearing matching rain ponchos. He wasn't confident Will, or cocky Gary, or sexually up-for-it Si. He lacked their front. Until that day, she told herself she looked for men with balls. She was a strong, independent woman. Any guy needed to keep up.

'How much of what she stands for do you believe in?' Lucy said.

If the question took her by surprise, it floored Colin.

'I... You know, I... What... Why would you even...'

She put him out of his misery. 'All of it, right? You do whatever she says.'

Colin leaned closer to the camera, his eyes narrowing as he scrutinised her features. 'Lucy-loo, I guess I got swept up in all the bullshit.'

She drew a deep breath, the weight of her decision settled. 'I'm sorry, Colin. I'm not going to marry you.'

The words hung between them, new but already unbreakable. She watched as his face changed, confusion morphing into something more unsettling, almost unreadable. He opened his mouth to speak, but she didn't wait.

She ended the call and poured herself a second gin—this time, without tonic—and pulled a blanket from the sofa, wrapping it around her shoulders as she moved to the window. People lived their lives behind all those windows and walls. Lives tangled in secrets.

Tomorrow, she'd dump a glossy pile of bridal magazines in the bins downstairs. Along with the veil she learned to love and then remembered to hate. She wasn't upset. That was the strange part. The ending didn't feel significant. It hadn't hit her in the way endings were supposed to. It was simply another moment, like any other.

In the kitchen, the dishwasher stood half-filled with mugs and plates from a week's worth of neglected chores. She pushed it shut with a satisfying snap, turned the dial, and listened as the soft swoosh of water sounded. Everything was being cleaned, washed away.

The bed was cool when she slipped between the sheets, the quiet of the room a gentle embrace. No more Colin. No more pretending to be someone she wasn't. Farewell Bridezilla Penrose. She closed her eyes, her body sinking.

For the first time, she had no idea what would come next.

And that was OK.

FADE TO BLACK

epilogue

```
INT. BIRMINGHAM CROWN COURT - DAY
An imposing Victorian edifice of red
brick and terracotta; its Gothic
revival architecture speaks to the
gravitas of justice. Ornate stone
carvings and pointed arches emphasise
its status as a cathedral of law.
```

Vicky stood tall, the weight of the moment pressing in but never overwhelming. This was it—the culmination of everything she had fought for, everything she had become. Tarquin Walker had insisted she act as advocate.

'This is your catch, Harper,' he'd said. 'Don't let some grubby barrister take home the spoils. That's no way for our next named partner to behave. Grab life by the balls.' He'd had the decency to blush. 'Not that I mean anything by that, obviously. Last thing I need is HR sending me on another training course.'

Her hand brushed over her dark suit, fingers steady, breath

measured. She took a sip of water to ease the tightness in her throat.

'Your Honour,' she began, her voice firm despite a million knots in her stomach, 'the evidence before you demonstrates a clear pattern of illegal activities.' She paused, allowing the words to land. 'True North, operating via Ravenswood Enterprises and an intricate web of shell companies, has systematically funded and organised hate crimes across this country.'

Her gaze swept to the gallery, to her family—not the one she was born to, but the one she'd chosen. Lucy and her father sat together, hands clasped, closer now than ever. Jake, clutching his notebook, research for his new column in *Queer Midlands* magazine where he turned grief into hope for others. Fred and Emma had taken the morning off work, despite hospital budget cuts and a massive window display deadline. Even Jenny from the outreach centre had squeezed in near the back.

Neat piles of evidence lay before her—financial records, digital communications, witness statements. There had been nights when she thought it might bury her. But Alex had kept her in coffee. He never questioned her drive, seeing past the lawyer to the woman who needed to fight this fight.

'These are serious allegations, Ms. Harper,' the judge said. 'Are you prepared for the consequences?'

She straightened, meeting his gaze. Every insult, every slap from her father's hand, every doubt and challenge had led to this. She had fought to exist, to be herself in a world that tried to silence her. This wasn't just about Rona and Harry Staples— it was about standing up, about chosen family protecting its own.

'Your Honour, the only consequence that matters here is justice.'

The courtroom held its breath. The judge studied her a

moment longer before nodding. 'Very well, Ms. Harper. We will proceed.'

She wanted to scream, to jump, to punch the air. Instead, she gathered her papers, catching her reflection in the glass of the courtroom door. The woman staring back had earned this moment.

Alex pushed through to whisper in her ear.

'I love you, Victoria Harper.'

Together, they emerged into bright Birmingham sunlight. She'd expected reporters and cameras, people hurling questions, asking for quotes. There was just some bloke smoking a roll-up and a woman bending down to bag dog poo.

But her friends were there. Two months ago, she had none. Now she had a family—a gang she could count on, And they were more than friends.

They were family.

And their story was far from over.

FADE TO BLACK

about mo fanning

Page Turner Award finalist Mo Fanning is a part-time novelist, part-time stand-up comic, and full-time ageing homosexual.

With a unique talent for blending darkness and light in intriguing settings, Mo is an emerging voice in the contemporary fiction scene, determined to make each book a little different from the one that came before.

He also has a passion verging on unhealthy when it comes to the Eurovision Song Contest and will happily discuss the waning value of a key change.

He currently lives in the West Midlands.

husbands

A gripping, dark romantic comedy, *Husbands* is an entertaining and fast-paced peek into the not-so-bright lights of Hollywood.

Wannabe actor Kyle Macdonald is down on his luck. Working as a supply teacher in an inner-city Birmingham school, he's single again at 28 and sleeping in his childhood bedroom.

Then comes a call claiming he drunkenly married top Hollywood director Aaron Biedermeier in Vegas six years ago. Could this be the golden ticket to the life he's always fantasised about? But the glamorous veneer of Los Angeles soon cracks, revealing a darker, corrupt underbelly to La-La Land.

Perfect for fans of Jane Fallon, Marian Keyes, Beth O'Leary, and Taylor Jenkins Reid.

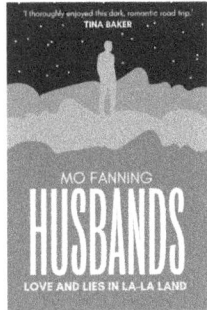

'I thoroughly enjoyed this dark, romantic road trip.'
TINA BAKER

MO FANNING

HUSBANDS

LOVE AND LIES IN LA-LA LAND

In Hollywood, every pavement star tells a story. Not all of them shine.

husbands

I've always believed that winning at life comes down to achieving the holy trinity: a fabulous job, great (and regular) sex, and a Sunday-supplement-worthy home. I'm a supply teacher in an inner-city Birmingham school, single again at 28, and sleeping in my childhood bedroom beneath a *Hard Candy* Madonna poster.

In some parallel universe, another version of me lounges in a daytime chat show green room, reaching past Dame Joanna Lumley for freshly baked pastries while trading stories of our respective recent sell-out West End productions. Joanna would call me darling and praise my courage for risking a one-man coming out confessional, and I'd explain how much it mattered to my art that I prove to all young gay men they too can evolve from a shy, acne-ridden ugly duckling into a graceful swan with good hair. A budding national treasure. Tipped to win the *Evening Standard* Most Promising Newcomer award.

A football hits my head.

It's my turn for playground duty at Oak Park Juniors, sheltering from the mid-morning drizzle next to a mildewed concrete fountain that Birmingham City Council drained for health and safety reasons.

'Sorry, sir.'

The apology comes from a Year Four boy, Lewis something-or-other. The Head of Year calls him a twat. His rough-as-a-bear's-arse father texts the school with illiterate complaints about his little prince's unfair treatment. Last week, his little prince broke a kid's arm and locked two dinner ladies in the netball cupboard. One of them has claustrophobia. Lewis grabs his ball and backs away, giving me a shit-eating grin. I'm ten years old again, hiding how I'm not like all the other boys, pretending not to mind when they call me poofter.

An uneaten sandwich sits on my lap. Cheese and beetroot. Mum started making the same packed lunch every day after I mentioned liking it. As the early evening weatherman finishes his forecast, she turns off the TV and totters to the kitchen to slice mild cheddar, and fish Sainsbury's own-label beetroot slices from a jar.

I liberate the sandwich from its cling film shroud. Damp white bread stained pink and curling at the edges, with a cloying note of sweet vinegar. I'll toss it in a skip near the sports hall extension and buy something from Pret. One more loyalty stamp, and I score a free coffee.

Except tonight, I'm not going straight home. I'm meeting a Grindr date for drinks—a 21-year-old Taiwanese kickboxer who thinks I look 23. I'm wary of anyone who suggests a late afternoon hook-up. They avoid evenings because they have a wife and kids or an electronic tag that puts them under post-sunset house arrest. This guy is cute, though, and mentioned having had a part in a recent action film.

Five years of teaching is enough. My true calling is acting, not sitting in a classroom that may or may not have asbestos in the walls. Last year, I scored a minor role in a period drama and worked as a body double for a soap star. A prosthetic nose fell off during a sex scene, and the intimacy coordinator lost her shit. I've played a mysterious monk in a gentle whodunnit and once featured in the audience for a taping of *Britain's Got Talent*. The producer zoomed in twice on my appalled face as an octogenarian crooned 'Danny Boy'.

Today marks three months of being a single man after ending a disastrous relationship with a compulsive liar who cheated on me with our Brazilian cleaner, Joaquim.

Walking across the playground, I mutter a pep talk about how dreams are worth chasing and tonight's hot date could start a new chapter. The school bell signals the end of break time, and kids form reluctant lines to head inside. There are three weeks until the summer holidays, and they're as sick as me of introductory algebra and hearing about the Irish potato famine.

Tonight, I'll step out of my comfort zone, embrace the unknown and inch closer to the life I've always wanted. I'll say yes when opportunity knocks.

———

A warm bottle of Czech lager sits on a rickety plastic table beside my phone, and I contemplate leaving a third message for my date. But how would that make me sound? Desperate? Needy? Pissed off? The sun beats down, turning my face the colour of boiled ham. Why do I never pack sunblock? Joan Collins swears by that, and a wide-brimmed hat—which I once tried, but a random woman tapped my arm and asked if I'd lost my carer.

The bar opposite is bathed in soothing shade, but I chose

The Pink Flamingo for its potential networking opportunities —BBC casting directors loiter here and scout for new faces. One of the ex-barmen now runs a second-hand book stall on Albert Square in *EastEnders*.

Surrounded by empty chairs and tables, I glance up whenever anybody emerges from inside. A cuter guy clearing tables keeps looking over, judging me, and writing me off as a loser. Rummaging through my backpack, I pull out a dog-eared copy of Stanislavsky's *An Actor Prepares*, my place marked by a folded-in-two prescription for lower back pain tablets.

The Head called me into her office as I was leaving.

'Are you happy here?' She peered over huge round spectacles like a constipated owl.

'Delirious,' I said, hoping she had an ear for sarcasm.

She fished a folder from a drawer. 'This morning, I had a conversation with Suzanne.'

'Right?'

'You're filling in while she takes stress leave.' She placed air quotes around the last two words. 'Suzanne won't be rejoining our merry band. The doctor recommends a total break, so she's moving to Telford to keep chickens.'

I held my breath as she slid papers across her desk—application forms for a full-time position.

'We'd love to retain your services, Kyle,' she said. 'The kids adore you.'

We both knew it was bull. The kids there see me as just another burnt-out teacher in an Ofsted failing school, but I come with Grade 3 piano skills, which makes me invaluable at morning assembly.

Every sensible bone in my body says to apply for the job, but what if my acting break happens? For one thing, it wouldn't be fair for the kids to lose a much-loved father figure midway through the term. And any casting director will ask if I'm employed and pick someone more available.

————

I consider firing off a third message to my date. He's well over an hour late. My first was casual, jokey even.

> Hey there. At the pub. Ordering lots of beer.
> See you soon.

Should I add a kiss? After all, he's a stranger, and I don't know his real name, though I do suspect it isn't CumDump64. Grindr dates are like petrol station milk. Usually, they're fine, but there's always a risk you might get sick and develop a nasty rash.

I wait another 20 minutes and try again. This time, leaving a voicemail.

We did say five o'clock, didn't we? Or did I get it wrong? Anyway, I hope you're OK and didn't get injured in a fight...or something. Call me when you pick up.

I considered adding how horny I was, but my sex voice is more creepy than thirsty. We've already traded dick pics, so he gets what kind of evening I have planned.

By the time I've drunk one and a half more overpriced bottled beers, the pub is getting busy for happy hour, and topless, tattooed bartenders have replaced the afternoon shift. A DJ takes over, and it's bottomless jugs of margaritas all round. Office girl gaggles descend, and a random asks to 'borrow' chairs from my table. Soon, it's just me, one empty chair, and two tall, skinny guys in shiny blue suits cut tight on the leg with estate agent hair, giving me stink eye, willing me to move.

I grab my phone.

'Milly,' I say when she answers. 'The tosser stood me up, and there's a half pitcher of watered-down cocktails with your name on it.'

———

Milly reaches for the jug, and ice cubes clink. The background music has reached shout-to-be-heard levels, and the after-work crowd is drunk-dancing and singing along with Kylie.

'The man is deformed.' She returns my phone. 'You had a lucky escape.'

A part of me wants to believe her. For one thing, she's right. Something weird is going on with his penis, but it could just be bad lighting. Nobody ever looks their best without an LED halo lamp.

We've moved inside and bagged seats at the bar. The Flamingo tries to pass itself off as a Birmingham gay institution, but it's seen better days. The walls are painted the same garish shade of purple as when I summoned the courage to duck past bouncers and order my first gay pub drink ten years earlier. The place even smells the same. Say what you like about Lynx Oriental body spray. It's a classic.

Kylie gives way to a four-on-the-floor beat of loud, distorted guitar and pounding bass.

An unread text notification appears on my phone. Most likely CumDump64 rescheduling.

Milly pays for our drinks. She never lets me settle bills because I'm a supply teacher, and she's a partnership fast-track lawyer with an expense account.

'Let me guess,' she says. 'His wife has COVID, and he's in charge of making sure the kids get their fish fingers and oven chips?'

I stuff the phone back into my pocket, wounded not from

Grindr rejection but by a ten-word text from Montgomery Casting. Two days ago, I auditioned for a non-speaking role of "man at party". The brief said: male, 18–30, six-foot-tall, dark hair, not too fat, not too thin, any ethnicity. It should have been a formality.

'They gave some other pretty boy actor the part,' I say, and she reaches to stroke my arm.

'You'll land the next one.'

'You said that last time and the time before. And when I made the final three to play a headless corpse in *Silent Witness*.

'You did that play.'

She means an experimental theatre piece I let myself be talked into by a man with swimming pool eyes and super-tight jeans. My character spent an hour on a stage locked in a box, making animal noises while someone dressed as Bo Peep called for lost sheep. On the opening night, we played to an audience of seven. There was no second performance.

My phone rings, but I don't react.

'Shouldn't you answer that?' Milly says. 'What if the casting people sent the wrong message?'

She's a proper glass-half-full kind of friend. We agreed if we're both still single at 35, we'll buy matching fuchsia sweaters and a bungalow. We'll join a choir and start rumours about the neighbours being swingers.

Tomorrow, she'll call and say she's booked us in for La Mer facials, followed by lunch at some fancy place with a two-month waiting list run by a TV chef.

She puts up with my wannabe actor shtick on the whole, but never shies away from suggesting the grass might not be as green as I imagine on the other side of fame.

The phone stops ringing, and she peers at the screen. 'That was a US number.'

Seconds later, a ping signals voicemail, and I act like it's no big deal. 'Probably some bloke to ask if I'm happy with my doors and windows.'

'Calling from America?' She lunges for my mobile.

'Fine.'

I play the message on speaker.

'This is Carlton Dupree. I work for Aaron Biedermeier. I must speak to you. Today, if possible.'

Milly wrinkles her nose, and I scratch my head, running through a long list of the men I've slept with since discovering my husband-to-be was a lying, cheating bastard. Had there been an American? I half recall an air steward with a New York accent.

'Biedermeier,' I say. 'Why do I recognise that name?'

She taps it into a search engine on her phone. 'Is this him?'

The face is familiar. Handsome, square-jawed, and rugged with dark brown eyes.

'He's a director,' she says. 'Remember that artsy bollocks film we watched? The one set in the French civil war? Everyone in the village lost their memory after aliens invaded.'

The pair of us sit through so many terrible films. It's our thing. A perfect Saturday night involves way too much Chinese food while streaming something that scored zero on Rotten Tomatoes, ideally with subtitles.

'*Paper Tiger*,' she says.

'That was him?' I stare at the picture. 'I figured the director would be Italian, with a bulbous wine-drinker nose and a penchant for underage girls.'

'Close.' She takes back her phone. 'I read in *Popbitch* about how this guy trades roles for sexual favours from wannabe movie stars. Male wannabe movie stars.'

I snort. 'Perhaps this is my break.'

'Except he prefers younger men.'

I'm at a loss for words. 'I'm 28, Milly. That's hardly old. CumDump thought I was 23.'

'So, you'd sleep with a man for a part in a film?'

I'm about to reply that yes, of course, I would. Who in their right mind wouldn't, when my phone lights up. It's Mum. For over a week, I've ignored hints the size of a boulder about how her choir group needs someone to fill in since their regular pianist booked a late saver deal to Lloret de Mar.

———

Early evening Birmingham city centre is always the same. The smells of food cooking fill the air, and music plays from open windows, a woman's soulful voice crooning, bass notes thumping. Crowds mill, talking, laughing, drinking, and enjoying good weather. A setting sun pastes warm shadows between high-rise buildings.

Someone calls out, and heads turn. A guy in his thirties with shaggy hair and a worn leather jacket raises a hand in greeting and forces a crooked grin. He plays an alcoholic doctor in an afternoon drama. Once, we got chatting online, and he sent a photo. Not of his face, obviously. I recognise a tiny tattoo on his wrist—Sanskrit for eternal flame.

'Where are you? Is that music playing?' Mum interrupts my pondering whether to go over and say hi, invite him to join me for a margarita, and swing the conversation on to whether the producer of his soap might need a six-foot-tall, moderately handsome geek.

'Drinks with Milly,' I say. 'Sorry, I missed your calls. We had a staff meeting after work.'

Mum holds a huge candle for Milly and me getting together, always pointing out how much we have in common.

When I first dated Chris, Mum showed him photographs

of our joint graduation, making him agree just how happy we looked. How well-suited we appeared. Two eggnogs later, and she was debating whose nose any future grandchildren might inherit.

'A man keeps calling.' The wobble in her voice suggests she hopes this doesn't mean a new boyfriend. 'I gave him your mobile number.'

'Did this caller have an American accent?'

'Yes, but he sounded friendly.'

'If he calls again, hang up. It's a scam.'

There's a long silence. Mum reads the *Daily Mail* and stays alert for scammers out to swindle away her meagre savings. She bought a special pen to obscure the address on envelopes and a commercial paper shredder for bank statements. She's ex-directory and has a device attached to the phone to show who's calling before picking up. If anyone knocks on the door, she demands identity and refuses to shop online.

'There's a number you call to report them,' she says. 'Hang on while I find it for you.'

The line muffles.

She'll be searching through the drawer in her special hallway telephone table.

'I'm about to jump on a bus.' Sometimes, I worry just how easily lies spring into my mind. 'I'll be late home. Don't bother doing me anything for tea.'

After typing Aaron Biedermeier into my phone, I scroll through photos of him and his super-buff husband-to-be, actor Noah Winters, frolicking in Venice Beach waves. Winters was tipped for an Oscar three years back for *Walter's War*, a Biedermeier Pictures production. The bastard was nineteen, and now he's 22 and engaged to the guy who made him famous.

The crowded city centre street feels too loud, too exposed for what could become my pivotal step on the yellow brick road to fame. Everything hangs off first impressions, and I need to sound like I get calls like this all the time. I glance around, seeking somewhere private. Somewhere that might pass for my dressing room on the set of a prestige BBC drama.

Narrow concrete steps lead to the nearest canal. Below street level, the air is musty and dank. Water laps against lichen-coated walls while early evening traffic rumbles overhead. Carlton Dupree's number rings, and the voice that answers is high-pitched and nasal.

'Who the fuck is this?'

'Kyle Macdonald.' I try to sound chilled. 'You left a message on my voicemail.'

Static crackles.

'Oh, hey... Kyle.' He sounds less frosty. 'Thank you for getting back to me. Especially given the circumstances. Kinda shitty, right?'

He's got the wrong guy. It's happened before. There's a Glasgow Kyle McDougall listed in *Spotlight*, and he's doing way better than me. Last month, he auditioned for a Jennifer Aniston show.

I clear my throat. 'When you say circumstances...'

'We here at Biedermeier Pictures can't begin to imagine what you must be going through. It has to be hard to hear your husband was attacked. Let alone that he's in a coma.'

'Can I check something?' I say, but he's not listening.

'You have such a great voice, Kyle. So distinctive and memorable.'

'Tell me again about the attack.'

He exhales. 'Aaron is in a bad way, and the doctors aren't sure if...well, I'm getting ahead of myself.' He leaves a pause. 'There's a flight leaving Heathrow in three hours, and I figured if I booked you a seat...'

'You've got me confused with someone else,' I say. 'I don't know anyone called Aaron.'

Papers rustle down the line.

'Am I talking to Kyle Rupert Macdonald? Born on the fifth of September in Stourbridge.' He pronounces it to rhyme with "drawbridge". Americans always do.

'Yes, but...'

'Jeez, you're hard to track down. Clark County gave me your name, date of birth, and the wrong telephone number. I spoke to some woman who kept asking if I was trying to sell double glazing. She passed on your details. It's not like I can ask your husband.'

It's the second mention of a husband, and now he's done the whole name, date of birth and embarrassing middle name. I feel I should ask quite what the hell he's talking about.

'You keep talking about me being married,' I say, and then snort like a cat coughing up a furball.

There's another long silence. More keyboard taps.

'Six years ago. You were in Vegas. April 2016.'

I think back. Vegas just isn't my kind of town. I've only ever been once for a stag weekend. One I got talked into and regretted within ten minutes of arriving at a hotel that made Blackpool Pleasure Beach look classy.

'Do you remember what you did on Saturday, April 9, 2016?' he says. 'To be fair, it was more like the small hours of Sunday, April 10.'

Like any Vegas stag weekend, things got messy fast. There were six of us, and we emptied three hotel room minibars, and proved the bottomless cocktails had a cut-off point, before hitting the casino, where I accidentally-on-purpose ducked into a gift shop to avoid being dragged to a strip club.

'Do you recall visiting The Little Less Conversation Wedding Chapel?'

My mouth runs dry, and I grab a railing to steady myself as my stomach rolls. I've long since buried the memory of agreeing to joke-marry a stranger I met in a casino. We were both falling-down drunk, and no overweight Elvis impersonator could join us in any legally binding way. Surely.

'We never collected the marriage certificate,' I say. 'So it didn't count. And the guy...' His name might have been Aaron. Or Alan. Or Adrian. 'He was going to call the chapel for an annulment.'

'I'm not here to judge. My job is to help.'

'Help with what?'

A bubble of sick rises, and at the back of my mind, a nagging voice points out how I should have double-checked that nothing ever came of that drunken half-night stand.

'Here's the deal. I work for Biedermeier and six years ago, you married my boss. Aaron loves doing impulsive things. It's a total ball ache keeping track of his lunch order.'

There's a pause. I should demand proof. A copy of the marriage certificate. The one that was going to be annulled.

'Are you certain about any of this?' I say. 'Because I never actually signed anything.'

Carlton Dupree sighs. 'Aaron just got engaged to some twink actor called Noah Winters. You may have heard of the guy. Nominated for an Oscar. Yadda yadda. And then...what with the attack and everything...'

'Hang on,' I say, 'tell me more about that.'

'A bunch of guys. Early morning. Downtown. I keep telling him to use studio drivers and security, but Aaron's a free spirit. Now he's in Cedars Sinai, hooked up to a bunch of machines. A guy from Legal was going through paperwork, and... well, that's how come we're talking.'

There's every chance I'll vomit. Like people do in TV shows when unexpected bad news breaks. Mum's biggest moan about *Coronation Street* is how, at the slightest hint of something going wrong, someone ends up bent double over a toilet bowl.

'Should I have changed my name?' I say, punch-drunk, confused. 'Should I be Kyle Biedermeier?'

'About that flight.' He ignores my questions. 'It's showing one seat remaining in First.' Clicks suggest he's typing again. 'You want me to specify a meal preference?'

Things are moving too fast. Why fly anywhere?

'My friend is a lawyer,' I say. 'You could courier the documents...'

Dupree sighs. 'You think I wouldn't be doing that if it was a possibility? The marriage was in Nevada. California has different laws.'

'I can't just drop everything.' I step to one side to let a couple with a border collie pass by. 'I have a job. Perhaps if I make some calls...'

'You've got a husband in the ICU.' Carlton's breathing gets heavy and unsteady, like a hissing kettle set to boil over. 'I'll take care of everything once you're here.'

Heathrow is four hours away. Tomorrow is sports day at school, and I'm in charge of the stopwatch.

'Are there no flights out of Birmingham?' I say.

'Birmingham, Alabama?' He sounds surprised.

'Birmingham, England.'

More clicks. 'OK, so I can route you through Amsterdam in business-class, with lounge access. How does that work for you? Can you make a ten-thirty flight tomorrow morning?'

I scan nearby bridges and buildings for TV cameras, suspecting a prank. Any minute, some minor daytime presenter will leap out and yell "surprise".

'This is a joke, right?' I say. 'Milly put you up to it.'

He ignores me. 'When you land in LA, look for a guy holding a board with your name. He'll bring you to the hotel.'

My phone pings with an email containing ticket details. Business-class seats and an executive suite at the Beverly Hills Hotel. In Hollywood.

———

Milly narrows her eyes. 'You're married to Aaron Biedermeier, and he's in a coma?'

I nod. 'This Dupree guy made it sound super urgent...like he could die any minute.'

She's tapping at her phone, checking the story. 'The coma part checks out. But I don't get why you need to be by his bedside. It's not like you stayed in touch.'

'We're married.'

Out loud, the phrase sounds dumb.

She folds her arms. 'You can't drunk-marry anyone. Not even in Las Vegas. It's the same the world over. Both parties must be of sound mind and able to exercise free judgement.'

A memory pops up. Of a hotel suite. Of some kid in another room. Bare-chested. Scared. Young.

'The woman at the wedding place said to go back the next day for our certificate,' I say, recalling fuzzy details. 'But my ticket was non-refundable, and I had to get to the airport. The guy...Biedermeier, I guess...he promised to sort everything out.'

'Jesus.' Milly slaps her palm on the counter. 'All this time, you didn't think to check? You get how I'm a lawyer, right?'

I stare at the floor, face burning. 'Isn't it like here where you get to divorce on the grounds of desertion? It's been six years.'

'How would I know, Kyle? I trained in UK criminal law. You need to speak to an expert in what to do when some feck-less twat gets wasted in Vegas and marries a total stranger.' She pulls out her phone. 'I have a girlfriend in San Francisco. Her boyfriend is a family lawyer.'

Milly always comes through, no matter how deep I wade into crap. She once convinced a furious Italian chef that I was a rare cheese connoisseur after I called his lasagne greasy. After the place closed for the evening, we sat through a tense cheese-tasting in his overheated kitchen, with me praising the Gorgonzola like it was the holy grail.

'Biedermeier's guy booked me onto a flight, leaving tomorrow morning,' I say.

She looks up. 'Don't you have to work?'

'I was going to say I tested positive for COVID.'

Milly's lips form a grim line. Her eyes narrow. 'How do you plan on explaining to your mum why you're taking a change of clothes and that you might be gone a while?'

'Last-minute inset training?'

I shift, avoiding her glare. This is my chance to prove the school bullies wrong. Revenge for every poofter, fag or queer jibe.

'Is it wrong of me to want this? How often does a Holly-wood director need you at their bedside?'

'What if all you get is hurt? Block the number. Move on with your life.'

Coma or no coma, Aaron Biedermeier has connections, and when he wakes, who's to say he won't remember our wedding night? And then, we'll catch up, and I'll let slip about having acting experience, and he'll call in favours. Things start small. A background role with no words. Or one line. A scene-stealing valet parking attendant who gets slapped by Julia Roberts. Milly waves a hand in front of my face.

'I got a text back from my friend with the lawyer boyfriend. He's going to call you tomorrow evening.'

'Does he need the hotel phone number?'
She looks crestfallen. 'So, you've decided?'

GHOSTED

Professional Santa Silas French fills out the same application as always for his regular stint at a New York department store.

Ellen Gitelman hangs her jacket behind the counter at the East Side Diner and smoothes out her waitress uniform as she waits for the coffee pot to stop percolating.

The fuck-it list meets the bucket list when fate conspires to book two unlikely allies on the MS Viking Gay Christmas Cruise.

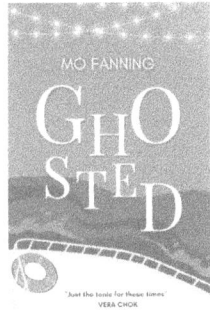

REBUILDING ALEXANDRA SMALL

Alexandra Small has it all—a thriving career, a beautiful home, and a loving family. And then—in the space of one awful day—she doesn't.

Sometimes rock bottom is the best place to start when you've climbed the wrong mountain.

THE ARMCHAIR BRIDE

Lisa Doyle keeps a list. Of everyone she knew at school. Of their husbands, wives and happy families. Lisa isn't on that list, because she's heading for 30. And she's single.

Logic would tell her to turn down the invite to the wedding of her childhood friend. Logic would tell her not to invent a husband and accept. But when the guest list includes the girl who made school hell for Lisa, the RSVP becomes a formality.

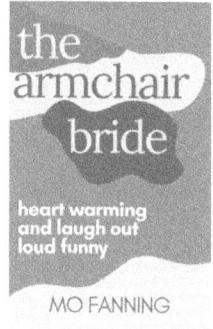

The brightest lights cast the darkest shadows.

www.ingramcontent.com/pod-product-compliance
Ingram Content Group UK Ltd.
Pitfield, Milton Keynes, MK11 3LW, UK
UKHW041848140125
453606UK00003B/31